IT ENDS WITH HER

A NOVEL

DEBRA WEBB

This book is a work of fiction. Names, characters, places, and incidents are the product of the author's imagination or are used fictitiously. Any resemblance to actual events, locales, or persons, living or dead, is coincidental.
Copyright © 2nd Edition 2024 Debra Webb
Cover Design by Vicki Hinze

All rights reserved. In accordance with the U.S. Copyright Act of 1976, the scanning, uploading, and electronic sharing of any part of this book without the permission of the publisher is unlawful piracy and theft of the author's intellectual property. Thank you for your support of the author's rights.

PINK HOUSE PRESS
Debra Webb, Fayetteville, Tennessee
Second Edition *It Ends With Her* Debra Webb December 2024
First Edition *Secrets & Lies Anywhere She Runs* Debra Webb 2019

This book is dedicated to my dear friend and twisted sister Peggy Webb—a beautiful soul inside and out and a brilliant author of some of the most amazing stories you will ever read! To many more, my friend!

IT ENDS WITH HER

CHAPTER ONE

Laurel, Mississippi
Sunday, December 17, 8:42 p.m.

"Jingle bell...jingle bell...jingle bell rock."

Danny Jamison lay in bed and hummed the Christmas song. He didn't know all the words, but he liked this one a lot.

His mommy had told him at breakfast this morning that in just eight more days it would be Christmas. Another good thing about today was that it was the last day of school for two whole weeks. The paper ornament he had been working on at school was on the Christmas tree. Pretty soon his mom would put some presents with his name on them under the tree so he could try and guess what was inside.

But the bestest part of all was the stories she told him every night. Some of the stories were about the elves and the reindeers. His favorite one was about how good little boys always got what they wished the hardest for at Christmas.

But she hadn't come to his room to tell him a story tonight.

His dad was in one of his moods.

More of the yelling made Danny put his hands over his ears. He didn't like when his mommy and daddy had fights. Tonight was scarier than ever before. His daddy was screaming real loud. Saying the meanest things. Meaner than the other times when he yelled.

"I told you not to let this happen! Damn you!"

Danny pressed his hands harder against his ears, but he could still hear his mommy crying and his daddy yelling. His daddy didn't like yelling. He told Danny so. It was always his mom's fault. She messed up too much. Just like his grandparents. That was why Danny hid sometimes when he went to their house. Then he didn't have to hear the yelling when they got mad at his daddy.

He wished he had a place to hide now. But his dad had warned Danny never to hide from him…for any reason.

"Now look what you've done! You've ruined everything!"

Danny tried to block the bad words his dad kept yelling by singing along with the Christmas music on the radio. "'Jingle bell…jingle bell…'"

His mommy screamed. Danny burrowed deeper under the covers but he could still hear her crying…crying and begging for his dad to please stop. Danny felt bad for her even if she had messed up again.

"There will be no princess in this house!" his dad shouted.

Something crashed. Sounded like glass. It was the same sound the kitchen window made when his baseball went through it last summer. His dad had been real mad about that, too.

The screaming and the crying stopped.

Danny dragged his hands from his ears. He lay still for a moment and listened to make sure it was really over.

No more screaming. No more crying. Just the Christmas music.

"Jingle bell time is a swell time…" he murmured.

Maybe if his mommy had fixed everything she would come tell him a story now.

"…to rock the night away…"

His bedroom door flew open, banged against the wall. "Danny!"

Danny bit his lips together to keep from crying out as his daddy jerked the covers off him. He didn't want his dad to be mad at him, too. He was supposed to be asleep. "You should be asleep by now, son."

His daddy sat down on the side of the bed. Danny tried not to shake or to cry for his mommy. That would only make his daddy more upset. Danny told his mouth to smile but his lips just kept shaking like he was cold.

"Don't be afraid, son."

His daddy smiled at him, but the smile looked funny with that red stuff smeared on his face. Why would his daddy have ketchup on his face?

"You don't have to worry about anything, son," his daddy promised. "No princess will ever take your place."

CHAPTER TWO

Huntsville, Alabama
Friday, December 23, 10:30 a.m.

The Christmas tinsel tickled her breast.

She shivered.

The shiny silver strands slid down her sweat-dampened torso. Over her belly button. Along her inner thigh. The tip of a deliciously wicked tongue followed that same path.

A sigh whispered from her lips. Man, that felt good. But she was so ready to get on with it. This guy was evidently going for a foreplay record.

Adeline Cooper propped up on her elbows and peered down her nude body at the red and white velvet hat. She couldn't believe she was about to say this. "Look, Santa, patience has never been one of my virtues."

Her lover lifted his attentive face from the task of tugging down her skimpy panties with his teeth. His brown eyes were glazed with the same anticipation currently throbbing in her veins.

"I'd like my present now." She crooked her finger. "Come on up here and show me what you've got besides that nifty hat."

His well-shaped mouth split into a grin as he crawled his way up her tingling body, all those gorgeous male muscles bunching and rippling with the effort. "Baby." He nipped her lips with his teeth. "I got the package you've been waiting for all year."

"Oh yeah?"

"Yeah," he growled as he nibbled her chin.

Pounding on the front door dragged her attention from his hungry mouth. *Damn.* "I should get that."

"It's your day off," he muttered between kisses.

"Yeah, well." She reached for the cuffs on the table next to the bed. "That's the thing about being a cop, there's no such thing as a real day off." She fastened one cuff around his wrist with a titillating click. "Now, don't move, because I'll be right back to interrogate you, Mr. Claus." While she plundered his mouth with her own, she attached the other bracelet to the iron headboard.

Adeline scooted off the bed and grabbed his shirt. She poked her arms into the long sleeves and hugged the warm flannel around her. At her bedroom door, she paused, surveyed his long, lean frame stretched out on her bed, and made a sound of approval deep in her throat. *Merry Christmas to me.*

"Hurry on back, now," he teased, "and you can unwrap your present."

She would definitely hurry back.

Another round of pounding echoed from the front door.

"Hold your horses," she shouted as she padded

through the house. "I'm coming." Or she would be if whoever was doing all the banging hadn't interrupted.

She yanked open the door. "What?"

"Morning, Cooper." The man in the FedEx uniform, Wesley McElroy, nudged his Ray-Bans down his nose and surveyed her from head to toe. "You look all relaxed this morning."

"It's my day off," she said. She sent a pointed look at the large, padded envelope under his arm. "That for me?"

"Yes, ma'am." He held out his electronic clipboard. "You need to sign for it."

She put her signature where he indicated. McElroy passed the padded envelope to her. "You have a nice day now."

"You, too." Distracted by the sender's address, she bumped the door closed with her hip and leaned against it. Though she didn't recognize the specific return address, the location surprised her. Besides her mother, there wasn't a soul in Mississippi who would contact her. Not by mail anyway.

Both Christmas and her birthday were coming up…maybe her scumbag uncle had finally decided to forgive her for doing her job nine years ago.

"Yeah, right. And hell just froze over." She stalked into the kitchen and placed the envelope on the counter.

"Santa's waiting!" her cuffed lover shouted from the bedroom.

She ignored him. Her well-honed cop instincts were revving up, overriding all else. Getting anything from anywhere in Mississippi was too bizarre to ignore—even for great sex. She dug up a pair of latex gloves and scissors. Pulled on the gloves and then slowly cut the envelope's flap free. Carefully parting the severed edges, she bent her head down and peeked inside.

Adeline jerked back. Her heart bumped her sternum.

"What the hell?" She tucked two fingers inside and pulled the item from the envelope. A white sheet of copy or printer paper with letters pasted across it.

More of that pulse-pounding adrenaline seared through her as she read the cut-and-pasted words.

Pretty, pretty princess. See her smile...see her die.

"Shit. Shit. Shit." Adeline dashed back to the living room, almost slipping on the slick hardwood, and searched through the stack of old mail on the table by the door. In her haste she sent junk mail and monthly statements fluttering to the floor.

Where the hell was that other letter? Unlike this one, the first letter had been hand-delivered to her mailbox at home. No return address, no postage. And no prints.

She'd nagged the guys at work, thinking one of them had been playing a joke on her related to her birthday and the fact that she was about to be promoted to lieutenant. She'd brought the letter back home that same day. It had to be here.

"Addy! What the hell are you doing?"

"Gimme a minute." She shoved a handful of hair behind her ear. The letter wasn't in the stack. Hand shaking, she yanked open the table's only drawer.

There it was.

She picked up the single sheet of plain white printer paper. Stared at the pasted on letters that formed the words which now carried entirely new significance.

She was born a princess for all to see. Her light was so bright that they could no longer see me.

Adeline returned to the kitchen to compare the two notes. Paper looked to be the same weight and shade of white. The way the words were pasted on the page, right side angled slightly upward, was the same. No continuity in the spacing.

She set the two letters to the side and looked in the envelope to see what else it contained. A newspaper clipping. Big article. Front page. She pulled it out. *Hattiesburg Press*. She read the headline.

City Attorney Cherry Prescott Missing

Heart rate rising, Adeline skimmed the article. Prescott served as Hattiesburg's city attorney. Four years older than Adeline, Prescott was married with two kids. A photo accompanying the article was in black-and-white, but the woman's smile was nothing less than dazzling—oozing self-confidence. Blond hair, pretty lady. According to the article she was a brilliant attorney with a great future in politics. Prescott had gone missing three days ago.

Adeline braced her hands on the counter, analyzed the details a second time. The woman's car had been discovered just outside Moss Point. Only a few miles from where Adeline had grown up.

There were no suspects as of yet. No ransom demand. Just the abandoned vehicle. Prescott's family was offering a sizable reward for any information that helped to find her and the person responsible for her abduction.

Frustration soared through her and Adeline threw up her hands. "What the hell is this?" Why would some perv send her these stupid princess letters and an article about a woman who'd gone missing near her hometown? A woman Adeline didn't know...had never even met? She shook her head. Didn't make any kind of sense.

And yet, there had to be a reason.

Instinct prodded her.

There must be some kind of connection here that she just couldn't see. This was obviously not just a joke about her thirty-first birthday.

This was…a piece of some kind of creepy puzzle.

After placing the newspaper clipping next to the letters, Adeline turned her attention back to the envelope and opened it wider to see if there was anything else she had missed.

A postcard or photograph was tucked deep into a corner. She frowned, then shook the envelope until the final item fell free and fluttered to the counter.

A Polaroid snapshot.

Adeline picked it up by the edges. Same woman, Cherry Prescott, pictured in the article. Only in this color snapshot her eyes were closed and she definitely wasn't smiling. No way to tell if she was dead or alive. No discernible injuries. Since only her upper torso and face were visible in the photo, there was no way to be certain of anything. Her makeup job was overdone, clownish, she wore a tiara and nothing else as far as Adeline could see.

She read the words scrawled in tiny print across the bottom of the photo. As the ramifications of the statement filtered through her confusion, a new kind of tension ignited in Adeline's veins.

One dead princess, two to go.

CHAPTER THREE

815 Wheeler Avenue
Huntsville Police Department, 12:45 p.m.

"The only prints are on the first letter and those are yours."

Adeline had expected that would be the case. "But it's the same paper. Same type of glue as the first letter."

Chief Burton Spencer nodded. "No question. The clerk at the FedEx drop-off center in Hattiesburg doesn't recall what the sender looked like, only that he was male. The street address he provided doesn't exist."

Adeline had called the chief en route. A lab tech had been standing by when she arrived downtown. Less than an hour later they had the results, not that she had needed a lab tech to tell her what she already knew. Both letters had evidently been created and sent by the same individual. Both were void of prints, other than hers on the first one, or any other trace evidence beyond the glue. And neither one gave the slightest hint at what the message had to do with Adeline.

"Cherry Prescott lives and works in Hattiesburg," Adeline went on, "but her abandoned vehicle was found near Moss Point. My hometown. I don't know her, but obviously the person who abducted her knows me."

The idea that this could have something to do with her family was almost ludicrous. *Almost.* Nine years had passed. Why the hell would that ancient history be coming up now? And what would the Prescott woman have to do with it? Why had she been in the area? Did she have family there? Was she investigating a case related to something going on in Hattiesburg?

Adeline had questions. Lots of questions.

"I know what you're thinking," the chief warned. "This may or may not have anything to do with your past. My immediate assessment would be that somebody's playing a game. Trying to muddy the investigation down there by dragging you into the mix." He leaned forward, braced his forearms on his desk. "Bottom line, this evidence could be crucial to the Prescott case. I've put in a call to the sheriff in Jackson County, Mississippi. When he calls back, we'll get his take on how this involves you and determine a course of action from there."

Adeline rolled her eyes. "I can just imagine what that old bastard has to say." The words were out of her mouth before she could stop them.

Spencer's expression turned to one of displeasure. "I understand that you have ample reason for despising law enforcement in Mississippi, but, as one of my detectives, you will show the proper respect as this situation moves forward. Understood?"

"Yes, sir." Adeline damned sure didn't want any more trouble. She'd gone through enough bullshit a few months ago with that internal affairs investigation into the last case her former partner, Kevin Braddock, and she had worked. Damn she wished Braddock was here now.

But he'd resigned and moved to Baltimore to be with CJ during the final year of her residency. The two were deliriously happy. No one deserved that kind of happiness more. Braddock didn't need Adeline dragging him into her personal problems.

Since Braddock's departure she'd spent most of her time as a "floating" partner, working with whoever needed her. She knew the deal. None of the older guys wanted her as a partner and the chief wasn't about to put some rookie's life in her hands until the dust had completely settled. She and Braddock had pushed the limits on the Nash/Abbott case, and they had paid the professional price.

But, by God, they'd gotten the job done and she would do it again if the need arose. Not a single prostitute had been murdered in this jurisdiction since Tyrone Nash got what was coming to him. Edward Abbott, well he was just a freaking psycho who had been no danger to anyone except to those who got in the way of his bizarre plans for CJ.

Honestly, it was a flat-out miracle Adeline was getting this promotion. Not everyone was happy about it. That was why the princess letter had felt exactly like sour grapes. She'd had no reason to suspect some dirtbag was planning to drag her into a case in Mississippi.

"I expect you to be on your best behavior while we see how this is going to play out," Spencer cautioned. "We'll get a whole hell of a lot more cooperation if we play nice." He tucked his reading glasses into place and glanced at his notes. "Besides, there's a new regime in Jackson County now. I understand the new sheriff's doing a damned good job."

Yeah, yeah, she got it. "You're the boss."

"Sometimes you appear to forget that fact," he reminded. "Case in point, if you received this letter four days ago, why am I just now hearing about it?"

"I told you." She shoved a hand through her hair, wished she had taken the time to put it into a ponytail before rushing over here. "I thought it was a joke." She shrugged. "About the promotion. And my birthday's next Thursday. I figured some of the guys were just giving me a hard time."

Spencer shook his head. "Obviously whoever delivered the first note and mailed the second one knows where you live. Perhaps is watching you. This is not to be taken lightly, Detective."

She got that, too. Didn't like it one damned bit. "The only person back home who knows my home address is my mother and she wouldn't give it to anyone. Whoever tracked me down went to a fair amount of trouble." All the more reason she'd assumed it was one of her colleagues. The initial letter hadn't seemed threatening...until now.

"Now we understand this isn't a joke," Spencer chastised. "This is serious."

Definitely serious. Though she couldn't imagine any of her Mississippi relatives going to the trouble of sending her a note like this. If one or more of them had decided to seek out a little delayed revenge, they would have simply attempted to put a bullet between her eyes. This kind of tactic wasn't their style.

The intercom on the chief's desk buzzed. "Chief," his secretary announced, "that call you've been expecting from Pascagoula is on line one."

Uneasiness slid through Adeline. She hadn't set foot in Mississippi—much less Jackson County or Pascagoula—in nine years. What the hell was this about?

The chief thanked his secretary and took the call. Adeline sat up straighter. Maybe now they would find out what was going on with the Prescott investigation and, hopefully, some clue as to what it had to do with her.

She bit her lips together to hold back an incredulous sound as the chief went through the usual good-old-boy spiel. How's the hunting? Pretty damned cold for December. Blah. Blah. Blah. Who gave a shit? Pissed her off that he didn't put the call on speaker.

Then Spencer explained the reason for the call. A lot of "uh-huhs" and "yessirs" later and her chief finally said, "We'll be happy to turn the evidence over to you for a look-see." A nod. "Absolutely. We believe it's quite significant. I'll courier it down right away."

Adeline waved her hands back and forth but the chief ignored her. "No way," she piped up when he continued to pay no attention to her objections. "This evidence isn't going anywhere without me." So much for the respect thing.

"Yes, sir," Spencer said with a glare in her direction, "that's my detective you hear in the background. Why, certainly. One moment." Spencer held the phone across his desk. "The sheriff would like to speak with you, *Detective.*" Spencer's eyes told her she had better not forget the warning he'd issued about three minutes ago.

Spencer was pissed, but that was too bad. No way was she allowing those yahoos down in Mississippi to get their hands on this evidence without answering some of her questions first. She knew the type who sought law-enforcement opportunities back home. Not only were they bullies, but they liked doing things their way. No outsiders allowed. They would take this evidence, and she wouldn't be permitted anywhere near their case. Nor would she get jack shit in the way of information. What the hell was the chief thinking?

She took the phone and settled it against her cheek. "This is Detective Adeline Cooper."

"You will surrender that evidence, Detective," the voice on the other end of the line ordered, "and you will not interfere with this investigation."

About a million or so memories bombarded Adeline at once. This couldn't be...

No way in hell. When she'd left Pascagoula, Mississippi, *he* had been a brand-new detective. He wouldn't have sold out to the politics and become a sheriff. No way.

He was still talking.

It was definitely *him*.

Feelings she hadn't experienced in almost a decade whirled around her, put a chokehold on her ability to respond.

The chief was staring at her funny. Probably because she no doubt wore the same expression as a vic slipping into shock from massive blood loss after a gut shot. Or maybe that face a person wore when they had just seen a ghost.

This man was a ghost from her past.

From a relationship that had been dead and buried for nine damned years.

"Have I made myself clear, Detective Cooper?"

As if nine years had not passed and they were sitting in the front seat of his souped-up old Firebird, she went off. "Don't even think about telling me what to do, Wyatt Henderson. You may be the sheriff down there now, but that just tells me you got bored or lazy. This is my evidence. Evidence connected to *me*. I may be obliged by law to turn it over to you, but I will be hand-carrying it to your office and I will be a part of this investigation."

Then, without waiting for his comeback, she leaned forward and shoved the phone back at the chief. Spencer could handle the damage control. She'd said all she had to say.

Spencer stared at her with just enough outrage to conceal the glimmer of pride she'd seen flash in his eyes as she'd said her piece. He might be talking the talk of full cooperation and respect, but he didn't want HPD left out of this any more than she did. Not when it appeared to involve one of his people.

Unable to sit any longer, Adeline got up and paced the chief's office while he smoothed things over with Wyatt. She didn't have to hear the other end of the conversation; she had an idea how it would be going.

Adeline Cooper did not need to set foot in the state of Mississippi. It had taken years for things to calm down in Jackson County after her departure. If she knew what was good for her, she would stay clear.

If Spencer tried that line of crap with her she would turn in her badge here and now. Whatever the person or persons who'd abducted Prescott wanted, Adeline had a right to be involved. She'd gotten a personal invitation, by God.

Spencer hung up the phone and settled his full attention on her. "That little performance was completely out of line, Detective Cooper."

"Sometimes stepping over the line is necessary," she said bluntly. She stopped her pacing to stand in front of the chief's desk. "Are you going to let them leave me out of this?" She leaned forward for emphasis, braced her hands on the edge of his desk, and looked him straight in the eyes.

He had the power to put-her on this case with regard to the sharing of evidence. Since the case apparently involved her, it wouldn't exactly be SOP to assign her to follow up, but he knew about her past. Understood how this would go down if she was left out. No one else in HPD would ever get past Cooper law. In Jackson County, Mississippi, Cooper law ruled. And it was rarely on the side of true justice.

She was the only cop on this force who had a snowball's chance in hell of protecting HPD's interests in this case. *Her* interests.

"Authorizing you to follow this investigation would be a mistake. Even you must see how that would look to an ethics review board."

Okay, he hadn't come straight out with a no. "Yes, sir. I am very much aware how it would look. But I also know how this will go down if you send anyone else. I understand how those people work." She left out the part about being one of them. Adeline had stopped being a Mississippi Cooper the day she allowed one of them to die instead of her.

Unless she took the bull by the horns, Sheriff Wyatt Henderson would relegate HPD's representative to a corner and that was where he'd stay until further notice. The idea that Wyatt was now the sheriff rattled her. Had her experiencing all kinds of crazy emotions. How the hell had this happened?

They had both despised the politics of the job. Maybe a wife and kids had sent him on a different path. After all, it had been nine years.

Somehow the idea of Wyatt with a wife...and kids...carried the same impact as a fist straight into her gut. What had she expected? That he would grieve the loss of her until now? That his sorry ass would still be groveling for forgiveness nearly a decade later? She had to be out of her mind.

"Forty-eight hours, Cooper," Spencer said. "You hand-carry the evidence down to Sheriff Henderson, check out the situation, and then you get yourself back up here. You can keep tabs on the investigation from right here." He poked his desk with his finger for emphasis.

"But, sir, that's barely enough time to—"

"Forty-eight hours," he reiterated. "Not a minute more. You don't get back here on time, I'll send Metcalf and Wallace down there to bring you back."

"Yes, sir." She could argue the point later, when she had both feet solidly entrenched in the investigation. Grabbing her jacket, she headed for the door.

"And Cooper."

She turned back to her boss. "Sir?"

"Don't go down there throwing your weight around," he warned. "Keep it low-profile. There are too many folks who'd still like to see you pay for what happened nine years ago. I don't want to have to do the necessary explaining or the paperwork if you get yourself killed."

"I'll do my best not to let that happen."

She had no intention of getting dead for anyone. That much she could promise Chief Spencer. Adeline Cooper planned on staying alive.

The thing she couldn't promise was exactly what she might have to do to stay that way.

CHAPTER FOUR

4718 Miller Road
Pascagoula, Mississippi, 2:30 p.m.

Irene Cooper perched on the edge of the sofa. She had waited ten minutes already. She'd run out of things to do with her hands. She'd twisted her purse straps every which way. She'd tugged at the hem of her skirt until it was out of shape. Then she had wrung her hands until her fingers felt numb.

This was wrong.

She'd made a terrible, terrible mistake.

And her daughter could never know.

Lord, Irene didn't even want to think what Adeline would say if she learned about any of this.

The squeak of wheels turning drew Irene's attention to the parlor doors. She should've known better than to come to him about this. His help always came with a heavy price.

But just like thirty years ago, the situation had been desperate.

Now things were out of control. Again.

How had she allowed fear to drive her to make the same poor choice twice?

Cyrus Cooper rolled his wheelchair through the double parlor doors. He looked old. Not just because of the wheelchair. He'd been a prisoner to the crutches and then to that thing for more than thirty years and that had never stopped him from doing a single thing he decided to do. Never once prevented him from looking powerful. And as mean as a junkyard dog if the need arose.

No, this was the cancer. He had maybe six or eight months at most.

And then he would finally be dead.

No other man on earth deserved to die more than Cyrus Cooper. Irene, for one, would dance on his grave the same day the old bastard was buried.

God forgive her for the thought...but it was true.

As had been the case for more than thirty years, she had no other place to turn. She was a prisoner to the decision she had made all those years ago.

"Irene." He rolled across the room, parked his ambulatory chair on the opposite side of the fancy coffee table from where she sat. Every piece of furniture in the room was a priceless antique. The man owned nothing that wasn't valuable, more often than not bartered in blood. "Is something wrong?" Those too-seeing brown eyes scrutinized her. "You look pale as a ghost. What's happened?"

A sudden burst of determination chased away the weaker emotions that had her hands sweating. "She's on her way here. I couldn't stop her."

His eyebrows winged up his forehead, accenting the

surprise that flared in his eyes. "I suppose her reaction is only natural. Considering."

Irene wanted to shake him. Though she didn't dare. "I want your word, Cyrus, that no one will bother her while she's here. My daughter has obeyed your decree for all these years, as have I. As you said, under the circumstances you can understand why she might not be able to hold to that agreement now." Irene summoned her sternest tone. "I mean it, Cyrus Cooper. I want you to swear to me here and now that she'll be protected."

"I sent her away nine years ago," he clarified. "That decree, as you call it, was to protect her. She knows it's not safe to come back here. Not even now. I'll do what I can to see that she's protected, but I can hardly make any promises, as you well know."

Her bravado gave way to fear and frustration. "This thing has gone all wrong." What in God's name had she done? "That woman is missing. That's why Addy's coming back. It has nothing to do with what happened nine years ago."

Cyrus nodded. "This is a terrible tragedy, there's no question. But one that's as big a mystery to me as it is to anyone else."

Irene searched his eyes. Tried to see the lie. "Swear to me, Cyrus. Swear on your baby brother's grave that you had nothing to do with that woman's disappearance."

"You came to me," he said, adding salt to her wounds, "and you asked for my help. I was more than happy to provide whatever assistance you needed."

"But not like this," Irene exclaimed. "I only wanted you to..." She shook her head. "To…"

"Make the problem go away," he finished for her.

Dear Lord, that is what she'd wanted. She had known before coming to him that this ending was a strong possibility. But she'd hoped, considering the cancer, he would handle things differently now. She should have known better.

"Sweet Jesus, Cyrus! It wasn't my intention for you to do something like *this,*" she argued. This was insane. Just insane. Did the man have no conscience at all? "This is—"

He held up a hand to quiet her. "You're getting yourself all worked up for no reason. Aren't you listening? This wasn't my doing. I sent Jed and Simon to talk to the woman," he explained, his tone uncharacteristically gentle.

Mercy, Jed Stovall and Simon Cook were pure hoodlums.

"Prescott was nowhere to be found," Cyrus went on. "They discovered her abandoned car, just like the police did a few hours later. My boys never even got to say boo to the woman. She was already gone, Irene. You have no reason to worry. Whatever misfortune has befallen the poor woman had nothing to do with you or with me."

Irene pressed her fist to her mouth. Didn't know whether to cry or to rejoice. What was she thinking? The woman may have been killed! God forgive her for the relief she felt even now...even knowing this woman's disappearance was clearly due to foul play. "Who could've done this?"

"I'm sure the police will be able to answer that question in time," Cyrus offered. "Prescott is an attorney, enemies come with the territory. I suppose someone she crossed in the past was just waiting for an opportunity to have revenge. Since her family's quite wealthy, the fact that there's been no ransom demand is a very bad sign, in my opinion."

Irene watched the news. The consensus was the same. "Whoever did this," she began, not sure how much she should tell him...he already knew too much, "sent a letter

IT ENDS WITH HER

to my Addy. That's why she's coming. She's bringing some kind of evidence for Sheriff Henderson."

Cyrus nodded. "I was informed of this turn of events a little while ago."

Of course he'd already heard. He knew everything that went on in this county. He likely knew Addy was on her way well before Irene did. The surprise he'd shown moments ago had been nothing more than for show…for her benefit. The bastard. Even now he played his games.

No matter what he claimed, he would have some inkling about the Prescott woman's fate. No one came into Cyrus Cooper's territory and took a breath without his knowledge.

Somehow Irene had to ensure Addy never found out…about any of this. "No one can know what we've talked about, Cyrus. *No one.*"

His gaze held hers. She wanted to look away, but she didn't dare. She needed him to promise despite knowing what that would mean.

"This will be our little secret, Irene."

Vomit rose in her throat. She would rather die than owe this man anything more than she already did. But she would likewise do anything to spare her daughter this particular truth. *Anything.*

"The Prescott woman appears to be out of the way for now," he went on. "Whatever she had hoped to accomplish by coming to you is irrelevant under the circumstances."

That was another thing Irene would have to live with. The idea that she had lied to that poor woman. Dear God. Had her lies sent Prescott in search of the truth elsewhere? Had that search ended in tragedy?

Irene had to get out of this house. She pushed to her feet, her legs unsteady. "Thank you for your time, Cyrus." She rounded the table, tried to veer beyond his reach.

She wasn't quite fast enough. He grabbed her hand as she passed. "Try not to worry, Irene." Those doughy fingers squeezed hers, making her shudder inside. "No one's ever going to know our little secrets."

She wrenched her hand free of his and rushed out the door. Managing to climb into her car before her knees gave way, she was halfway down the mile-long drive before she had to slam on the brakes and open the car door.

The bitter bile strangled her as she retched it from her throat.

She'd made a pact with the devil...

There would be a hefty price to pay. Just like before.

Irene prayed that Cherry Prescott had not been a part of that price.

CHAPTER FIVE

Jackson County Sheriff's Office
3104 Magnolia Street
Pascagoula, Mississippi, 7:20 p.m.

Adeline sat in the dark for a moment.

She studied the four-story courthouse. Christmas lights were strung in the windows and wreaths hung on the doors. As a kid, she'd gone to the courthouse many times with her dad when he had business to take care of. The marble-floored main lobby with its soaring ceiling had enthralled her. During the Christmas season a towering tree stood in the center of the main lobby. Sometimes Santa would hang out there and give away lollipops.

Despite her curiosity, the deputies walking around with their guns on their hips had sent her hiding behind her daddy's legs. She'd been certain that bad people lived in the courthouse even though Santa had made it one of his regular annual stops.

Funny, she'd found out much later that, to some extent, her childhood theory had been all too true. Even at twenty she hadn't fully realized that truth. She'd been so damned excited to make the cut as a deputy for the Jackson County Sheriff's Department. At the time she was only the second female to accomplish the feat. She'd been damned naive. Truth and justice had been her ideals. Her father had finally come around and at least pretended to be happy for her. He'd wanted her to succeed. He just hadn't wanted it to be in law enforcement. His approval had been her ultimate goal in spite of her fierce independence.

When she'd made the switch from tutus and tights to uniforms and service revolvers, he hadn't been anywhere near ready to see it happen.

My little angel can't be a cop.

A smile tugged at her lips. She'd always been her daddy's little angel. All the Cooper men hereabouts had boys. Adeline was the only girl for three generations. The only Cooper offspring with blond hair and blue eyes, too. Her mother had insisted that Adeline had gotten the blond hair and blue eyes from Great-aunt Joan on her side of the family.

Long before becoming a cop, the frilly dresses and fancy bows her mother had insisted she wear as a child notwithstanding, Adeline had spent a whole hell of a lot of time trying to prove she could do anything the Cooper boys could do. At eight she'd cried her eyes out because all the boys had gotten guns and holsters for Christmas and she'd gotten a damned baby doll.

In school, she had found her way into more than her fair share of scrapes and scuffles, gotten caught smoking behind the boys' locker room. All much, much to her daddy's dismay. To top it off she'd given up her virginity at the ripe old age of seventeen to Wyatt Henderson.

Tall, gorgeous. Captain of the football team. Wyatt had been the hometown hero who always carried the team to victory. She and her little world had worshipped him.

She blinked away the past, allowed her gaze to refocus on the courthouse. *He* was in there. She stared at the first-floor windows, the only ones still lit by more than strung-up holiday lights past the five o'clock hour. Wyatt was waiting for her arrival.

During every minute of those six hours of hard driving she'd played out how this would go down in about five hundred different ways. She would be her usual cocky self. Nine years had passed. They were both adults. She'd had plenty of sex with other men in the intervening time.

She was a cop. He was a cop.

There was an investigation to be dealt with.

What was the big deal?

Yet, she sat here, her palms sweating and her pulse hammering as if it was Saturday night and she was still a sophomore anticipating her first kiss from the senior who just happened to be captain of the football team.

"That's truly screwed up, Cooper." She shoved the cell phone into her coat pocket and grabbed the sealed evidence envelope. The sooner she got this initial awkwardness over, the sooner they could get down to the business of investigating this case. She wasn't here to reminisce.

She climbed out of her Bronco, pushed the door shut with her shoulder. It wasn't even eight o'clock and already the streets of downtown Pascagoula were rolled up for the night. No one could deny the city's Southern charm, with its lovely old antebellum homes and the sea as its lifeblood. Even with industry hovering in the background amid the live oaks laden with Spanish moss, Pascagoula had all the quaint appeal of the fishing villages that dotted the New England coast.

Only this was the Gulf of Mississippi, where the drug trade thrived in that same sea, providing its coastal villages with crucial lifeblood. The trouble wouldn't be seen in the light of day when those who lived and worked in Pascagoula swathed themselves in the city's quiet dignity. The devil's work started after dark, deep in the bayous along those twisting riverbanks. All the dirty little secrets and ugliness of living on the Gulf were played out in the places the sun never reached.

Drugs. Murder.

Most of it transpiring under the direction of Cooper law.

Adeline glanced over her shoulder twice as she crossed the street. Being here was a direct violation of that unwritten law. She might be a Cooper but she wasn't welcome this side of the Alabama line.

She didn't have to wonder if Cyrus Cooper knew she was here. He would know. And he wouldn't be pleased.

That was tough.

It wasn't like she'd come back because she wanted to.

She'd gotten a personal invitation. One she couldn't decline, much less ignore.

The ground-floor door on the west side of the building that led directly into the sheriff's department was unlocked. Usually by this hour it was locked and all but the folks on night duty had gone home. A buzzer allowed anyone with an emergency to make their presence known.

He had left it unlocked.

For her.

The department's cramped lobby was empty. A small Christmas tree in the corner twinkled with colored lights. A few gifts lined the green skirt beneath it, giving the impression that the department operated like one happy little family. And maybe it did...now. But that hadn't been the case a decade ago.

The once gray walls had been painted a pale blue that reminded her of the sky on a clear day. That was one thing she missed about living on the Gulf. The sky was a canvas that the weather spilled nature's most vivid colors onto—far more vivid than any back in Huntsville. The clouds seemed closer to the ground here. As if God had purposely lowered heaven toward the earthly inhabitants along the Gulf. Too bad the influence had done little to keep those inhabitants safe from the scum that flocked here, much less the tragedies like Hurricane Katrina.

Nothing like being back in paradise.

In the corridor beyond the small lobby the first door to the right opened into the office of the sheriff's secretary. Adeline walked straight through the empty office and into the boss's inner sanctum. The large, padded envelope she carried bumped the wreath on his door and she stalled, reached out to right it.

Wyatt looked up from a pile of folders on his desk.

She'd made it to his desk and placed the package there by the time he stood. "Took me a half hour longer than I expected," she said by way of greeting. "Traffic on I-10 through Mobile was hell."

"Addy." He nodded, sized her up a moment. "You...look good."

The pained expression on her face told her that wasn't exactly what he'd intended to say. "You, too, *Sheriff* Henderson." And he did. His coal-black hair was a little shorter. He'd gained a couple more laugh lines around those hazel eyes. Looked a few pounds heavier, not quite as wiry as he had been as a kid. The official uniform was crisp, but then he'd always managed to be able to keep that freshly dressed look all day. She never could.

He gestured to the package. "Let's get this to the conference room—that's where we've set up our command center—and have a look."

"First you gotta sign." She tugged the chain-of-evidence form from the top of the package and placed it on his desk. "I'm officially turning the evidence over to you. Something happens to it, it's on you."

He signed the form, the pen strokes bold and efficient. Then he passed a copy of the form back to her. "Now we're *official*."

"Thank you." She folded her copy and stuffed it into her coat pocket.

"I'll show you the timeline we've set up. Believe it or not, we know how to play by the rules down here, too."

She didn't rise to the bait. Her insistence that he sign the form wasn't a personal jab. It was business. She had a chain of command. One internal affairs investigation this year was more than enough.

He reached for the envelope at the same time she did. Their fingers brushed, eliciting a series of warm pulses along her limbs. The traitorous reaction jacked up the tension already interfering with her ability to focus.

Ultimately she let him take the damned package. He'd signed for it, after all. Mainly she hoped like hell he hadn't heard her breath catch or seen the widening of her eyes when they touched. Stupid and immature. Giving herself grace, she acknowledged that those letters—or coming back here; maybe both—had her more than a little off balance.

She followed him from the room. "You were going to bring me up to speed on where your investigation is," she prompted. That was part of the deal. He'd assured her chief that he would give her a full-on briefing as soon as she arrived. No details withheld.

"We've established a timeline through our interviews. We don't have much," he confessed, then confidently added, "Yet. At this point we have the usual. Interviews with friends and family. I've got three volunteers taking calls around the clock. We've had a couple of hits from folks who saw her in town the day she disappeared. Several hundred volunteers have been combing a five-mile radius around the scene where her vehicle was discovered. About half an hour ago we called off the search for the night."

"Any marital problems?" Adeline had the presence of mind to ask as they moved along the corridor. It felt surreal being here...with *him*...listening to his voice. She was having far more trouble maintaining a professional bearing than she'd anticipated. "Spouse been cleared of suspicion?"

"No marital or family problems. Nothing out of the ordinary at work. Her husband is, of course, still a person of interest, but I don't think he had anything to do with her abduction." Wyatt paused at the conference room door to let her enter before him. "According to her friends, Cherry Prescott has the perfect life."

"Nobody has a perfect life," Adeline muttered. She'd been a cop far too long to believe that was even remotely possible for any human. "You just haven't pushed the right friend hard enough yet."

"I'm interviewing a couple of her closest friends for the third time tomorrow," Wyatt said, his tone on the defensive side. "I'm familiar with the drill."

"Girlfriends?" she guessed. Those were the ones who usually knew the most and held back any secrets the longest. A good, solid female bond was hard to crack.

Wyatt nodded. "I don't have anything conclusive, just a hunch."

Which meant he thought one or more of the friends was holding out on him.

The deputies poring over the material stacked along the conference room table glanced up as she and Wyatt entered the room. Adeline recognized Deputy Rex Womack from before. The female at his side, she didn't.

"Womack," Wyatt announced, "you remember Detective Cooper?"

Womack nodded. "Looks like you went and grew up, little girl." Womack had been on the force since Jesus crossed over from Louisiana and hailed the plot of ground between it and Alabama as Mississippi...or so the story went.

"And you look exactly the same, Rex," she offered with a genuine smile. Rex Womack was one of the few who hadn't completely turned on her nine years ago. He'd been a wary sort of mentor to her despite the fact she was a woman when it wasn't cool to be a woman in uniform in the Jackson County Sheriff's Department. Womack was as thin and wiry as ever. His thick head of hair had surrendered to age, gray claiming what male-pattern baldness hadn't.

"Deputy Charlene Sullenger," Wyatt said as he indicated the female deputy next to Womack, "is new to the department, but damned indispensable."

Charlene fluttered her long lashes. "Thank you, Sheriff." Her goofy smile told Adeline that she had a major crush on her boss—which could be part of why she was so indispensable.

Retract the cat claws, Adeline. It's unbecoming.

"You Tom's little sister?" Adeline asked Sullenger. The girl looked a whole hell of a lot like her brother and that wasn't exactly a bad thing, but it wasn't a compliment, either. The Sullenger nose was her most prominent feature, but the big-ass boobs likely kept anyone male from noticing much else. Strawberry-blond hair and green eyes. Couldn't be over twenty-two or -three.

Just stating the facts.

Charlene cocked her head and eyed Adeline. "I sure am. Tom told me all about you, *Detective.*"

Adeline would just bet that he had. Tom Sullenger belonged to Cyrus Cooper. If he was still in this department, then little had changed in Jackson County, Mississippi.

"Let's see what we've got here," Wyatt said, dragging Adeline's attention back to him. He deposited the padded envelope on the conference table and pulled on a pair of latex gloves.

While he got a look at the evidence and the analysis reports she'd delivered, Adeline studied the timeline that had been created on a long chalkboard-style white board. Prescott's vehicle had been discovered at 5:17 p.m. on Tuesday. Her husband had been contacted two hours later. No purse, no cell phone found in the car.

The next item on the board stopped Adeline cold. The cut-and-paste letter. Why the hell hadn't Wyatt mentioned this?

She was born a princess for all to see. Her light was so bright that they could no longer see me.

"Did she receive this letter by mail or anonymous delivery?" Adeline tapped the letter, which was safely encased in a plastic evidence bag and mounted with double-stick tape to the whiteboard. According to the date and time annotated, Prescott had received her letter three days before Adeline's had been left in her mailbox.

"Anonymously delivered about a week ago, her husband believes." Wyatt joined Adeline at the whiteboard. He posted the evidence, including the Polaroid she'd brought, and logged the appropriate information. "When did you get yours?"

"The first one, about four days ago. The rest came today, as the chief explained on the phone." She opted not to make a fuss that he hadn't told her this before. This was already difficult enough.

Wyatt studied the Polaroid. "Damn." He shook his head. "This makes it hard to hold out hope."

"Definitely lessens the likelihood of finding her alive," Adeline said, giving voice to what she knew he was thinking—what she herself was convinced of. "He wants us to know there's a strong chance she's dead and that there's nothing we can do about it."

"I briefed the family after our conference call."

The desolation in his tone tugged at long-buried emotions Adeline was determined not to feel. Relaying that kind of news was the hardest part of being a cop. "It never gets easier, does it?"

Wyatt shook his head then looked from the Polaroid to her. "You know of any connection whatsoever between you and Prescott?"

"Nope." Adeline studied the family photo that had been posted amid the other evidence. Prescott, her husband, and two kids. Wyatt wanted to keep the idea that the victim was a wife and mother, a daughter, in front of all the cops working the case. "But that's why I'm here. I intend to find out."

"You aren't honestly considering staying for the duration?"

Adeline turned to face him. "Of course I'm staying." When he would have interrupted, she held up both hands and plowed on. "I'm not going any damned where until this is finished. You can exclude me from the investigation, but that won't send me away. I'll work my own investigation. With or without your blessing."

Wyatt glanced at the other deputies, who had stopped their work to listen to her rant. "I think we should have this discussion in my office."

"Doesn't matter where we have it, the result will be the same."

She knew the ploy. He was buying time to regroup. He'd likely planned exactly what he would say if she stuck by her guns on the issue, but he hadn't actually believed she would do it. Now he was having second thoughts about his original game plan. Not only would she be in his way, he would have to answer to Cyrus for allowing her to be a part of the investigation.

Just because this was Wyatt—a man she'd once loved with her entire being—he would not be immune to the old bastard who owned this part of Mississippi.

Once they were back in his office Wyatt closed the door. "When Cyrus's boys find out you're here, the shit will hit the fan. You know this. This case demands all my department's resources. I don't have time to work this investigation and protect you."

Adeline crossed her arms over her chest. "I don't need your protection."

He laughed but the sound held no humor. "When you left, I believe the exodus order from your uncle went something like, set foot in Mississippi again and you're dead."

"That's right," she agreed. "But I'm not afraid of my uncle. I never have been. I haven't stayed away because of Cooper's law. I haven't been back to Mississippi before now because there was nothing to come back for."

Wyatt flinched.

Victory tore through her. She'd nailed him with that

one. "Let's get this straight once and for all," she warned. "I'm here until this is done. Deal with it."

Five, then ten seconds elapsed before the color of outrage faded from his face. He took a deep breath and said, "You'll be staying with your momma?"

"No. I don't want my presence to bring any trouble to her door. I'll stay at the Shady Oaks over on Delmas."

"Not a good idea." He shook his head. "That place is even more of a dive than it used to be. There are other places." He named a couple of the chain motels that had moved into the area since she'd left.

"I won't be spending much time there so it doesn't really matter. A quick shower, a few hours' sleep." She shook her head. "Not a big deal. I'd rather be close to downtown." The Shady Oaks was only a few blocks from the courthouse.

"Does your momma know you're here?"

"I let her know I was coming, if that's what you're asking. She isn't expecting me to stay at the house. The house is on Cooper land. She knows I won't come there."

He shoved the files on his desk into a drawer. "It's been a long day. I'll escort you to the motel and we'll convene at eight tomorrow morning to kick off the search and then we'll go over the case."

"You said you planned to conduct a couple of interviews."

He rounded his desk, reached for his coat. "That's right."

"I'd like to sit in on those."

"I'll consider the request."

Great. He wasn't going to make a single aspect of this easy. "Do you mind if I take the file and read up on the interviews conducted so far?"

"I had a copy made just in case you asked." He went back to his desk and picked up the numerous pages held together by a binder clip.

He'd gone to the trouble to make the copy but hadn't offered to share until she asked.

Perfect.

Outside, the air was cool. But not as cool as back home in Huntsville. The Gulf weather was great in the winter, but in the summer it would be muggy as hell and the mosquitoes would carry your ass off.

Her stomach rumbled, reminding her that she hadn't taken the time to eat today. She would pick something up later. It wasn't like the Shady Oaks Motel had room service, but there was probably someplace close that delivered. She would check once she had a room. No way would she ask Wyatt and have him insist on joining her for a sandwich. If she mentioned food he would feel compelled to do the gentlemanly thing.

Too bad he'd fallen down on the job nine years ago.

If she hadn't been so deep in the past, she might have recognized something was wrong. But she'd been way down memory lane and hadn't gotten her head out of her ass until she was halfway across the street.

Wyatt drew up short first.

Adeline halted as the reality of what her eyes saw was absorbed by her brain.

Her big old four-wheel-drive Bronco was her baby. Thirty-six-inch tires. Six-inch suspension lifts. Roll bar. Bad-ass exhaust pipes. The world knew she was coming well before she turned a corner. She had spared no expense on her baby.

She snapped out of the disbelief and sprinted the rest of the way to where she'd parked. Walked all the way around her vehicle before she could speak. "Son of a bitch!"

All four tires had been slashed.

"Welcome home, Addy," Wyatt muttered.

CHAPTER SIX

4718 Miller Road, 8:45 p.m.

"This is not a good idea."

He'd said that about half a dozen times already. "Just wait in the car, Wyatt." Adeline wasn't going over this again. She reached for the door handle.

"I'm going in with you."

"That's not necessary." The old bastard knew she was coming. He was probably watching out the window at that very moment.

"The hell you say." Wyatt got out.

Adeline rolled her eyes and did the same. She slammed the door of the SUV to show her displeasure.

Cyrus Cooper's place stood about halfway between Moss Point and Pascagoula. The Coopers owned the land for as far as the eye could see. Nothing but woods butting up to the river. Too lazy to farm any of it. Too ornery to develop a single acre. Cyrus's only brother, Adeline's father, had owned the adjoining farm. Her mother had lived there alone since his death ten years ago.

Adeline hadn't set foot on either place in nine years. Had sworn she never would again.

Right now she was too pissed to give one shit what anyone thought of her change of heart.

She climbed the steps to the old plantation-style house that had been in the Cooper family since before the Civil War. Ancient live oaks populated the yard, Spanish moss dangling from the long limbs. Every square foot of the house, inside and out, was meticulously maintained. And yet, with the looming trees and its hurricane shutters closed over the windows, the place could easily be mistaken for something out of a horror flick.

Adeline walked straight up to the door and banged hard.

Wyatt took his time reaching the door. He'd called Cyrus to let him know they were coming. Most likely to prevent being shot by some of his hired guns. Folks knew better than to show up unannounced on Cooper land.

The door opened and a tall, thin man stepped back for Adeline to enter. "Mr. Cyrus is expecting you," he said. "He's waiting in the parlor."

"Thanks." Adeline didn't hesitate. She strode across the entry hall to the double doors leading into the parlor, slid the pocket doors apart and stepped inside. Wyatt didn't permit her to get more than two steps ahead of him.

Cyrus sat next to the sofa, his legs and lap covered with a blanket that couldn't disguise the fact that he was seated in a wheelchair. The wheelchair was new, so was his butler, man Friday—whatever the hell he was. When Adeline had last had words with Cyrus, he'd been quite mobile on crutches. No more apparently. That he had himself a Jeeves spoke volumes about just how incapacitated he was.

Adeline hated to feel glee from anyone's misery but she did just the same.

The fact was this part of Mississippi would have been a better place if the old bastard had died in the car accident that had stolen his ability to walk without assistance thirty-some years ago. Apparently his damaged back had finally given in to mere human frailty.

"You're just as beautiful as your mother said," Cyrus declared. "Your daddy would be proud."

What the hell was he doing talking to her mother?

"I didn't come here to exchange pleasantries, old man." Fury throbbed in Adeline's veins. How dare this old bastard try to talk family shit with her!

Next to her, Wyatt shifted. "Mr. Cooper, Adeline only just arrived in town and already there's been some trouble."

Cyrus stared at Adeline, didn't bother so much as flicking a glance at the sheriff. "I can't imagine you were surprised by that reaction, Addy. You left a bad taste in a lot of folks' mouths nine years ago."

She had hoped he would say something like that. Scarcely able to keep the smirk off her lips, she turned to Wyatt. "We need a minute alone."

He was shaking his head firmly from side to side before she'd finished making the statement. "It's my job to keep the peace in this county. I'm not about to step out of this room and have you two go at it."

"No need to be concerned, Sheriff." Cyrus held up both hands. "I'm unarmed. You may check beneath my blanket if you feel the inclination. Addy is my niece. I'm certainly not afraid of being alone with her."

"One minute," Adeline snapped. That the old bastard referred to her as his niece made her want to kick something. "Just step out into the hall, Wyatt." She lowered her voice to a fierce whisper. "One damned minute, that's all I'm asking for."

Hands on hips, Wyatt held his ground several seconds—just long enough to piss her off even more. Then he turned and walked out of the room.

When the doors had closed, Adeline settled the full weight of nine damned years of fury on Cyrus Cooper. "Now you listen to me, old man. A woman is missing, most likely dead. I'm here to help determine what happened to her and I'm not going anywhere until I know all the facts. So you call off your dogs until this is done and we won't have a problem."

Those squinty eyes held hers. A few years ago he would have gone toe to toe with her even if only by means of the crutches. But no more. The idea that he was so helpless gave her a warm, fuzzy feeling all over again.

The seemingly patient and kind expression he'd worn for the sheriff vanished. A long-simmering bitterness tightened his features. "You're still as full of piss and vinegar as ever, aren't you, girl? Still flaunting that self-righteous attitude your daddy took to his grave."

The comment about her father obliterated the glee she'd momentarily experienced. Hatred charged through her. "Did you hear what I said?" Adeline stepped closer, glared down at him with all the loathing that writhed inside her. "I'm sorry as hell Gage is dead, but I didn't kill him. Your son killed himself by being involved with drug smugglers. So if you're still holding that against me, it's time you got over it."

"You are my baby brother's only child." Cyrus lifted his saggy chin and studied her, the bitterness abruptly replaced by something akin to sentimentality. "He and your mother loved you more than life itself. That's the reason you didn't die when my Gage did. *The only reason.*"

"I didn't die," she countered, "because I was on the right side of the law."

"This thing that happened," Cyrus confessed, the ferocity going out of his voice and his expression with the same abruptness as the bitterness, "was a long time ago." He braced his elbows on the padded metal chair arms and steepled his fingers. "At the time, I asked you to leave Mississippi and never come back. As long as you didn't, I promised not to seek my vengeance for what you did to my son."

Whatever else she said on the subject would be a waste of time and energy. "Do you have a point?"

"My point is," he offered, "things have changed. I no longer have any interest in seeking revenge."

"Then why the hell were my tires slashed?"

"I can't control what others do," Cyrus explained wearily. "There are a lot of folks around here who are still deeply grieved by what you did to Gage and to Sheriff Grider."

"Grider was a piece of shit who sold out his office to help the people your son was working with. People *you* were working with."

"I won't argue about the past with you, Addy. I'm *dying*."

The word rang in the silence that followed.

Why the hell hadn't her mother told her about this? Adeline gritted her teeth against the slim thread of emotion she shouldn't have felt. This bastard didn't deserve her sympathy. "If you're expecting me to say I'm sorry," she offered, "that's not gonna happen."

"I don't expect you to feel remorse for my situation."

That was good, because she sure as hell didn't.

"I have cancer. They say I have eight months tops. Life

looks very different when you're viewing it from this angle."

Whatever. "Are you going to tell your people to leave me be?"

"I'll tell them," Cyrus granted, "but I'm doubtful that it will carry much weight. Since my cancer was diagnosed, Clay does what he pleases with or without my blessing."

Clay, the scumbag, was Gage's younger brother. He was probably the one who vandalized her Bronco. "Maybe you've got everyone else around here believing you're no longer in charge, but I know better. Clay does exactly what you tell him, just as his brother did."

"Things really have changed, Addy." Cyrus held her gaze, probably selfishly searching for some glimmer of the sympathy he claimed he didn't want. "More than you know."

"Did you send me the photo?"

The old bastard frowned. "What photo?"

"Did you cut and paste words onto a page and send it to me?"

He shook his head. The confusion was seemingly genuine. "I have no idea what you're talking about."

"Then that puts you in the same boat as everyone else around here. Nobody knows shit. I'm here to see that the job gets done right since it involves me somehow. So keep your dogs off my back." That was all Adeline had to say.

She headed for the double doors. She'd spent as much time breathing the same air space as this creepy old bastard as she intended to.

"Was Ms. Prescott blond?"

Adeline hesitated. What the hell kind of question was that? "You don't read the paper or watch the news?"

"Not anymore. My vision's too poor since having the chemotherapy treatments. On Sundays Everett reads the paper to me. Keeps me abreast of the important headlines as they appear."

"Then why don't you ask him?"

"I'm asking you."

Adeline turned to face Cyrus. He really did look old and frail. Nothing like the powerful son of a bitch he used to be. She was glad. She hoped he withered up completely before that black heart ceased to beat. "Yes, Cherry Prescott has blond hair." It wasn't lost on her that he asked the question in the past tense. "Why do you ask?"

"Just curious. That's all."

Bullshit. "Stay out of my way, Cyrus, and I'll be out of your territory before you know it."

She glided the doors open, pushing the heavy slabs into their wall pockets. Wyatt stepped aside as she burst into the hall.

He followed her out the front door and down the steps without saying a word. Was he going to do this the whole time she was here? She wanted to turn around and tell him to back off. But she didn't. Instead, she climbed into the SUV and let her fury recede enough to regain her composure.

"Why did he ask you if Prescott was blond?"

"I don't know. Maybe to freak me out. He's an asshole like that."

"I called Tony Laughlin. He'll take care of repairing or replacing your tires." Wyatt glanced at her as he guided his SUV down the long gravel drive. "The county will pay for the damages."

"I have insurance." Adeline pulled her seat belt into place. "You don't need to do me any favors."

He didn't respond for a moment, just drove. Finally he spilled what was on his mind. "So this is the way it's going to be."

What did he expect? "I'm here for the investigation, Wyatt, not to mend fences." She stared out into the darkness. She didn't want to look at him. Didn't want to hear his voice, especially not in the dark. After nine years that shouldn't have bothered her, but it did. It bothered her a lot. The sooner she was at the motel and away from him the happier she would be.

The five miles back into town were driven in total silence. There was nothing else to say. Even now, after all this time, she understood what Wyatt wanted. He wanted forgiveness. For the first year after she'd left, he had tried to make things right. But he didn't understand. There was no way to make what happened right. Nothing he could say or do would change the choice he had made any more than it could the choice she had made.

She didn't belong here. Whatever they'd once shared had died as surely as Gage Cooper had that day nine years, three months, and four days ago.

A final turn off Delmas Avenue and they were at their destination. An antiquated neon sign proclaiming the establishment as the Shady Oaks Motel stood proudly in a seriously neglected lake of cracked and faded asphalt. The rundown row of rooms was dark, but a dim glow beamed from the office window. Hourly rates were written by hand and posted beneath the window. Not exactly a welcoming sight. The Chevy pickup parked in the lot likely belonged to the manager.

Trees, naked for the winter, towered behind the rooms, but there wasn't a shrub or sprig of grass in front. Just the disintegrating asphalt and a narrow band of sidewalk lining the row of equally decrepit rooms.

Definitely worse than she remembered.

"This is a bad idea." Wyatt shoved the gearshift into park and shut off the engine. "Anyone who drives through will see your Bronco in the lot while you're here. It's not like you can miss it."

"I'll be fine." She hopped out, opened the back passenger door and reached for her bag. "You don't need to worry about me. I can take care of myself."

"Like you did nine years ago."

Adeline pushed the SUV door closed and headed for the office. She wasn't going to discuss nine years ago with him. Not tonight. Not ever.

Wyatt didn't drive away until Adeline had gotten her room key and gone inside room number 10. She watched from the window as he pulled out of the parking lot. When his taillights had disappeared, she closed her eyes and let go a weary, disgusted breath.

She was not going to let him get to her.

How the hell could she still be susceptible to him on any level after all this time? It didn't make sense. Nothing about this situation did.

She tossed her bag onto the bed and surveyed her digs. Definitely the lowest of low rent. Same wallpaper with the big gold flowers that had been here when she was a wild and fearless teenager and had partied with friends in this dump. At the time, they hadn't cared. Privacy away from the parents was all they had been looking for. A whole group of friends would rent a room to party. At the time there had been a different manager but he'd had the same attitude—as long as the law didn't show up he didn't care what happened.

The thinning green and blue shag carpet needed a serious shot of Rogaine. She wasn't sure she wanted to see the bathroom. One peek past the door and she confirmed her worst fears.

"There should be a biohazard warning." But for a few nights it would do.

She plopped down on the bed and dug the file Wyatt had given her from her bag. Twenty-six interviews had been conducted with friends, family, and colleagues. Adeline read each one. The shared themes were "no problems" and "loved by everyone who knows her."

Adeline picked up a candid shot of Cherry Prescott with her family. "Someone didn't love you, Cherry. Who was it?" The husband? A lover? What had brought her to the Moss Point area? No one seemed to have a clue why she was down this way.

According to her colleagues, Prescott hadn't been working on a case that might have lured her to the area. No known friends or family lived here.

But there had to be a reason for her visit.

A reason someone wasn't happy about.

The husband and closest friends didn't have a clue why she had received the princess letter. Unlike Adeline, her birthday was months away. No known enemies. Nothing.

Adeline's cell vibrated. She pulled it from her pocket and accepted the call. "Cooper."

"Addy, you were supposed to call me when you got here."

"Hey, Mom. Sorry. I got distracted." The idea that Adeline's baby was sitting in some garage awaiting new tires pissed her off all over again. Telling her mom about the incident was out of the question.

"I hope you're being careful," Irene fussed. "I'm very worried about your being here."

"I'm fine." How many times did she have to say that? "I carry a big-ass gun, Mom. No one's going to mess with me." Not and live through it anyway.

"It's Clay that concerns me."

"I warned Cyrus to keep his offspring off my back."

"You talked to Cyrus?"

There was something in her mother's voice. "Yes, I did." Adeline turned over the inflection she'd heard...fear, maybe? "He told me about the cancer." *And you didn't,* she thought but didn't say.

"You and I never talk about him. In the past when I've brought up anyone or anything around here you didn't want to hear about it."

That was true. Adeline could scarcely blame her for not mentioning Cyrus's health issues.

"If I have time we'll have lunch tomorrow, okay?" The last thing she wanted was her mom fretting over every step she took.

"You could come here," her mother ventured.

Adeline considered the idea for a moment. She hadn't set foot in her childhood home in more than nine years. Staying there was out of the question but dropping by for lunch...maybe. It would make her mom happy. "We'll see," she hedged.

"Please be careful, Addy. Your father...worried so about you being in law enforcement. *I* worry about you."

"I'm always careful, Mom." Not exactly true but her mother did not need to know that.

After another minute or two of awkward conversation, they said good night.

Adeline stared at her phone a long moment after the call ended. She was home. And it felt acutely weird. She'd gone to school a few miles from here. Her father was buried in a cemetery just down the road.

And the man she had loved with her whole heart still lived here. He didn't wear a wedding ring. Hadn't really changed that much.

Adeline pushed up from the bed and walked over to the mirror on the back of the closet door. She hadn't changed, either, not really. Still thin. Her hair was exactly the same. Long. Wild and thick. Drove her nuts most days.

What did *he* see when he looked at her?

The same wild girl who'd loved him so madly?

Or this older, jaded woman who knew him for what he was?

A man fully capable of betrayal.

The man who had betrayed *her*.

CHAPTER SEVEN

11:05 p.m.

She was here.

He'd known she would come. Watching her as often as possible during the past few weeks had confirmed his conclusion. She took her work very seriously. Seriously enough to defy the long-standing threat to her safety.

If ending her life had been his only goal, he could have killed her numerous times before now. While she slept or showered. Even one as vigilant as she let her guard down from time to time. But luring her here was essential to the finale he had planned.

A smile tugged at his lips.

It was fate…just as it had been centuries ago. He closed his eyes and let the death chant whisper through his mind. He'd planned every moment. Not a single step could be skipped. Each step, no matter how small, served a purpose too important to bypass or to ignore.

Especially now. He opened his eyes, his jaw tightening with fury. The police had taken his son. And the bitch who'd ruined everything was still alive. He'd intended to see that she was good and dead as he had the last bitch who'd attempted to destroy him. But his son had still been awake. By the time the boy had gotten to sleep trouble had shown up. The bitch had called 911 behind his back. He'd had no choice but to leave. The unexpected adjustments were a nuisance but he had a plan in place for those, too. It would all come together in the end, just like a finely orchestrated battle.

Until the enemy had been silenced once and for all.

It would finally be finished.

Rage ignited deep inside him, churning and building like an inferno. The past had to be set to rights first before his future could be protected.

Before his son would be protected.

He had been wrong to believe that the past could be ignored...disregarded. The signs had all pointed to this. He had to be strong and fulfill his destiny.

Movement in the window drew his attention back to the woman in the motel room. He sat in the darkness of his car and watched. Occasionally he saw her shadow through the drapes.

Of all the princesses, she would present the greatest challenge.

But he was prepared for that challenge.

He would not fail.

He would not be free—his son would not be safe—until the last princess was silenced forever.

CHAPTER EIGHT

Saturday, December 24, 4:00 a.m.

She held her breath.

Adeline struggled to escape. Flung her arms outward to knock free the restraint keeping her beneath the water.

She couldn't hold her breath much longer! Why didn't somebody help her?

Help!

Her lungs burned.

She couldn't resist any longer. Her lips parted and water rushed into her throat.

Adeline bolted upright.

She gasped. Coughed. Fought to catch her breath.

Her skin was damp...her T-shirt soaked.

She peered through the darkness. Struggled to regain her bearings.

"Damn."

She rested her face in her hands and waited for the calm to replace the fear.

The dream.

Same one she had suffered her whole life. She was under the water. It was too murky to see what was holding her down. Something strong...heavy...sat on her chest, making it impossible to rise up or to get away.

She flung the covers back and got out of bed. Her body shivered as the cool air in the room rushed over her sweaty skin. The digital clock on the table next to the bed mocked her: 4:01. It wouldn't be daylight for another couple of hours. No one she needed to talk to would be out and about yet.

"Dammit." She turned on the bedside lamp, then rummaged through her bag for clothes.

A shower to wash away the lingering funk that held on after those damned dreams would be good. Back when she was a kid she used to climb into bed with her mom to chase away the icky feeling of dying. Later she had...

Stop. She didn't want to think about that.

The bathroom looked just as crappy this morning as it had last night. Maybe worse. Dark spots on the wall behind the toilet warned that something related to a long-term water leak was flourishing. The wallpaper had curled and drooped around the ceiling. But the fixtures looked clean enough. The fake stone linoleum floor had seen way better days.

"Could be worse." She grabbed a white towel that looked and smelled clean and slung it over the shower curtain rod. After adjusting the spray of water, she stripped off her T-shirt and panties, then stepped beneath the welcoming heat and dragged the dingy curtain into place.

Memories of showering with Wyatt barged their way

into her head. She opened her eyes and forced the images away.

"What's the deal here?" She gave herself a mental shake.

For most of the nine years she had been gone from this godforsaken place she'd done a stellar job of not thinking about him. It had been hard at first, but then her career had gained momentum and she'd started to date other men and eventually it had become a lot easier. Adeline had finally succeeded in tucking him into the farthest reaches of gray matter—where he'd obediently stayed. She actually hadn't thought about him in ages.

How could seeing him after all this time make such a totally screwed-up impact on her willpower? Have her reliving the past so vividly?

Maybe it was that whole closure thing.

They hadn't talked since that last day. He'd called and left messages that she had erased without listening to. He'd spoken to her mother and attempted to pass along more urgent messages.

Ignore. Ignore.

How could something that happened a decade ago still matter? At all? "Stupid." She swiped the water from her face. "Just totally stupid."

She rinsed her hair and skin, then shut off the water. What difference did it make if she forgave him or not? They had been over like...forever. She had moved on. If some rogue brain cell was still clinging to the idea of closure, then that cell needed to screw off.

Adeline didn't need closure or anything else from Wyatt Henderson. Well, that wasn't entirely true. She needed him to do his job and to find the facts related to this investigation. And to stay out of her way.

As she dried off she studied her face in the mirror. She

still looked young. Turning thirty last year hadn't been the end of the world. She kind of liked being in her thirties. She felt stronger and more confident. Her twenties had been too full of turmoil and making a new life. As a cop and a woman she'd always felt secure...it was the whole relationship thing where she had fallen below the mark. Some would say her life was pretty damned dysfunctional on a personal level. Her father had died within weeks of her twenty-first birthday. Her mother refused to leave "Cooperville" except for rare visits to Huntsville. No one Adeline had grown up with or gone to school with remembered her fondly.

Why the hell should she care what those people thought of her?

She didn't.

She didn't need this place or these people. Nothing about being back here was going to make her feel uncertain about who she was and what she did. "No way."

She dried her hair, took forever with the worn-out dryer provided by the motel. She wiggled into her panties, said to hell with the bra, then pulled on her jeans, blouse, and sweatshirt. Who needed a bra under all this? She'd never been blessed with big tits. Unlike Deputy Sullenger. The woman's cup size was likely the only reason she'd gotten the job.

There you go again...what's up with the jealousy thing?

Socks, sneakers. Adeline was good to go.

5:12 a.m.

Damn. Still too early to accomplish anything useful.

She strapped on her utility belt, tucked her cell and weapon into place, and grabbed her jacket. There was a pancake house a couple of blocks over on Watts Avenue. She could have coffee and wait for daylight.

Grabbing her creds on the way out, she made sure the door locked and headed across the parking lot.

The town was dead. Like rigor mortis dead.

She could never live here again. Maybe there had been a time when she had fit in, but no more.

She hated the way the refinery and chemical corporation had horned in on the natural way of life here. Pascagoula was about dredging the seas for its bounty while protecting the environment. That simpler way of life had been overtaken by progress and accessibility. The port and various waterways had long ago lured lucrative import/export business to the area, but the accessibility had also brought drug trafficking.

Funny, Hurricane Katrina had devastated many homes and too many businesses to count, though you could scarcely tell it now, but it hadn't done a damned thing to slow down the flow of drugs. Adeline had been keeping tabs on the area since her mother refused to leave. Otherwise she would never have looked back.

The December air was crisp, the pavement damp. She hadn't realized it had rained. Maybe the rain had triggered the dream. Rainstorms in particular had done it in the past.

The one shrink she'd made the mistake of spilling her guts to had insisted her dreams were related to childhood trauma. Adeline hadn't bothered telling him that as childhoods went, hers had been as close to idyllic as was possible. Things had been just great until she'd hit eighteen and she'd learned the truth about what and who her uncle was. Life hadn't been the same since. Unlike her father, she hadn't been able to just pretend it didn't matter and move on with her life.

She'd fought the wrong as if she'd been born to that one crusade.

Problem was, she hadn't been able to fight it alone.

Eight cars were jammed into the small parking lot of the River City Pancake House. Not a chain joint, just a rinky-dink independent mom-and-pop operation that had been in the same spot and run by the same family for about fifty years. A large snowman and smaller snowflake clings adorned the plate-glass window. Colored lights forming the words HAPPY HOLIDAYS flashed and flickered in time with the jolly Christmas music wafting from inside.

The bell jingled over the door as she entered. The waitresses along with the dozen or so patrons stopped chatting and turned to check out the latest arrival.

Adeline walked to the far end of the serving counter to ensure a view of the door and mounted a stool. A good cop never sat with her back to the door. "Coffee," she said to the waitress who lifted an eyebrow in her direction.

The hum of conversation resumed as did the shoveling of grits and bacon into hungry mouths.

Coffeepot in one hand, the waitress strolled over and plopped a stoneware mug on the counter. "You here about the Prescott case?"

Everyone knew everyone in a town this size. A strange face would automatically be connected to the latest gossip or news event. Adeline had been gone plenty long enough for the average citizen to forget what she looked like or that she'd ever even lived here. If she were lucky, it would stay that way until this was done.

"I am." Adeline sipped the warm brew. It had a definite kick but tasted as smooth as any she'd picked up at Starbucks back in Huntsville.

"Anything else I can get you?"

"This'll do it." Adeline glanced at her nametag. "You new around here, Leslie?"

Leslie waved the half-empty coffeepot. "Moved to Pascagoula," she pursed her lips and thought about it a moment, "about three and a half years ago." Then she harrumphed. "Been working right here since day one."

Adeline nodded and savored more of her coffee.

"You working with Sheriff Henderson?" The glint in Leslie's eyes when she asked the question was unmistakable.

Ah. Another fan. "That's right."

"Whatever happened to that lady," Leslie leaned across the counter and spoke for Adeline's ears only, "the sheriff will find her. He never lets the folks around here down. He's a damned fine man."

"Good to know." Adeline wasn't surprised to hear the adoration. Wyatt had always been good at his job. Being a cop defined him. It was on a more personal level where the flaw lay...hidden beneath all that fine Southern-boy charm. A too familiar bitterness churned in her gut.

Don't even go there.

"He comes by here about six for coffee." Leslie straightened and patted her meticulously arranged bundle of platinum curls. "Black coffee and a cheese danish. Every single morning."

Wyatt had always been a cheese danish man. The jingling of the bell over the door drew Adeline's attention there. Even without the weathered leather jacket and the cowboy boots, she would have recognized the man immediately. Tension wired her nerves.

Clayton Cooper. First cousin and first-rate jerk.

He'd been a kid when she left, almost fifteen. Despite his youth at the time, his heartlessness and bullying tendencies had manifested themselves in all that he did. He was expelled from high school twice as a freshman. Got his girlfriend pregnant that same year. A real piece of work.

That he could have been watching Adeline and had followed her here was a strong possibility.

He swaggered across the room, straddled a stool, and propped his arms on the counter. "Morning, Miss Leslie. How 'bout a cup of that outstanding coffee?"

Adeline resisted the urge to gag. Same mousy brown hair and squinty brown eyes as the rest of the male Cooper clan. Exactly like his older brother. All charm when it came to wooing the ladies out of their panties, pure asshole when it came to anything else. She didn't miss the sudden burst of avid murmuring at the tables or the fact that the patrons seated at those tables were not so subtly dividing their attention between her and Clay.

As if she'd called his name, Clay's attention swung to Adeline's end of the counter. "Well, well, if it ain't my dear cousin Addy."

He made the statement dispassionately enough, but there was no mistaking the sheer hatred on his face—not even from this distance.

Adeline gave him a salute with her mug, then finished off the last of the coffee. Leslie hurried to provide a refill. Even she looked nervous. Maybe one of the others had whispered Adeline's identity to her. There was no more efficient means of rapid communication than a small town's grapevine.

"My daddy says you're here about that lady lawyer who's missing," Clay announced, holding the attention of everyone in the place. When a Cooper talked, people listened. They were afraid not to. "I guess that means you're still playing at being a cop."

He was baiting her. She wasn't biting.

"You believe that?" Clay turned around on his stool to

face those seated around the room. "Getting my brother killed and running away wasn't enough to prove she had no business trying to be a cop. Wonder who she's gonna get killed this time?"

Adeline could leave. Just get up and walk out. The courthouse was only a couple short blocks away. Someone would be in the sheriff's office. All she had to do was ring the buzzer and identify herself.

But she wouldn't give this sawed-off little bastard the satisfaction.

"Maybe you were too young to remember," Adeline said, when she should have just let it go, "your brother got himself killed dealing drugs. A DEA agent put a bullet right between his eyes. I witnessed the whole thing."

Fury tightened her cousin's lips. "First off, my brother's association with those people was never proven in a court of law. And," that furious mouth slid into a sneer, "the way I heard it, that bullet missed its mark." He laughed as he turned back to the counter and picked up the mug of coffee Leslie had delivered. "But fate has a way of catching up with those who slip under its radar. No matter how fast they run."

"You think?" Adeline cocked her head and studied him. "I don't know." She shrugged. "That's a nice theory, Clay. But I never put much stock in fate. I prefer to make my own destiny." She didn't bother to pick up on the remark about running. Maybe she had run...but she'd had more reasons than this piece of shit knew about. Her motivation hadn't been his business nine years ago and it wasn't his business now.

"You might want to be careful around here, cuz." The look that passed between them left no mistake as to the intent of his words. "A lot of folks have long memories and they don't like what they remember."

"I appreciate your concern, *cuz.*" She shouldered out of her jacket, let him see the holstered weapon she wore on the belt at her waist. "But just like nine years ago, I'm more than capable of taking care of myself."

The grill sizzled beyond the serving window, underscoring the hush that had fallen over the room. She held the bastard's gaze, dared him to clarify that threat in front of witnesses. Dared him to make even the slightest move of aggression. If he thought he could make her flinch, he was crazier than his half-dead old man.

The bell jingled. Clay broke the stare-off.

"Morning, Sheriff," Leslie enthused.

The murmur of conversation and clink of forks on stoneware resumed as if the past few minutes hadn't happened.

Wyatt chatted with the citizens seated at the tables he passed as he made his way in Adeline's direction. Freshly starched uniform. Matching jacket and cap. There wasn't a female in the place who wasn't drooling.

Beyond him, Clay Cooper slid off his stool, threw down a couple of bills, and walked out. He glanced back once as he stomped away.

Adeline hadn't seen the last of him.

"Morning, Addy." Wyatt settled on the stool next to hers. "You sleep okay?"

He knew she hadn't. It had rained. He would remember that she usually had the dreams when it rained. He'd held her and soothed her to sleep afterward enough times.

"I read the interviews." She wasn't interested in small talk. "Cassie Elliott and Jessica Huff the two you plan to interview again?" Adeline had picked up on the minor discrepancies in their statements.

"You nailed it."

Was that approval she saw in his eyes? Or surprise? She was a good cop. She'd been a good one nine years ago.

Leslie placed a steaming mug of coffee and a fresh cheese danish before her idol. "There you go, Sheriff." She beamed at him. "I warmed up your danish in the microwave. Just the way you like it."

"Thank you, Leslie." He flashed one of those wide, killer smiles that made his hazel eyes twinkle and the female hearts flutter.

"I aim to please." The attentive waitress turned to Adeline with a little less enthusiasm. "Are you sure I can't get you anything else, hon? We have a special on those whole wheat pancakes."

"I'm good. Thanks."

When the awestruck waitress had scurried out of earshot, Adeline turned to Wyatt. "There's one thing we haven't discussed."

His gaze collided with hers. "There are a lot of things we haven't discussed."

That wasn't what she'd meant and he knew it. "About the case."

He cradled his coffee in both hands, stared into the cup as if he would rather look anywhere than at Adeline. "What specifically have we not discussed?"

"The message he wrote on the photo."

" 'One dead princess, two to go,' " Wyatt acknowledged.

Adeline nodded. "Assuming Prescott is the *dead* princess and I'm one of the two to go, that means there's another victim out there."

"Agreed, but there's no way to know who she is. I've worked up a list of the similarities between you and the victim." Wyatt set his mug aside and pulled a notepad from his jacket pocket. Every cop carried one. "Both in your thirties. Blond hair, blue eyes. Same general body type and size. Both born in Mississippi. Prescott's an attorney, you're in law enforcement. And that's where the similarities end. That doesn't give us a lot to go on as far as narrowing down potential victims."

"Then we focus on what we have. Serial offenders typically hunt in familiar territory, which would make him a local or someone who comes through the area fairly often."

Wyatt scratched a note on his pad. "With the movement of goods in and out of our port, we get plenty of repeat visitors."

Yet Adeline just didn't see this as a classic serial offender case. There was no clear strategy to his work. Not yet, anyway. "Why pick me? I live several hours away in a whole other state. I haven't lived in Mississippi in a hell of a long time. It's not like I'm the only blond, thirty-something, female cop between here and Huntsville."

"We have to assume," Wyatt suggested as he cut a piece of danish with his fork, "that there are other similarities between the two of you that we're simply not aware of or that only he sees."

Adeline hated that she watched with such interest as he popped the bite of cheese danish into his mouth. *Focus, dammit!* "I want to know why Prescott was here. Where I grew up. That point has to be significant somehow. I didn't get an invitation to come *here* for no reason. The place is relevant somehow."

"With that in mind," Wyatt said, setting his fork aside, "logic would dictate that the third victim has or will soon receive the same type of invitation."

"She could be here already. A resident of the area. Someone who was drawn here by the news. A reporter or staff member of a newspaper or magazine." Adeline didn't have to ask to know that an influx of reporters and curiosity seekers would be or had been hanging around town. The other so-called princess could have been lured here in some similar manner. If that was the case, the would-be vic had apparently been smart enough to stay at one of the other lodging options. Adeline remained the lone guest at the Shady Oaks Motel.

"We find the connection between you and Prescott," Wyatt reasoned, "and we'll know where to look for the third vic, maybe even for the perp."

"If he doesn't nab her first." *And kill her.* Adeline hoped like hell that Cherry Prescott was still alive, but her instincts were saying otherwise. If Prescott was alive, she wouldn't be for long. Until someone else was reported missing or they heard from the perp, Adeline had no way of knowing if she was next on his agenda.

Whatever the case, there was another victim out there...somewhere.

CHAPTER NINE

8:30 a.m.

Wyatt watched Adeline as she paced the perimeter of what had been the Prescott crime scene. The yellow tape was gone now since multiple sweeps by the forensics techs had revealed nothing in the way of evidence.

It was as if the lady had gotten out of her car and disappeared into thin air.

No signs of a struggle. Her car had been parked on the side of this lonely stretch of road deep in the woods. The one detail that stirred suspicion was the open driver's side door. When she'd gotten out—or was dragged out—of her car, she'd left the door open. That was likely the sole reason one of his deputies had called in the parked vehicle that rainy evening. A car left on the side of the road wasn't necessarily an indication of foul play. With the price of gasoline, drivers attempting to stretch every gallon often ran out. Other times mechanical problems required that the vehicle be left behind for a time. Wyatt suspected that the door had been left open on purpose, to ensure notice was taken well before the vic would otherwise have been reported missing.

There had been no blood inside the car. No indication of foul play whatsoever. The keys were in the ignition and the vehicle had started without hesitation. The tank had been more than half full.

The driver had simply vanished.

Adeline crouched down to inspect something on the ground. She'd scarcely changed at all. Same wild mane of blond hair. Same intense blue eyes and sharp tongue. Still as ornery as ever. Tough as hell in spite of her size. No more than five four and a hundred pounds.

His gut tightened. He knew every inch of her body by heart.

She pushed to her feet. He braced...as if she might have heard his thoughts. She strode farther along the perimeter. A smile haunted the corners of his mouth. Still walked like a man—or tried to. She couldn't really pull it off considering that cute little butt had a sashay entirely of its own.

Adeline stopped abruptly and turned toward him.

Heat rushed up his neck. "Told you there was nothing to see."

She braced her hands on her hips and surveyed the area for about the fifth time. When her attention landed on him, Wyatt felt himself holding his breath.

"I want to see the car."

He shrugged. "Four different techs have been over the vehicle. The last search was conducted with the husband. There's nothing there that shouldn't be. Nothing missing." That was another thing she'd always done. Questioned every damned step taken by anyone involved in an investigation. Never took anyone else's word for anything.

"Indulge me."

He supposed there was no harm in that. He'd gotten the search under way as scheduled this morning. The phones were ringing off their hooks with tips on sightings, most of which, so far, had proved to be cases of mistaken identity.

"No problem," he said at last. "Multi-jurisdictional cooperation is my specialty."

Their gazes held for another moment or two...as if there was more she wanted to say. She broke eye contact and headed for his SUV.

He ordered himself to relax and followed.

There were things he wanted to say to her. Things he wanted her to say to him—or to yell at him. This thing had festered between them for far too long.

About nine years too long.

But now wasn't the time.

A woman was missing.

Whether her abductor was a killer or merely some sick bastard trying to prove a point, he had an agenda and Adeline appeared to be on that agenda.

Wyatt had let her down all those years ago.

He wasn't about to let her down this time.

Pascagoula Sheriff's Department, 11:05 a.m.

Wyatt liked watching Adeline. Maybe a little too much. He

had to hand it to her, she had a way about her when interviewing persons of interest.

Cassie Elliott squirmed in her chair. "Like I told you before, I can't think of anything that was bothering Cherry. She was happy. Really happy. I don't know what else you want me to say."

The woman looked Adeline straight in the eyes as she spoke but all the signs of lying were there. She looked away as she completed her statements. Couldn't appear to get comfortable in her chair. Kept her fingers tightly laced in her lap.

Adeline had walked around the room a couple of times, but the woman's hands never moved from her lap. She was working hard to conceal her outward display of nervousness.

Elliott was thirty-five. Graduated from the same high school as Prescott. Brown hair that she wore short, brown eyes. A little on the chunky side, unlike Prescott who looked quite fit in all her photographs.

Adeline settled in the chair next to Wyatt on the opposite side of the table from Elliott. Adeline had insisted on using the interview room when he hadn't wanted to since these ladies weren't suspects and the whole concept was demeaning on some level. Small-town sheriffing would do that to a guy. Made him forget it was about the investigation not the comfort of the persons of interest. Even if they weren't actually suspects in the investigation.

He suspected Adeline felt relatively certain the ease with which he'd cooperated with her so far was more about trying to make up for the past than about what he believed to be the best decision for proceeding.

Whatever. He just wanted to get through this.

Adeline exhaled a heavy breath. Wyatt remained silent

but kept his attention fixed firmly on Elliott. Another tactic Adeline had requested.

"Look, Ms. Elliott," Adeline began, leading up to something he worried she hadn't run by him first. "We already know what was going on with Ms. Prescott. Her other friend told us just a few minutes ago." The woman's eyes got wider and wider with each word Adeline spoke. "All we want from you at this point is confirmation of certain specific details."

Wyatt held his surprise in check. If this maneuver got the job done...

"I...I don't know what you mean." Elliott looked from Adeline to Wyatt.

Wyatt didn't waver.

"What did Jessica tell you?" Elliott asked.

Though Adeline hadn't mentioned Jessica Huff's name, the two had arrived at the same time for the interview. Deputy Womack had promptly separated the two, but not until after they had seen each other—which was the point, Wyatt realized. Elliott knew Huff was being questioned, as well. No doubt Adeline was wagering the two had gotten their stories straight before coming in this morning. But neither one had likely thought to have a plan B just in case the police attempted to trip them up.

Wyatt could see how this routine would work, particularly with those who'd never been a part of an investigation before.

"I'm afraid I can't discuss her statement with you, but," Adeline said, nodding knowingly, "if we can confirm the details she shared, we might have a chance at cracking this case and finding your friend."

A beat of silence had Wyatt jumping in.

"That's the thing," he said, his voice low, but firm, "I don't think you understand that Cherry's life could be at stake here. What you're withholding could make the difference in whether we find her in time or not."

Cassie Elliott visibly trembled. Her wide-with-worry eyes filled with emotion—the kind that would roll down her cheeks any second. "I don't know what was going on. All I know is that something was wrong. It started about three months ago when her little girl turned four." Elliott licked her lips and tried again to get comfortable in her chair.

"What started?" Adeline pressed. "We'd like to hear your version. The absolute truth is critical."

Elliott's face scrunched with confusion. "Some kind of nightmares. Cherry kept talking about being afraid to take a bath. The water scared her to death. It was bizarre. She reacted so strongly...as if the dreams were real somehow."

Tension visibly claimed Adeline's posture. Wyatt had never forgotten the nightmares she had...especially when it rained.

"Had she been uncomfortable with water events in the past?" Adeline asked. "You know, swimming, skiing, that kind of thing?"

Elliott swung her head side to side. "That's what's so crazy. She was a great swimmer. Good diver, too. It was weird. Like she was going through some kind of crisis. I've never seen anything affect her like this. But she stopped talking to me when I suggested she see someone." She shrugged. "You know, a counselor. It was just so strange. I guess she opened up to Jessica. They've been friends the longest. Makes sense, I suppose."

Adeline stood abruptly. "I...have a...call..." She walked out of the room without a backward glance.

Wyatt stared after her then grappled for what to say to the woman seated on the other side of the table. He finally settled on, "Thank you, Mrs. Elliott, for your cooperation."

CHAPTER TEN

Every muscle in Adeline's body quivered. She walked straight to the ladies' room. Wanted to run but didn't dare. Didn't make it to the toilet. Barfed in the sink.

The dreams Elliott had spoken of had haunted Adeline her entire life...for as long as she could remember. She had forced herself to learn to swim. But she had never been a water sports fan. Every time she drove over a body of water she told herself she wasn't actually afraid of the water...it was the stupid dreams that made her feel uncomfortable.

But that had always been a lie.

She was afraid of the water.

No. Not afraid...terrified.

Adeline rinsed her mouth and the sink then stared at her reflection. What the hell was going on with her?

She washed her hands, leaned down and rinsed her mouth again under the tap, then snatched a couple of paper towels.

"To hell with this." She banished the fear, tossed the wad of damp paper, and stormed back into the corridor.

Wyatt waited for her. "You okay?"

She wasn't talking about it. "Huff in the other interview room?"

"She is. But, Addy—"

Adeline held up a hand to stop him. "Don't."

Wyatt conceded, gestured for her to lead the way. Adeline walked past interview room 1 where Elliott had opened up enough to confirm there was something she and her friend weren't telling, took a breath, and entered room 2.

Jessica Huff looked up, then past Adeline. "Sheriff Henderson, can you please tell me what's going on?" She glanced at her watch. "I really don't have a lot of time today. I've already been waiting here for over an hour."

"This won't take long," Adeline assured her as she took a seat. Wyatt sat down next to her. "Why don't you tell us about Cherry's abrupt fears related to water?"

Huff blinked but not quickly enough to hide the surprise and the first inkling of uncertainty. "I don't know what you're talking about."

Wyatt didn't speak, as promised, just watched the woman.

"Let me explain something to you, Ms. Huff." Adeline leaned back in her chair and folded her arms over her chest. "We know about the problem. The fact that you're concealing information that may have something to do with why Cherry's missing makes you a suspect."

Outright fear replaced the uncertainty. "A suspect?" She looked to Wyatt. "How can I be a suspect? Cherry and I are like sisters. The idea that I would do anything to harm her is ludicrous." Huff lifted her chin in defiance. "I should call my lawyer if what you say is true."

Adeline reached into her pocket and pulled out her cell

phone. "Be my guest." She slid it across the table. "Of course, we were hoping to keep this out of the media."

Huff's eyes rounded with uncertainty. She drew her hand away from the phone as if it were contaminated. "This can't get out. Cherry would..."

"Cherry would what?" Adeline held that worried gaze, let the other woman see that this detective was not happy.

"She would be mortified."

"Ms. Huff," Wyatt spoke up, "if we can deal with this here, get all the facts, then perhaps no one else will need to be involved."

Good move. Adeline resisted the urge to smile. "Otherwise," she countered before the woman could catch her breath, "this could get pretty ugly. You know how the media twists things."

Huff caved. "Okay." She closed her eyes and took a breath. "Cherry will be extremely upset that I told you this, but," she met Adeline's gaze once more, "if it'll help find her, that's all that matters."

Well, yeah. What the hell was wrong with these people? "Why don't you start from the beginning?"

"Three months ago, Chastity, Cherry's daughter, turned four. It was as if some long-slumbering phobia triggered. Cherry started feeling anxious all the time. Having nightmares. She refused to take a bath, something she'd loved doing, with her daughter." Huff flared her hands. "She has this big Jacuzzi tub and she loved running a big bubble bath and playing with Chastity. She called it girl time."

More of that too familiar tension knotted in Adeline's gut. "Did she ever describe the nightmares to you?"

Huff nodded, her expression resigned. "She said she kept dreaming that she was holding Chastity under the water." Tears welled in the woman's eyes. "It terrified her.

She was scared to death...that she was having some sort of breakdown."

"Did she recall any other elements of the nightmares?" Wyatt asked.

Huff shook her head, then stopped. "Not until she got that."

Adeline's breath was trapped in her lungs. "The cut-and-paste letter?" She was careful not to mention the contents, though from Huff's comments in her previous statement she evidently had seen the letter.

"Yes." Huff swiped the tears from her cheeks with meticulously manicured fingers. "She and her husband had called Chastity their little princess since the day she was born. Cherry would go nuts every time Ron, her husband, called her that...*after* the letter came. Ron just figured it was because of the letter."

A frown nagged at Adeline's forehead, ushering forth the distant ache that threatened to turn into a full-fledged skull breaker. "Wasn't it because of the letter?"

Huff shook her head. "It was because of something else she remembered from the dream."

Jesus Christ. Could the woman get to the point any more slowly? "Something else?"

"In the dream," Jessica said hesitantly, "while she was holding her daughter under the water, she would say something like 'no more princesses'."

The full impact of what Huff was saying suddenly hit Adeline's brain. "Her older child is a boy."

"Chad," Huff confirmed. "He's nine."

Those deep spasms started in Adeline's gut once more. "So you believe that Cherry was afraid of hurting her daughter? That she feared the dreams somehow might become a reality?"

"She started doing all this research," Huff explained.

"She was convinced that the dreams were connected to some childhood trauma. But her parents assured her that wasn't the case." Huff leaned forward. "She even started to question whether or not her parents were really her *parents*. Is that ridiculous, or what? I felt so sorry for her. I was literally watching my best friend fall apart."

Adeline fought the tension clamping around her throat. "Did she talk about this to her husband?"

Huff moved her head firmly from side to side. "No one but me. She didn't even tell Cassie. She was afraid she might be going…you know…over the edge."

"What did Cherry do about her concerns?" Adeline felt as if she were poised on a cliff and that the woman's next words might send her plummeting over the edge.

"I don't know."

Shit. "What do you mean, you don't know? You're her best friend. She told you everything. Things she didn't tell her husband."

"She wouldn't talk to me about it." Huff's expression reflected her certainty. "But she was doing something. Every time I called her she was busy. When I couldn't catch her at home, her husband would say that she was tied up with work research."

"But you didn't believe that," Wyatt suggested.

"No. I called her office. She was taking a lot of personal time. Her secretary thought she was going to physical therapy for back pain."

"And you're certain she wasn't." Adeline pushed Huff for clarification.

"If Cherry ever had back pain in her life," Huff confided, "I never heard about it. No, I think she was trying to find answers."

"To the dreams?" Adeline asked.

Huff nodded. "She didn't want anyone to know. Not

even Ron. And that was totally weird. They have a perfect relationship. She never hid things from him. Not in twelve years of marriage."

"You believe she was looking for the childhood trauma that had provoked the dreams?"

"Yes. I think maybe her parents were keeping something from her."

"Are you suggesting that Cherry had seriously considered the idea that Mr. and Mrs. Bowden might not be her biological parents?" Wyatt ventured.

Adeline stared at him. Not because what he asked wasn't perfectly logical—Huff had just said as much—but because that same question had been hovering in the back of Adeline's mind. Only it wasn't about Cherry.

"I can't imagine why she would have actually considered such a thing," Huff argued vehemently. "She looks just like her mother, and they have tons of photos of her as a baby. Cherry and I attended school together from day one of kindergarten. There are no secrets in her family's past. Our families have known each other forever."

Adeline searched Huff's face. Zeroed in on her eyes. "What do *you* think happened to Cherry?"

Huff didn't speak for a long moment, but she didn't break the eye contact with Adeline. "I think she ran away."

Now there was an answer Adeline hadn't been expecting. "Why do you believe that?"

"I saw the fear in her eyes." Huff's tears spilled past her lashes once more. "She was scared to death that she'd hurt her baby. She didn't tell a soul she was coming here. She just up and left and then disappeared. She took her purse and her phone."

"But she didn't withdraw any money from the bank," Wyatt countered. "Neither her credit cards nor her cell phone have been used since her disappearance."

"Cherry kept a petty-cash fund at home. A few hundred dollars. Maybe she took that," Huff offered. "And she has a lot of sorority sisters from law school. Any one of them could be giving her refuge."

"You're certain this has nothing to do with her husband?" Adeline asked.

"It's not about her husband." Huff shook her head. "It always comes to that. When a woman goes missing, everyone suspects the husband. Trust me," she looked from Adeline to Wyatt and back, "her husband is amazing. If he weren't, Cherry would never have left her kids with him."

The woman was telling the truth to the best of her knowledge. Adeline had no doubts about that.

"Please don't tell Ron I said this," Huff went on, "I don't want him to know I kept this from him." A sob tore from her throat. "If I'd thought for a second that any of this might save her from some monster, I would have told you. I swear. But I don't think there's a monster involved here. I believe it's the nightmares."

"You don't believe Cherry was abducted?" Wyatt asked for clarification purposes.

Huff shook her head, her lips trembling. "I don't. I'm convinced that Cherry is running from this," she flared her hands as if she didn't know how to explain, "thing that's happening to her." She took a deep, fortifying breath. "She won't come back until she's sure it's safe for her daughter. I can guarantee that."

CHAPTER ELEVEN

Prescott Home
Hattiesburg, 3:50 p.m.

Charles Ronald Prescott was home with his children. His mother-in-law had sequestered her grandchildren in the family room and was reading to them so as not to expose them to any police talk regarding their mother. The husband had closed down his dental office the day after his wife disappeared. Four times per day, like clockwork, he checked in with the Hattiesburg police as well as with Wyatt.

Wyatt hoped like hell he wouldn't have to end up delivering the news that his wife's body had been found.

Addy had introduced herself and interviewed Ron. Thankfully with a good deal more finesse than she'd used with Huff and Elliott. Wyatt had kept his comments to a minimum as she requested. As if he hadn't gone over these same details with her already, she first explored the master bedroom, closets, drawers, and then inventoried the home office, family computer, files—everything—along with the husband. She'd asked about the petty-cash fund Huff mentioned. The money was in his wife's lingerie chest, tucked into a sock.

Adeline would find exactly what Wyatt and his team had found.

Nothing.

But that knowledge hadn't kept her from touching the things Cherry Prescott had touched. Her clothes. Jewelry...the pillow where she'd laid her head at night.

Wyatt's desire to watch every move she made warred with his frustration. He wanted to be annoyed that she thought she had to go over every step he'd already taken. But watching her do so was nearly worth the irritation it generated for him as a cop. Truth was, she had gotten more from the victim's friends than he had. What she'd learned could change the scope of the investigation—except for those damned letters, the same letters that had been sent to Adeline.

And the nightmares.

"The folks from the state forensics lab took the home computer," Ron explained, repeating what Wyatt had already told her. "They've checked her cell phone records. All electronic communication devices here and at her office. No calls to or from anyone she didn't know. No e-mails. No Internet searches of interest. Nothing."

The husband had followed their every step from one room to the next. Not that Wyatt blamed him. The man's wife was missing.

"Mr. Prescott." Adeline picked up the framed family photo positioned on the corner of the desk in the couple's home office. "Did your wife mention being afraid of anything at all during the final weeks before the disappearance?"

Ron shook his head. "Nothing." He collapsed in a chair by the bay window. "I mean, I sensed that she was anxious about something but she insisted it was only next year's elections. As the city attorney, she was subject to stress during any change in the administration."

Adeline returned the photo to its original position. "Any trouble interacting with you or the children?"

Wyatt watched the husband's reaction to the seemingly off-the-cuff question. Surprise. Confusion. Both cluttered his face before the veil of sheer grief he'd worn for four days now fell back into place.

"Absolutely not."

"Mr. Prescott," Adeline nudged, her tone gentled, "you need to be aware that we've gotten conflicting reports from some of your wife's friends which suggest there was, in fact, a problem of some sort."

Uncertainty claimed the man's expression. "Well, maybe a little. Nothing really." He lifted his shoulders ever so slightly in a beaten-down shrug. "She seemed nervous about bath time with Chastity. She told me the last time she bathed her, the baby had slipped and fallen beneath the water and it scared her to death. But that's completely understandable." He shook his head, irritation needling its way into his expression. "I can't imagine why anyone thought that was a big deal. Do you have children, Detective?"

Adeline shook her head. "No, sir. But I can see where that sort of incident would unnerve the best parent."

"Exactly. You worry yourself sick that you'll make a mistake and you try your best. Sometimes your child gets hurt anyway. Cherry is a wonderful mother."

"I'm sure she is," Adeline agreed. "Your home tells me

a lot about both of you. Caring and loving. Don't mistake my questions for doubt in that area."

Ron looked around. "Right now it's a pretty sad place to be. I don't know how much longer I can keep the kids away from the news." His voice quavered. "Or keep explaining away their mother's absence. I've been afraid to send Chad to school since...she disappeared."

"Understandable," Adeline sympathized. She walked over and sat down in the chair next to his. "Again, my questions are not a lead-in to any sort of accusation. You have to appreciate that we're looking at even the most remote possibilities in an attempt to get a handle on why anyone would have taken your wife. Of course, her kidnapping could be a random act of violence, but we have to rule out all the possibilities to find the motive behind this crime. Finding your wife is dependent upon every step we take, no matter how painful or seemingly insignificant."

"You have no idea how badly I wish there was something I could tell you," Ron offered, surrendering to the defeat once more. "I want my wife found, alive and unharmed. But I just don't know why this has happened. There were no warning signs...no unusual events. Nothing. Just that weird letter."

"How was the relationship between your wife and her parents?" Adeline asked, venturing into sensitive territory. "Did you sense any tension between them?"

"I can answer that question, Detective."

Wyatt turned toward the voice. Patricia Bowden stood in the doorway.

"I'm sorry, ma'am," Adeline offered, pushing to her feet, "I didn't want to disturb you and the children."

Ms. Bowden walked into the office and closed the door. "My granddaughter is napping. Her brother is occupied with a computer game of some sort." Mrs. Bowden went to her son-in-law and stood behind him. Her hands settled reassuringly on his shoulders. "My daughter and I are close, Detective Cooper. Very close. Her husband is correct, something was bothering Cherry but she didn't want to talk about it. She chalked it up to work whenever I asked. I cannot believe that if something was going on with my daughter on a personal level, she wouldn't have come to me about it. She always has."

"Ms. Bowden," Wyatt interjected. He hated to stir up emotions, but this had to be asked. "Why didn't you mention this during your previous interviews?" He split his attention between the two. "There's nothing in either of your statements to indicate you felt there was a problem."

Ron dropped his head, stared at his hands. "We talked about it." He lifted his gaze back to Wyatt's. "Patricia, Howard, and I. We were terrified that if the police thought Cherry was having some sort of midlife crisis or issues with motherhood, you wouldn't treat the case as seriously. Please understand," he said, looking from Wyatt to Adeline and back, "we're desperate. We weren't trying to hide anything or lie to you...we're just desperate."

Sadly, this was exactly the sort of miscommunication that stalled far too many investigations. Not to mention that it sent the cops looking in the wrong direction way too often. Wyatt stifled the frustration. This family was, as the husband said, desperate.

"I'd like all three of you to revise your statements," Wyatt urged, trying not to let his impatience show, "we need every detail, no matter how seemingly insignificant. And you have my word that we will continue to work hard, no matter the circumstances, to find Cherry."

"Any additional information," Adeline put in, "could make all the difference. The slightest detail could be the one that makes or breaks the case."

Prescott nodded. "You have my word, Detective. All we want is Cherry back home safe and sound."

Adeline stood as if she'd heard all she needed to hear. Wyatt wasn't quite finished, but before he could ask the question related to Huff's revelations that nagged at him, Adeline spoke up again. "One last question, Ms. Bowden." Cherry's mother stared expectantly at Adeline.

"Is Cherry your biological child?"

Prescott appeared completely stunned by the question. His mother-in-law, on the other hand, looked downright offended.

"Why on earth would you ask such a thing?" Patricia Bowden dabbed at her eyes, her hand shaking. "This is exactly the sort of thing we're trying to protect Cherry from. If the press were to get wind of such a ridiculous suggestion..."

"Ms. Bowden," Wyatt prompted, "we're not trying to make this any more difficult than it already is. But," he pressed, "we do need you to answer the question."

"Cherry is my daughter," Bowden stated firmly, anger clearly having overtaken the weaker emotions. "In every way. I have her birth records as well as family photos if you need proof."

Adeline studied Bowden long enough to make even Wyatt feel uncomfortable. "That may not be necessary, ma'am. We'll see where this goes. If the need arises, we'll pay you a visit at home."

The tension in the room followed them out the door. Wyatt couldn't shake the guilt that settled on his shoulders. He hated what these kinds of investigations did to the families.

Outside, Adeline suggested, "Let's check the public library."

"If Prescott was looking for something in her past and

didn't want anyone at home or at the office to know," he said, following her reasoning, "she might use the Internet at a public place, like the library."

"That's what people do," Adeline said as they reached his SUV, "when they have something to hide."

CHAPTER TWELVE

Hattiesburg Public Library, 4:50 p.m.

"You're sure she was always alone," Adeline pressed. The librarian on duty was a little reluctant to talk about Cherry Prescott at first, but eventually opened up.

"Yes, ma'am," the young woman said with a pointed look. "She came during her lunch hour several times. Never checked out any books, just used the computers." She nodded toward the rear of the library. "Right over there. Station one. She always used station one."

"Do you recall the last time she was here?"

"The same day she," the woman glanced around, "disappeared," she whispered. "I remember because I couldn't believe it. I'd just seen her at lunchtime. When I watched the news the next morning, I was shocked."

The answer to the next question was essential. "Do you know how often your servers are updated?"

"Every Thursday night."

Damn it. "Thank you, Ms. Vincent." Adeline pulled a business card from her pocket. "I'd like you to call me if you remember anything else. Anything at all."

Vincent nodded.

Adeline headed for the front entrance. Damn it. Damn it. That would make finding what Cherry Prescott had been researching a hell of a lot more difficult.

Wyatt caught up with her on the front steps. "I can check with the state lab. They have a cyber division. It would take a warrant, but I don't think that'll be a problem."

That could take days. They didn't have days.

Adeline climbed into the passenger seat. "You should do another press conference." She had watched footage of his previous two press conferences. He hadn't mentioned the princess letters in either.

He started the engine and looked over his shoulder before backing out of the parking slot. "We don't have anything new to report to the public. What would be the point?"

Adeline grabbed hold of her patience with both hands. Why wasn't he on the same page with her about this? "There's another victim out there, Wyatt." She turned to stare at his profile. As she did his jaw hardened, a sharply defined muscle starting to tic. "Two to go, remember?"

He apparently took a moment to get a grip on his patience, as well. "I agree that there is possibly another victim. However, we have no known *relevant* connections between you and Prescott. What am I supposed to say? If you have blond hair and you're in your thirties call us if you've gotten a cut-and-paste letter about a princess?"

"What's wrong with that?" Adeline didn't see the problem. That was what they had. Why not make it public knowledge and see what kind of reaction they got?

She turned her attention to the street, inventoried the numerous Christmas displays, and marveled at the idea that it was Christmas Eve and she hadn't thought about that fact once today. "Besides, there is a connection between me and Prescott."

He glanced at her. Didn't say the words, but he knew. She hadn't missed the look he'd shot her when Huff admitted that Prescott was having *water* nightmares. As much as she hated to say the words, she reminded him, "The nightmares she started having related to her daughter is a definite connection."

"So you're saying," he said, while making the turn that would put them on 1-98, "that you believe there's some sort of past traumatic event involving water that connects you to Prescott?"

"That's what I'm saying." It was bizarre, no question. Maybe even a little irrational. But it was the only significant lead they had.

"Prescott grew up in Hattiesburg," he said like she didn't know. "She spent six years at Ole Miss. You said yourself you'd never, to your knowledge, met her. Are we talking about a psychic connection? Because that's sure as hell what it sounds like."

Now he was just trying to piss her off. "You know damned well I'm not talking that shit." Jesus Christ. "I could talk to my mom. Maybe we knew the family somehow when I was a kid." Frustration caught up with her. "How the hell should I know? There's a connection, Wyatt. We just have to find it. Meanwhile someone else out there has or is about to get a letter. If we don't do something she's going to disappear the same way Prescott did."

"You didn't."

Adeline took a deep breath and counted to ten. He was

right. Damn it. "Yet," she reminded, "the piece of shit who took Prescott could be watching me at this very moment."

"I have a more realistic scenario."

Adeline dropped her head against the seat. "Spell it out for me, *Sheriff*."

He sent her a fierce glare. She didn't have to look to know that it wasn't pleasant.

"You were a cop here for more than a year. Maybe this has something to do with someone you pissed off during that time, someone who Prescott just happened to piss off as well in her capacity as an aspiring attorney. This could be about revenge for some perceived wrong from the past."

"Clearly." Of course revenge was what it amounted to. "I can go along with the part about me pissing someone off. Take your pick of the residents in Jackson County, particularly if their last name happens to be Cooper. But Prescott would have been a student at Ole Miss at the time. Seems a stretch that we both pissed off the same guy."

"But not impossible. Womack is working on that theory. He's cross-checking anyone you arrested or hassled against the students registered at Ole Miss at the time. If he comes up with a list of names related to your work, and he will, we can then check to see if anyone on that list had a class with Prescott or might have known her."

Adeline had to admit that she hadn't even considered that line of thinking. "I'm impressed, Wyatt. I guess you are taking this connection seriously."

His jaw turned to stone once more. She'd hit a nerve.

"Cherry Prescott may very well be dead. That would make this case a homicide." Fury simmered in his tone. "But whether she's dead or just missing, I take every case seriously. I don't appreciate the implication, Cooper."

Cooper. Yeah, he was pissed. "Seriously enough to go to the press and let them get the word out?"

The silence thickened for ten full seconds before he responded. "Let's give it twenty-four more hours. If my people can't come up with a tie that connects you and Prescott to a possible suspect, then we'll go to the press."

Before she agreed to his offer, Adeline needed to know one thing. "Why the reluctance? The media can be your friend." Occasionally, she didn't add.

Another of those long silences. "I promised the family that I wouldn't let this investigation turn into a circus. Prescott is a public figure. The family has received dozens of crank calls since her disappearance made the news. It's painful, Addy. It makes an already bad situation almost unbearable."

He would know. Nine years ago, when he'd let her down, the press had had a field day with it.

FRATERNIZATION ON THE FORCE LEADS TO INCOMPETENCE

INTERNAL AFFAIRS INVESTIGATION REVEALS GRUDGE

Wyatt Henderson hadn't had any trouble talking back then.

She didn't have any trouble doing it now.

"When we get back to Pascagoula," she said, keeping her attention on the passing landscape, "just drop me at the motel. My Bronco should be there by now."

"It's Christmas Eve, Addy."

What the hell did that have to do with anything? "So it is." She would call her mom. Maybe join her for dinner somewhere in town. No big deal. Holidays weren't really her thing. Maybe that made her a bad daughter, but a cop's work didn't revolve around the federally recognized dates on a calendar.

"My family always has dinner on Christmas Eve night. I thought you might want to join us."

He had to be kidding. "I don't think your family would appreciate an unexpected last-minute guest, particularly one named Adeline Cooper."

"You know better than that." He glanced at her. She refused to meet his eyes. "My family adores you."

"You family adored me nearly a decade ago, Wyatt." She did turn to him then. "Before the shit hit the fan. Lines were drawn, in case you've forgotten. Sides were taken. There weren't too many folks who took mine."

The hollow roar of the tires on asphalt filled the lapse in conversation for a minute or more. What she had said was the truth. He couldn't deny it. Couldn't change it.

And she did not want to talk about it.

Now or ever.

"I'm not taking no for an answer on this, Addy. I'll pick you up at ten before eight," he announced. "If your mother would like to join us, we'll pick her up, too." When she started to argue, he cut her off. "You're in my jurisdiction now, *Detective*, and that's an order."

The chief had made her promise to show respect. She wasn't so sure that included family dinners. But, what the hell? It was Christmas.

CHAPTER THIRTEEN

Forrest General Hospital,
Hattiesburg, Christmas Eve, 6:00 p.m.

Danny sat in a chair in the corner of his mom's room. It scared him to look at her. She couldn't open her eyes and she couldn't talk to him. The machines around her bed made funny noises.

This whole place smelled funny.

He wanted to go home.

Where was his daddy? Danny was worried about him.

His grandma and grandpa stood by his mom's bed talking to her. She didn't answer. Danny didn't understand why they kept talking. It was kinda dumb. It made his chest hurt when his grandma cried.

It wasn't supposed to be sad at Christmas. His mom wouldn't like everyone being sad. He wished his mom would wake up so they could go home and find the presents she had hidden. Every time Danny asked to go home his grandma would cry. So he didn't ask anymore. If he asked when his dad was coming to get him, his grandpa told him not to talk about his dad.

This was the worst Christmas ever.

Danny stared at the people passing in the long white corridor outside his mom's room. Bunches of people. Not many kids, though. Lots of nurses and doctors. And people who looked sad like his grandma.

Nobody paid any attention to Danny. Kids were supposed to be at home getting ready for Christmas tonight. He wondered if other moms told their kids stories the way his mom did. He sure wished she could tell him a story now. He smiled, tried to remember what her voice sounded like. The way she smiled and tapped him on the nose with her finger when she told him a story.

The policeman who had been sitting in a chair outside his mom's room when Danny got here had smiled and asked what Santa was bringing him for Christmas. Danny told him the truth, he didn't know. That made Danny start to wonder what would happen after he went to sleep tonight. Would Santa really know that Danny wasn't at home? Would his presents get dropped off at his grandparents' house?

He didn't want Santa to forget his presents.

Maybe Santa would take them to Danny's house whether he was there or not.

Danny wished the policeman would come back from getting coffee. Maybe he could tell Danny what Santa would do. He didn't want to bother his grandma or grandpa right now. They were real upset over something the doctor said. Danny didn't understand what a hematoma was. The doctor had said his mom might need surgery.

It must be bad 'cause his grandma was crying again. It made Danny's stomach hurt even more.

A man stopped outside the open door. Danny couldn't see anything but his back. His head was shiny. He didn't have any hair. Probably a doctor since he wore one of those white coats and had one of those funny little hats in his hand. Danny wondered if Santa stopped at hospitals. If he did, he sure wouldn't be wearing that kind of hat.

Danny wanted to go home. He wished his mom would wake up and tell his grandparents to take him home right now. If she woke up, maybe she could go, too.

The bald man in the white coat outside the door turned around. Danny looked up at him and the man winked.

It took another wink but then a smile stretched across Danny's face. *Daddy!* He had known his daddy would come! He started to jump out of his chair, but his daddy shook his head and put a finger to his lips.

Danny didn't move or say a word. Even tonight Santa would know if he didn't obey his parents. Especially his daddy. He always did exactly what his dad told him to do.

His daddy pointed to his eyes, then his chest, and then at Danny.

I love you.

Danny nodded. He pointed to his eyes, then his chest, and then his daddy.

I love you, too.

His daddy put his thumb and finger to his mouth and traced them across his lips. He had told Danny over and over that it was very important to remember what that meant so nobody would find out their secrets. Danny hadn't forgotten.

Don't tell.

CHAPTER FOURTEEN

Wiggins, Mississippi, 6:50 p.m.

Penny Arnold parked in the driveway and just sat.

Exhaustion clawed at her. She couldn't remember ever being this tired.

Through the arched window adorning the front wall of her living room she could see her sweet boys on the couch. Her husband would be hidden away in their bedroom frantically wrapping the last of the Christmas presents. A job that was to have been Penny's.

He was angry with her.

And rightly so.

She'd been gone four whole days and three nights.

It was past six o'clock on Christmas Eve and she was only just now getting home.

Once the kids were in bed the arguing would start in earnest. She didn't have the energy to fight tonight. But her husband wouldn't let that stop him.

Her work took up too much of her time. Every argument began with that theme.

What kind of mother allowed her boss to send her to a real estate conference so close to Christmas?

The truth was Penny had volunteered to cover the Phoenix conference. Even more damning, the conference had ended yesterday. Penny had chosen to stay an extra night and day to get in a few career-boosting brownie points with the conference leader.

And to avoid *this*.

She closed her eyes and exhaled a heavy breath. Her husband didn't understand her need to succeed as a Realtor. Why wasn't selling a house now and then enough for her? he would demand. Getting her own agency shouldn't be her goal. She had two boys in elementary school. A husband who worked hard and made a sufficient living. Why couldn't she be satisfied with her life?

He didn't understand that she wanted to succeed in her own right. Why was that such a difficult concept to grasp? Penny didn't want to be like her mother or her younger sister, both of whom relied solely on their husbands.

Penny wanted her financial independence.

She wanted to be her own boss.

It wasn't that she didn't trust her husband to provide for the family—he would throw that in her face, too. Certainly it wasn't that she didn't love him and her children. But what in the world was wrong with being successful in addition to being a mother and a wife?

Nothing. There was absolutely nothing wrong with what she wanted. This was the twenty-first century. These days, more women worked than stayed home.

Most families needed dual incomes to survive.

No use putting it off any longer.

Dread welling to a fever pitch, Penny opened the car door and got out. She reached back in for her briefcase and purse, then closed the door. Her luggage would have to wait.

The dread she felt at walking into her own home heaped more guilt onto her already burdened shoulders. Why couldn't she just be glad to be home and go inside and enjoy a joyous welcome home?

Because she knew what was coming.

"Just get it over with, Penny." She trudged up the walk, then climbed the four steps.

At the front door she hesitated. An envelope had been tucked into the storm door. She pulled it free, read the name printed on the front. *Penny Arnold.*

Not handwritten, she realized. The letters spelling her name had been cut from printed material then pasted onto the envelope.

The dread and guilt morphed into fear. Her pulse started to race. Her hand shook.

Penny dropped her briefcase on the porch and quickly tore open the envelope. She removed the sheet of white paper and unfolded it. Her heart thumped harder and harder with each movement. A piece of folded up newspaper slipped out, fluttered down to her feet.

She told herself to bend down and pick it up but the words on the page held her frozen.

Pretty, pretty princess. See her smile...see her die.

This was...like the last one, only the message was different. Who would send such a statement? Why to her? She'd thought the last creepy letter was some kind of sick joke someone had misaddressed. Or the nasty work of her cutthroat competition. That bitch who owned the Property Shop didn't think Wiggins was big enough for yet another real estate agency. Penny wouldn't put this sort of thing past her.

What did this mean?

Grappling for composure, Penny bent down and picked up the newspaper clipping. She unfolded it and read the headline that had been highlighted.

CHERRY PRESCOTT STILL MISSING

The blood hurtling through her veins turned to ice. Penny couldn't read the words fast enough...a voice in her head kept screaming. *No! No! This can't be real!*

The Prescott woman had come to Penny's office. Penny had been too busy getting ready for Phoenix to deal with the ridiculous story the woman had been insisting she believed to be the truth. The encounter had been unnerving. Particularly when Prescott had thrown all those questions at Penny—none of which had made any kind of sense.

Did Penny have dreams about drowning? Did she have a daughter? Had anyone ever called Penny or her daughter a princess?

Penny had been certain the woman was nuts. Not only did she not have a daughter, she hadn't ever been called anything even remotely close to princess.

...until now.

She blinked. Read the headline again. Now Prescott was missing.

Her attention turned to the bizarre letter once more.

What was this all about?

The door suddenly opened. "Mom!" her youngest shouted. "Mom's home!"

Penny dropped to her knees and hugged her precious children. The guilt surged once more, diminishing the other emotions. It was Christmas Eve, she didn't have time to deal with this now. She shoved the envelope and its contents into the purse hanging at her side. Monday she would look into the Prescott thing. Maybe even talk to the police. If Prescott's disappearance had anything to do with Penny someone would have called or...something.

A couple more days wouldn't hurt.

It was Christmas after all.

CHAPTER FIFTEEN

4720 Miller Road, Pascagoula, 8:15 p.m.

Irene sat on the sofa, the family photo albums spread on the coffee table in front of her. Addy was disappointed Irene had begged off the invitation to the Henderson dinner. But Irene just couldn't face Wyatt Henderson tonight.

The Prescott woman was still missing.

How could Irene possibly look the sheriff himself in the eye, particularly if the subject came up? And it would come up. Everyone was still talking about it. The newspaper printed something about the ongoing case every day.

She had to change the channel each time an update appeared on the news. It was just too painful. All the local channels were avidly following the investigation.

Knowing that woman could be hurt or dead tore at Irene's heart. She prayed a dozen times a day for Cherry Prescott's safe return.

If this was her fault.

Irene closed her eyes, fought the tears. Please, please, don't let this be because of what she had done.

Dabbing at her eyes, Irene opened the oldest of the photo albums. A smile spread across her trembling lips. Addy had been such a beautiful baby.

The pictures of Carl holding her were some of Irene's favorites. Her husband had been afraid to hold the baby at first. Addy had looked so small in his big hands. From day one she had been a daddy's girl.

Irene's heart ached. She wished Carl were here now. He would know what to do.

Don't you worry none, Irene, it's all going to be fine.

How she wished she could hear him say those words tonight.

These last ten years without him had been so very difficult. Many times she had considered doing exactly as Addy wanted and moving to Huntsville. Living near her daughter would be so much better than staying here in this lonely old house.

But *he* would never stand for it.

Irene couldn't go.

She was a prisoner.

That was what happened when a woman allowed herself to make deals with the devil.

She sentenced herself to hell.

CHAPTER SIXTEEN

712 Canal Street, 9:30 p.m.

Wyatt couldn't take his eyes off Adeline. She'd worn her usual, jeans and a tee. Didn't matter to her that everyone else wore their Sunday-go-to-meeting clothes, including him. Addy was Addy and she didn't change who she was for anyone.

Right now, she was deep in conversation with his mom and sisters-in-law while they cleaned up the kitchen. He'd offered to help but his mother had insisted that no men were allowed in her kitchen. Watching from his position in the living room where the men were lamenting the latest political scuttlebutt and drinking spiced cider, he smiled as Adeline gestured magnanimously. She never had been able to talk without her hands.

The Christmas music playing in the background prevented him from overhearing the women's conversation. But that didn't really matter; watching her was entertainment enough. More so than what she wore, her hair had held him mesmerized since he'd picked her up at that shabby motel. She'd worn it down and his fingers had itched all evening to tangle into that long mass and just get lost.

God, how he'd missed her. He'd tried not to. Especially after that first year. For nine long years he had focused on his work to prevent obsessing about her. He'd been successful, for the most part. He'd dated. Even had a six-month relationship a couple years ago. But he just hadn't been able to make himself feel for anyone else what he had—no—what he still felt for Adeline Cooper.

His brothers and father had urged him to move on. To get her out of his system. His mom was the only one who'd understood how he felt. She glanced at him now and smiled. He knew what she was thinking, but Wyatt was relatively certain that getting her hopes up was a bad idea. A really bad idea for all concerned.

Adeline…Addy—he'd called her Addy back then, he might as well now. She refused to talk about the past. As a cop, she was still the same in many ways. Like when he'd taken her to the impound yard to see Prescott's car. She'd climbed in and sat behind the wheel—just sat there—for long enough to have the staff whispering among themselves. But that was Addy. She liked to get the feel of a case firsthand. Liked to touch the things the victim had last touched.

In the beginning of her career, the other deputies had made fun of her seemingly bizarre need to feel the evidence and the scene. Wyatt had exchanged heated words with more than one of his colleagues when Addy hadn't been looking. He would have done anything to protect her.

Then he'd let her down in the worst way. But it had been the only way to save her.

"So." His older brother clapped him on the back. "Addy defied her uncle and came back here to work this case. Interesting."

Wyatt shot him a look. Jason had questioned Addy during dinner. How were things in Huntsville? Was she engaged or married? Divorced? Any kids? What were her thoughts on the Prescott case? His older brother might not be a cop but that didn't stop him from utilizing less than polite interrogation tactics.

"I think you've asked enough questions for tonight," Wyatt commented, a clear warning in his tone. "This isn't your boardroom."

Jason shook his head, probably the same way he did when he was about to chastise his top executives at Chem Corp. "It's been nearly a decade, buddy. And you're still obviously hung up on her. What're you going to do when she leaves again? You going to follow her this time? Go rushing after her wherever she runs?"

Wyatt went nose to nose with his brother. "I don't want to hear your—"

Thomas, the youngest, pushed the two apart. "This is not the time." He glanced toward the kitchen. "It's Christmas Eve, for Christ's sake. Can't you two stop the bickering for one night?"

The Henderson patriarch joined the huddle. "Listen to your brother, gentlemen." He looked from Jason to Wyatt. "This has gone on too long as it is." His gaze settled on Jason. "Wyatt has enough on his mind right now without you getting into his personal business."

"Yes, sir," Jason acquiesced. He bopped Wyatt on the shoulder with the side of his fist. "I should learn to keep my mouth shut where certain subjects," he sent a look at the women in the kitchen, "are concerned. I just worry about you, that's all. You know I do."

Wyatt released his frustrations on a big breath. "I guess that's what big brothers are for." A pain in the ass.

Thomas lifted his mug of spiced cider. "To family," he offered.

"Hear, hear," his father agreed, clinking his mug against his youngest son's.

Jason and Wyatt did the same.

It was Christmas Eve. And for the first time in a very long time, he was spending it with Addy.

What're you going to do when she leaves again?

His brother's admonition echoed inside Wyatt.

Wyatt would simply do what he'd been doing for nine years.

Miss her.

10:37 p.m.

"Jason doesn't like me very much, does he?"

Wyatt slowed for the turn into the Shady Oaks parking lot. "What makes you say that?" He damned sure wasn't going to volunteer any information. But Addy was no fool. She'd sensed Jason's disdain.

A good kick in the ass was what his older brother needed. This—*Addy*—was none of his business.

"Oh, I don't know." She reached under the seat for her weapon, then for the door as he parked in front of her room. "Maybe it was the way he glared at me for most of the evening. Or the heated looks he sent your way every time you said a word to me."

Damn it. She'd noticed more than he'd suspected. "Jason's just—"

Addy climbed out before he could finish the statement. Wyatt shut off the engine and caught up with her at the door to her room.

"You know how older brothers are," Wyatt commented, playing off the whole notion as if it were no big deal.

She shoved the key into the lock, then looked at him. "No. Actually I don't."

Addy didn't have any brothers of her own, but she had male cousins. "You know what I mean."

"I know what I felt." She twisted the key, then the knob. "G'night, Wyatt."

"We should talk, Addy." This was enough with dancing all around the past.

She sighed. "You keep saying that but," she shook her head, "there's nothing to talk about. It's been a long time." Addy looked at him then, really looked. "There's nothing to say. Too much water has gone under the bridge. It's all irrelevant at this point."

"Addy, wait." He nabbed her by the arm before she could go inside. "There are things that need to be said, no matter how much water has gone under the bridge. And it damned sure isn't irrelevant."

"Fine." She turned her face up to his. "Then say what you have to say. If that's what it takes to put this behind us, just get it over with so we can focus on the case."

He wasn't sure saying the words would ever be enough for him. "I was wrong." His chest cramped. "What I did was wrong. I've had a long time to consider what I should have done. And I should have backed you up."

"Yeah." She nodded. "That's what you should've done.

But you didn't. Okay." She reached for the door again. "I'm glad we had this little talk."

He didn't let go, pulled her back around and manacled her other arm to keep her from jerking out of his hold. "So you're never going to forgive me?" The feel of her hair draped over his hands almost undid him. He wanted to release her and thread his fingers through that sexy mane.

"I'm done talking, Wyatt." She flattened her palms against his chest and gave him a push to get him out of her personal space. He didn't budge.

"Maybe I don't deserve your forgiveness," he went on, fury pulsing through him. "But I don't want you to think I haven't paid a price."

"Oh, gee, that's too bad." She tried to shake off his hold. "I hate to think you've suffered all this time. Let's see." Her lips pinched in fury. "My own family threatened to kill me if I didn't leave. Only because my boss, the damned sheriff, had plotted to have me killed and it didn't work out. I had to move away from everything I'd ever known." Fury blazed in those blue eyes. "Oh, and let's not forget how the man I loved kept his mouth shut when he knew the truth. I think maybe I paid a little more than you, wouldn't you say?"

Her lips trembled and he lost any hold whatsoever on his sanity. His mouth covered hers. It was a mistake, he knew. But he had to kiss her. She fought him at first, but then she gave in and kissed him back. So many times he'd dreamed of kissing her again. Had awakened with his heart pounding after dreaming of touching her.

His fingers released her arms, plunged into her hair the way he'd longed to do all night. He cradled her head, kept her mouth fixed firmly against his when she tried to pull away. Then her body relaxed and she surrendered to the kiss. No more thinking. He reached out with one hand and opened the door. They stumbled into the room. He kicked the door shut behind him.

Her fingers were fumbling with the buttons of his shirt. He carried her to the bed. They fell onto the mattress together.

"What the hell?"

He froze. "What?"

She lifted a handful of garments. "What's this?"

The light on the bedside table was dim, but there was sufficient illumination for him to see that the garments she held were ragged—no, torn or cut.

Wyatt pushed up onto his hands, stared at the jumble on the bedspread beneath and around her. Her clothes, jeans, T-shirts, underthings, were scattered over the bed. Not just scattered...ripped apart and then scattered.

Addy scooted away from him and off the bed. She reached down, picked up a bra. The straps had been torn off. The cups were shredded. "What is this shit?"

Wyatt backed off the bed. "Don't touch anything else," he warned. "I'll be right back."

He raced out to his SUV and dug through the console for a couple pairs of latex gloves. Closing the door with his hip, he put in a call to Rich Baggett. He'd gone to school with Rich. Trusted him. He was the best forensics tech in this part of the state.

Addy waited for Wyatt at the door. He thrust a pair of gloves at her. "You called a tech?" she asked.

Wyatt nodded, then followed her back inside. "Rich Baggett, you remember him?"

"Yeah." She turned back to her room. "He still one of the good guys?"

Anger lit deep in Wyatt's gut, obliterating the other lingering heat. "Yeah, he's one of many good guys in my department." How did he get it through her head that things weren't the way they used to be?

Cyrus Cooper didn't run Wyatt's department or him.

She picked through her damaged clothes, held up a Bon Jovi tee. "Damn. This was my favorite." She dropped it back onto the bed. "I got it at his last concert in Nashville."

Wyatt checked the lock on the door for evidence of forced entry. Maybe if he lingered long enough Rich would arrive and provide a much needed buffer. Right now, Wyatt just needed an excuse not to have to look at her.

They'd almost had sex.

What the hell had he been thinking?

Focus, dumbass. The lock. Of course there was evidence of forced entry. Lots of it. There likely wasn't a single room at the Shady Oaks that hadn't been broken into at least once. For someone with the know-how it wouldn't be that difficult. A damned credit card would no doubt do the trick.

"Shit. The Def Leppard shirt got it, too." She stared down at the scraps of fabric on the bed.

Wyatt dared to step away from the door he'd been examining. "I guess your taste in music hasn't changed." Seemed a safe enough topic until Rich arrived.

Yeah, right. Wyatt gave himself another mental shake. He was pretty sure he'd lost his damned mind.

"Lot of things about me have changed." She stood back from the bed and considered the room a moment. Then she looked him up and down. "I'm not that girl anymore, Wyatt. I'm a woman. Maybe you didn't notice." Then she headed for the bathroom.

There was no way to verbalize his response to that. Oh, yeah, he'd noticed...every damned thing about her.

"Well, well." She jerked her head for him to come to the bathroom door. "Check this out."

Adrenaline sent a second charge into his veins. He stopped in the doorway. Fury chased the adrenaline through his bloodstream. This wasn't just a random act of vandalism by some jerk from the past.

The bastard every member of law enforcement in three counties was looking for had been in her room.

Glued to the mirror was another cut-and-paste note.

Are you ready to die, princess?

"That's it," Wyatt snapped. "You're not staying here another minute."

She glared at him for three beats before turning her attention back to the mirror. "If he'd wanted to kill me, he would have paid me a visit while I was actually in the room. Clearly, murder wasn't on his schedule for tonight."

Wyatt's frustration meter topped out. "You are the most hardheaded woman—"

A knock sounded at the door before he could finish sticking his foot completely in his mouth. He turned away from the woman driving him absolutely crazy and strode across the room. He opened the door for his colleague. "Thanks for coming so quickly, Rich."

"Not a problem." Rich Baggett, his bag of tricks in hand, leaned his head toward one shoulder to see past Wyatt. "That can't be Adeline Cooper."

"Hey, Rich." She swaggered up to him and thrust out her gloved hand. "Long time, no see."

"You ain't kidding." He bypassed her hand and gave her a hug.

Wyatt grabbed their jackets from the floor. *Shit.* He hoped like hell Rich hadn't noticed.

"Somebody doesn't like my taste in clothes." She gestured to the bed.

Rich blew out a long, low whistle. "Looks that way."

"I doubt it'll do any good," Wyatt cut in, "but you can check the relevant areas of the room for prints." It would probably be a waste of time, but maybe they'd get lucky.

"Gotcha." He set his bag on the floor and knelt down to get the tools he would need for the job.

"There's also a message on the bathroom mirror," Wyatt told him. "I'm particularly interested in whether or not the glue used is the same as what was used on the princess letters Prescott and Adeline have already received."

"Whether it is or not," Addy piped up, "this is not the work of the same guy who sent the letters."

Her claim took Wyatt aback. "We can't be sure until—"

"I'm sure." She turned and headed back to the bathroom.

Wyatt followed, trying his level best not to stare at her sweet ass.

"Take a look at how the words are lined up." She drew a line in the air beneath the message. "Perfectly straight. Exactly the same distance apart. The letters, mine as well as Prescott's, were not so meticulously arranged. The words weren't so perfectly straight, a little upward tilt on the right as if the perp had trouble maintaining a straight line." She shrugged. "Hands weren't steady enough or maybe a vision problem." She pointed to the spacing between the words then. "These words are spaced precisely, like the guy took a ruler. Not so with the letters from our perp."

Wyatt considered the validity of her points. "Could be that having them on the mirror right in front of his face enabled him to be more accurate with the spacing and the lining up of the words." If the glue was the same, damn it, then it had to be!

Maybe. Damn it!

"That's possible," she admitted. "But why tear up my clothes? It's not consistent with his actions related to Prescott's abduction."

"Not that we're aware of," he countered. Addy was in way too much of a hurry to dismiss this situation. Bottom line, he didn't care who had come into her room. She wasn't safe here, especially not alone.

"Does management maintain video surveillance here?" she asked.

Wyatt laughed. "No surveillance, and if the manager's asked if he saw anyone hanging around, the answer will be no. But we'll ask, just the same."

Addy folded her arms over her chest and eyed the message on the mirror. "Next time I'll have a surprise waiting for this bastard."

"There won't be a next time," Wyatt informed her in no uncertain terms. "You're not staying here another night. No negotiations."

She turned to face him in the cramped bathroom. "I thought we'd gotten past that. You don't own me, Wyatt, so stop acting like you do. I can take care of myself."

Enough. "We don't have a single clue as to this perp's identity," he reminded her. "No fingerprints. Nothing. We're forced to wait for him to act and to hope that this time he'll make a mistake and leave us something."

"It's not the first case like this you've had to deal with," she countered. "Probably won't be the last. Sometimes it's just the way it goes."

"You are the one link we have to him." That was the part she was glossing over. "I'm not about to let anything happen to our one shot at getting this guy." That didn't come out the way he'd intended but he got the point across. The subtle shift from cocky to mildly uncertain in her expression was telling.

"You're saying this is business," she said warily, "not personal."

"That's right." A muscle in his jaw throbbed irritatingly. There was no reason for her to know any differently. "Strictly *official* business."

She laughed. "Good. I thought maybe you just wanted to finish what we'd started." She squeezed between him and the sink but stopped shy of the door. "Because that's not going to happen."

CHAPTER SEVENTEEN

Wiggins, Mississippi
Christmas Day, 7:00 a.m.

She was here.

The corners of his lips tugged into a smile. He'd been concerned she wouldn't come.

Good little real estate agent. She didn't want to miss out on a sale. It might look bad on her record. Especially since she had such lofty aspirations. So what if it was Christmas? The kids could wait.

That was just like a princess. Thought of no one but herself. *Bitch.*

Penny Arnold parked her car in the newly poured drive of the recently completed home in the highest-end development on her list of properties.

She'd worked so hard to get the builder to take her on. He had listened to one of her lunch meetings with the man. She hadn't suspected for a moment that the quiet gentleman at the next table was there, not for lunch, but to learn what she was up to. To confirm his conclusions.

Poor Penny had practically begged for the opportunity.

She had assured the developer that she understood that there were others in the community with far more experience and considerably more clout, but no one would work harder than her. She would be available twenty-four/seven. Princess Penny had gotten the contract.

Good for her.

Too bad she wouldn't need it.

Not after today.

Merry Christmas, princess.

CHAPTER EIGHTEEN

1708 Monroe Street, Pascagoula, 8:30 a.m.

Wyatt had bought a house.

Adeline shouldn't be surprised. She'd bought one, too. But it just felt *weird*.

He was even cooking breakfast.

He never cooked. They'd lived on take-out and frozen entrees. The only home-cooked meals they'd gotten were the ones her mom or his had prepared.

Adeline still didn't cook. Had no desire to learn the culinary arts.

Hell no.

At some point today she had to check in with her chief. He was a man of his word. If she wasn't back in forty-eight hours—or had a damned good excuse—he would send Metcalf and Wallace down here to collect her.

Adeline straightened the covers on the guest bed she'd

slept in last night. She'd been pretty pissed at Wyatt when he'd pushed the issue of her ending her stay at the Shady Oaks. There were plenty of other accommodations around town, but he'd insisted on bringing her home with him. Wasn't going to let her out of his sight, he'd proclaimed.

She fluffed the pillows. 'Course she could have simply said no. But she hadn't.

That made her a bigger fool than even she had known.

She looked across the room, studied her reflection in the mirror. A hot shower last night and one of Wyatt's shirts had kept her from going naked while her clothes were being laundered. He had a washer and dryer, too.

Freaky.

She wiggled into her clean jeans and tugged on her T-shirt. Plopping down on the bed, she grabbed her creds case from the bedside table and shoved it into her back pocket. After making quick work of her socks and sneakers, she bounded for the door. Between the smell of freshly brewed coffee and whatever he was cooking, she was ready to hit the kitchen.

Just after midnight last night Baggett had called in the results of the analysis he'd performed. The glue used to attach the words to the mirror was the same as on the letters she'd received.

But it wasn't the same guy. Adeline was certain.

Mulling over the possibilities, including her asshole cousin, she wandered to the kitchen door and leaned against it. His back turned to her position, Wyatt stirred the scrambled eggs. A plate covered with steaming biscuits obviously straight from the oven sat on the table. Smelled yummy.

But not nearly as yummy as watching her host for a minute without his knowledge. It would be a nice change.

He was usually too aware of his surroundings to be sneaked up on like this. Why not enjoy the anomaly?

Her mouth watered. The delicious smells would make anyone's senses stand up and pay attention.

Wyatt had forgone his uniform this morning. Just a plain white tee and faded jeans. She cocked her head to see past the table. Barefoot, too. A grin slid across her lips. He had really nice feet for a man.

And long, heavily muscled legs. She wondered if he still ran those four miles every morning. She had kept up her personal routine. The past couple of mornings were the first ones she'd missed in months. Not since all those twenty-four-hour days on the Nash/Abbott investigation.

Wyatt had maintained that lean waist. Her gaze trailed up his back to those broad shoulders.

Her body heated just thinking about that tumble onto the bed at the motel last night.

Sex with Wyatt had always been great.

Maybe that was why she'd allowed herself to get carried away.

She'd been primed and ready, no denying that.

In the end, the perp had done her a favor. Kept her from allowing Wyatt back inside her. It had taken several years for her to adequately evict him the last time. Last night would have undone a lot of hard work.

And pain.

She couldn't let herself forget the pain just because she was standing here looking at his fine backside. Which was a dumb idea.

"Morning."

He glanced over his shoulder as she pushed away from the wall. "Morning. You find everything you need?" He turned back to the stove and scraped the eggs onto a plate.

"Yep." Her skin smelled like him. Earthy, like leather and herbs. She loved his soap.

"Hungry?"

"Yep." The smell of freshly brewed coffee overwhelmed the other scrumptious scents. "Coffee ready?"

"Yep," he said, repeating her responses.

She strolled to the counter where the coffeepot stood next to the sink. A rumble of pleasure sounded in her throat as she filled the empty mug he'd set out for her. Caffeine would hit the spot. One quick sip of the steaming brew and her taste buds exploded with the just-ground flavor.

"When did you start grinding your own coffee beans?" God, it was good. She downed another swallow. Too fast. Burned her tongue.

"That's the only way to get really fresh coffee." He shot her a knowing look. "I hear folks in Huntsville think fresh coffee only comes from Starbucks."

"That's where I get mine." He'd already set the table. Adeline pulled out a chair and took a seat. "But," she lifted her mug in a salute, "I have to say this is every bit as good as what I pay the big bucks for."

He settled the eggs on the table next to the biscuits. "It was either figure out how to do this or starve after I bought my own place." He passed her a napkin. "OJ?"

"No, thanks." Careful not to touch those long fingers, she accepted the napkin. "You sticking by your promise to keep what happened last night off the record?"

The surprise in his eyes told her he'd misunderstood. He blinked it away. "Rich is the only one who knows. We'll keep it that way for now."

"Good." If any of his deputies were involved, she wanted them to wonder why there hadn't been a reaction. A reaction from whoever hacked up her clothes was exactly what she wanted. She bit her lip to prevent a little smile at the idea that Wyatt had at first thought she meant the *other* thing that happened last night.

She had to hand it to him. He was still the best kisser she'd had the pleasure of locking lips with. Considering the number of men she'd dated in the last eight or so years, that was saying something.

Wyatt pulled out a chair and lowered that tall frame of his into it. "Merry Christmas, Addy."

She blinked away the unexpected reaction to the way he said her name. He'd said her name plenty of times since she got here. Why the sudden burst of shivery heat?

Do not let him get to you like this.

"It is Christmas, isn't it?" A few more swigs of coffee kept her from having to linger on the subject.

"Dig in." He gestured to the goods he'd gone to the trouble of preparing.

That she could do. After scooping a heaping pile of eggs onto her plate, she grabbed a biscuit. It was still hot. He scooted the tub of margarine in her direction, obviously recalling that she liked to slather her bread in fat even if—she glanced at the brand of margarine—it came from vegetables.

The eggs were cooked just long enough, still moist and soft. The biscuits. Dear God, the flavor burst in her mouth. She ate. Ate every damned speck from her plate.

"More?" He'd cleaned his plate, as well.

Adeline leaned back in her chair and rubbed her tummy. "Couldn't hold another bite."

He had that look. The one that said he was going to open a can of worms, and she wasn't interested in fishing. Adeline sat up. Stuffing her face had permitted her to avoid conversation, but that was over.

"I'll clean up." She stood, sending her chair scooting across the wood floor.

"We need to talk about last night."

Oh no they did not. "What's to talk about?"

He brought his plate and fork to the sink. "There's still something between us, Addy. No point denying it. Last night was undeniable evidence."

She finished rinsing her plate and elbowed him out of the way so she could put it in the dishwasher. Wyatt had a dishwasher. Jesus. What else? Then she straightened and faced him. "It's called hormones, Wyatt. You're a man, I'm a woman. We got carried away. It only means that there was chemistry brewing."

She grabbed his plate, rinsed it, and tucked it into the sleek dishwasher. The forks went next.

"If not for the perp having vandalized your wardrobe we would have had sex," he said as he braced one lean hip against the counter.

She shrugged. "We're both adults. So what?"

He smiled, but there was no amusement in the expression. "Let's not play this game, Addy." He moved his head slowly from side to side. "We both know last night was about more than raging hormones."

"You're right." She walked around him and grabbed the skillet from the stove. "Some asshole broke into my motel room and ruined my shit." Reaching for the pot scrubber and dish detergent, she flashed him a smile—one just as fake as the one he'd shown her. "I'm pissed."

"Not just some asshole," he corrected. "Baggett said the glue was a match. The wording, not to mention the method of communication, was too similar. We haven't released any information related to the letters. This can't be a copycat. This was *him.*"

She wasn't going to waste her breath reminding him

that just because they hadn't released the information didn't mean it hadn't gotten out. Happened all the time.

"This guy is watching you."

"Probably." She scrubbed out of the skillet. This was the bad part of scrambling eggs in something nonstick. The cleanup.

"Then why don't you believe he was the one who came into your room?"

A quick rinse and she placed the skillet in the drainer, then dried her hands. "Because it wasn't him. I explained that last night."

Wyatt dropped his head back and blasted out a frustrated breath. "And I explained how those differences may have occurred organically."

"Organically?" Mirth furrowed her brow. "Really? I tell you what, let's put the letters Prescott and I received alongside the mirror," which was now logged in to evidence, "take a long, hard look at them lined up together." She moved back to the table and pushed in her chair. "My logic will be more obvious that way."

"You going to call your mother?"

"Sure. It's Christmas." What kind of daughter did he think she was? A bad one, evidently. She knew that about herself but she didn't need him reminding her. "We're doing lunch." She backed toward the kitchen door. "All the more reason to get a move on. Let me grab my jacket and I'll be ready when you are."

She hustled to the guest room, strapped on her belt, and nestled her weapon in place on her hip. She gathered her jacket and cell phone. The sooner she was out of this house the more comfortable she would feel.

Catching a glimpse of herself in the mirror, she made a face. Damn, she needed a rubber band or something for her hair. Bathroom. Though she couldn't imagine why

Wyatt would have a ponytail holder of any sort, it couldn't hurt to look. Maybe there was something usable in there.

She checked the hall bathroom. Didn't find anything. Next she banged on his bedroom door. "I need to get into your bathroom."

He opened the door. "What's wrong with—"

She squeezed past him. "I'll be ready in half a minute." Since it was Christmas or maybe because it was Saturday, he'd kept the jeans and added a dark green shirt. The color would bring out the green in his eyes. It wasn't necessary to look, she knew his eyes as well as she did her own.

Nothing in the two drawers. She crouched down in front of the vanity and opened the doors.

"What are you looking for?"

She glanced up. "Something for my hair." She shoved a handful of the wild stuff behind her ear.

He loitered in the doorway, wedging those massive shoulders from jamb to jamb. "I don't think—"

"Here we go." She held up a ponytail holder. Black in color. *Hmm.* "You have a girlfriend with black hair?"

Frustration lined his brow. "I don't have a girlfriend."

"Really?" Adeline held up a neatly folded pad in its flowery wrapper. "When did you start using these?"

Their gazes held for a few drama-filled seconds. The kind where you're scrambling to come up with what to say or do next. The reality of what her feminine finds meant had abruptly sunk into her brain.

It felt intensely strange. He had a girlfriend. She'd had plenty of guy friends. Sex whenever she wanted. No real relationships but plenty of repeat dates. Nine years had passed. Of course Wyatt had been with other women. Maybe even moved one into his place—which was exactly what this felt like. What had she expected?

Adeline blinked first, looked away. She tossed the unused pad back into the vanity and stood. "This'll work fine." She slid the holder onto her wrist, fingered her hair into an acceptable bunch and tugged the stretchy holder into place. She checked her work in the mirror. Ignored the fact that Wyatt was watching her in that very mirror.

She turned to the door and the tall frame blocking her path. "I'm ready. You?" He looked ready. All the way down to the boots.

"Her name was Rita. She works in the courthouse."

He swallowed. Adeline's gaze followed the tense movement.

"You don't need to tell me this." She took a breath. Did not want to hear about his sexual escapades. "Let's just go."

He continued to stand there, staring at her. The building tension seemed to push all the oxygen out of the room. She'd been right about his eyes. They looked greener with the shirt. Somehow that fact prevented her from breathing at will.

"I don't want to…" He shook his head, his mouth a firm line, those eyes full of regret or sadness. "I can't just pretend the past didn't happen. Maybe you—"

Music drowned out his words.

His cell phone.

She relaxed marginally, grateful for the reprieve.

He pulled his phone from the holder on his belt. Read the screen. Frowned, then answered the call. "Henderson."

Adeline managed to suck in a lungful of scarce air.

Wyatt listened another moment or two. "I'll be right there."

He ended the call, the look in his eyes giving her the details before he said a word.

She guessed, "The second princess has been taken." Her gut clenched.

"Real estate agent over in Wiggins." He slid the phone back into its holder. "She got a call early this morning, went to meet a client."

"On Christmas?" Adeline thought she was the only female who made that sort of socially unacceptable sacrifice.

He nodded. "She promised to be back within the hour. When she wasn't back, her husband started calling her cell. She didn't answer so he loaded the kids up and drove to the property she'd gone to show. He was pretty pissed since it's Christmas."

"He found her car," Adeline guessed.

"No sign of her or the cell or her purse."

"Any message?" Adrenaline was pumping through her veins, shocking her heart into a frantic rhythm.

"On the windshield of the car. The message instructed whoever found it to call my office. Dispatch just got the call."

"Come on." Adeline pushed him away from the doorway. "We'll take the Bronco."

He argued all the way out of the house. She ignored him, hurried down the drive, past his SUV, to where she'd parked her Bronco.

She stalled.

An envelope was tucked beneath a wiper blade. She was at the vehicle and climbing onto the running board before he caught up with her.

"Don't touch it, Addy!"

She froze. He was right. She took a breath. Ordered her hands to steady.

Wyatt poked around in his SUV then walked over with a pair of latex gloves.

She tugged on the protective wear and reached for the envelope. She hopped down, opened the unsealed envelope. A single sheet of white paper...like the others. She unfolded the paper and stared at the words pasted on the page.

Merry Christmas, princess. You're next.

CHAPTER NINETEEN

Wiggins, 12:05 p.m.

Wyatt asked one of the officers at the scene to escort the husband back home to his children. An aunt had picked the boys up a couple of hours ago.

Penny Arnold's husband was still in shock. He'd answered every single question without hesitation and yet neither his expression nor his tone had altered in the slightest. Not even once. The man was terrified that he'd lost the woman he loved forever.

Wyatt's attention swung to where Addy sat in Penny Arnold's car. The lab boys were ready to take the vehicle away as soon as Addy had finished doing her thing.

If anything happened to her...

All these years the only good part about her being gone was that he knew she was safely out of reach of the danger here. That band of uncertainty that had been wrapped around Wyatt's chest since the moment he heard her voice during that call with Huntsville's police chief tightened a little more. She'd been here two days and already the idea of losing her forever—again—was gnawing at him.

You're next.

Having her go back to Huntsville when this was over was one thing, but having some bastard do this—he surveyed the crime-scene tape draping the area—he couldn't let that happen. Somehow he had to protect her.

Who the hell was this son of a bitch? Unless they came up with something from Arnold's friends or coworkers, there wasn't a single connection between her and Prescott.

After five days of looking for Cherry Prescott they still had nothing. Now, the same steps would be taken for Penny Arnold. Wyatt had assured the Wiggins chief of police as well as the Stone County sheriff that his department would assist in the search. He'd called in six of his deputies already.

Wyatt scrubbed a hand over his face. The fear in Trent Arnold's eyes haunted him. Why the hell couldn't they get a single lead on this bastard?

The perp had left not one tire-tread imprint or shoe impression, much less a latent print. No trace evidence. The only certainty so far was undeniable proof that the perp was one careful asshole. The words cut from printed material had come from a dozen different magazines and newspapers that could be picked up on any sales rack. The glue was one available for purchase at all Walmarts and dozens of other places. Same with the paper and the envelopes. The phone call made to Penny Arnold's cell was their one hope. But Wyatt wasn't holding his breath. This guy had proven far too cunning so far. The probability that he would screw up with something as simple as a phone call was highly unlikely. The search of the Hattiesburg's Library's computer server had given them nothing.

"One of the deputies has already interviewed a couple of Arnold's close friends," Addy announced.

Wyatt jerked to attention. He hadn't realized she had gotten out of the vic's car and walked over to him. "Anything relevant?"

Addy glanced back at the car as if something about it nagged at her. "Maybe." She met Wyatt's gaze. "Do you have any idea how focused the vic was on making the dream of owning her own agency come true?"

"The husband mentioned that was her goal." Wyatt surveyed the upscale housing development. The model home Arnold had come to show was the first completed construction at the site. "She considered getting this contract a major coup."

Addy chewed on her bottom lip. She did that when she was mulling over what she intended to say next. Wyatt's throat went dry. His lips burned at the memory of kissing her.

"She has notes posted on every day of the calendar she keeps in her car." Addy flared her hands. "You know, the inspirational stuff. *No one can stop you but you. There is no time like the present. Persistence is the key*. The husband didn't want her working so much outside the home." Her gaze searched Wyatt's. "But she wasn't stopping for him or anyone else. I found out that conference she went to in Phoenix actually ended the day before she came home. But she stayed an extra day despite the fact that it was Christmas Eve and her kids were back home waiting for her."

"You think it was all work or was something else going on? An affair maybe?"

Addy gave her head a quick shake. "No, I don't think there was anything like that happening. The lady was just determined to make the right impression on the people with the power to authorize the opening of her own agency. According to her husband and her friends, she wanted that bad."

"You have no doubt the letter found at this scene is the work of the same man who sent yours and Prescott's letters?" She was still insistent that the break-in at the motel was unrelated. He wasn't a fool. He understood that it was possible someone in his department had leaked the information, but it hadn't been reported in the media. One generally went hand in hand with the other.

"None at all. The random spacing and cockeyed alignment of the words are consistent with the note I received this morning and the one found on Arnold's car."

"You do realize," Wyatt voiced what they both already knew, "that the only persons who would want to vandalize your possessions are those connected to your uncle? That greatly narrows the scope of who may have leaked the information." All the way down to his department, in fact. He didn't want to believe that possibility was real, but it was his job to follow all leads, even when he didn't like where they were going.

"I do." She kept those baby blues fixed on him. "It came from your department, Wyatt. Face it. There are still a lot of people here who have a grudge against me. Passing on the info to Clay or some of his thug friends would be the perfect way to get a little vengeance."

Wyatt wanted to be madder than hell at the whole notion. But he couldn't. She had too valid a point. No one, including him, wanted a dirty cop on his force. "If I learn that's the case, I'll be collecting badges."

Addy turned away from him and headed for the Bronco. He fully understood that she wanted no part in the collection of badges. She'd been there, done that, bought the T-shirt. She was here for the case. Not to rehash the past. How many times had she said that?

She climbed into that big old Bronco and settled behind the wheel. She'd had that damned thing since she turned sixteen. Her father had bought it for her. He figured that was why she'd kept it all this time—especially considering the price of gasoline. When that monster-sized vehicle rolled up to a parking slot, no one expected a waif-like blond chick like Addy to climb out. As pint-sized as she was, she could hold her own in a shoot-out or a brawl. Yet her heart was every bit as huge as that big old Bronco.

So was her sense of justice as well as her discernment of people.

Wyatt wanted to believe the break-in at her room was about the case, but if she said it wasn't. . . he'd wager it wasn't. Addy possessed an uncanny cop intuition. He'd always envied that keen ability.

He just hoped like hell that intuition could keep her out of this bastard's clutches.

For now, another talk with Cyrus was in order. If his errant son was planning any more theatrics, he'd better think twice. Wyatt would love nothing better than to put him in lockup.

For the rest of his sorry life.

First, however, there was one housekeeping detail he couldn't put off.

Jackson County Sheriff's Office
3104 Magnolia Street
Pascagoula, 3:15 p.m.

Wyatt waited for one of the three men sitting across from his desk to break.

An hour and counting. He'd called these three deputies into his office as soon as he'd returned from the Arnold crime scene.

Brett Guthrie. Lance Cochran. Dillon Swift.

Three holdovers from the old regime. Good deputies but loyal to the end to former Sheriff Zeke Grider. All three were buddies with Jed Stovall and Simon Cook, men who worked for Cyrus Cooper and his no-good spawn, Clay. If there was anyone in Wyatt's department—and that was a big-ass if—who would leak details of an investigation related to Addy, it would be one of these three. Before a single one walked out of this office, he would know which one, if any, it had been.

"Sheriff, it's Christmas," Cochran said, breaking the silence. Tall, skinny red-haired guy who typically followed the lead of the men sitting on either side of him. "My kids are probably wondering why their daddy's not home. How long you going to keep yanking our chains with this nonsense?"

Wyatt turned his palms upward. "We can all leave as soon as I have the truth. Otherwise," he said, reclining in his chair, "I've got all night. My family had Christmas dinner last night."

Addy and Womack were going over the new interview reports that Robert Cummings, the detective in charge of the Arnold case, had faxed over. Comparing any comments by friends and family to what they had in the Prescott case. He didn't want her to know about this little tete-a-tete.

For more reasons than one.

Guthrie stood. "Fine. You want someone to speak up, I'll do it." He hitched a thumb toward the door. "You let *her* come back here after what she did. You're working with her like none of that stuff ever happened. That's what's wrong here. We haven't done a damned thing wrong, Wyatt. You're the one who's making this department look bad."

Wyatt checked the immediate reaction. No need to let the man see he'd hit a nerve. That would only confirm his accusation. Guthrie was the oldest of the three. He'd been closest to Grider. Like a brother. But he was a third-generation cop and he hadn't wanted to give up his badge despite his indignation over the events that had transpired nine years ago. At fifty, his hair had grayed and he needed glasses for reading, but age hadn't slowed him down when it came to taking care of the business of being a cop. Wyatt understood that despite his loyalty to the badge, Guthrie's hatred for Addy ran deep.

Fierce emotions were involved. Maybe Addy was more right than he wanted to admit.

"Sit down, Guthrie."

His deputy defied him for about two seconds before lowering his bulk back into his chair.

"This isn't about whether or not you agree with my decision to allow Detective Cooper to be involved with this case," Wyatt explained. "This is about breaking the law. Violating the department's trust. If one of you passed the details of those letters along to anyone else who might have let it get out, I need to know. Now."

Swift wouldn't meet his eyes. Hadn't since he'd learned the topic of this meeting. He was the one Wyatt had pegged for the infraction. *If* there had been an infraction.

"Tell him," Cochran said with a fierce glare at the man beside him. "I'd like to get the hell out of here before Christmas is over."

Swift glared right back at his fellow deputy.

"Are you saying there's something to this?" Guthrie jumped to his feet once more, sent a glower first at Cochran, then at Swift. "Dillon Swift, I've known you since you were a snot-nosed kid. If you did this you'd better fess up, buddy. You do not want me to find out some other way."

Swift launched to his feet and stuck his finger in Guthrie's face. "I didn't do nothing," he snarled before sending another drop-dead glare at Cochran.

Swift was the youngest and most hotheaded of the three. He'd joined the department the same month Addy had. They'd been rivals of a sort from the beginning.

"He and Clay Cooper have gotten to be pretty big pals," Cochran said to Wyatt, cutting to the chase.

"Asshole!" Swift shouted.

"You better settle down, boy," Guthrie growled. Swift held his ground. "You may not agree with the sheriff's decision but you owe him the respect that goes with the office. Now sit your skinny ass down and explain yourself."

After Swift had taken his seat once more, Wyatt gave him a moment to pull himself back together. "Start at the beginning," he instructed, the fury simmering deep inside him making his teeth clench on each word.

"Me and Clay are buds, that's right," Swift boasted. "It's a free country. I chill with him and the others from time to time."

"The others" meaning Stovall and Cook. "Did you share any of the details of this investigation with him?" Wyatt asked, working hard to keep his cool.

"No, sir," Swift shot back, "I did not."

"Tell him," Cochran grumbled.

Swift's shoulders shook with fury.

"What's he talking about, Swift?" Wyatt demanded.

"Clay was bragging about how his cousin was finally

gonna get what she deserved. Said he had some inside information." Swift raised his chin in a defiant gesture. "That's it. He didn't say nothing else."

Wyatt mulled over the admission, then zeroed in on the points Swift had bypassed either inadvertently or by design. "During that discussion or since, did Clay make any reference to where he'd gotten his inside information or if it was related specifically to this investigation?"

Swift shook his head, adopted one of those this-is-a-waste-of-time expressions. "When I asked him what the hell he was talking about, he just laughed and said 'You'll see.' He never brought it up again."

That fury he'd managed to keep in check so far threatened to break into a boil. "What was your response to that comment?"

"That he'd better not break any laws or you'd throw his ass in jail."

Good answer. "You understand that you should have reported this incident to me immediately."

Swift nodded. "I figured he was just running off at the mouth. He'd knocked back some serious JD and was all worked up over something his daddy had done." The deputy shrugged. "I didn't think no more of it."

There was a fine line to be walked here. Wyatt had no reason to believe Swift was lying to him. If he overreacted, all three of the men sitting in front of him would understand that it was personal. This had to be by the book.

"I should put you on administrative leave."

"Sheriff." Swift's eyes went wide. "I—"

"But," Wyatt said, cutting him off cold, "I'm going to give you the benefit of the doubt. *This time.* Under two conditions."

The three deputies stared at him expectantly.

"You will all," Wyatt ordered, "treat Detective Cooper

with the same respect you treat any of your colleagues. And," he added before any one of them could speak up, "you will keep your ears open where Clay or his cronies are concerned. This could turn into a very bad situation very fast. My department will not look the other way for Clay Cooper, his father, or anyone else crossing the line in this jurisdiction. The only law in this county now is the one represented by the uniforms we wear."

"Yes, sir," Guthrie and Cochran said simultaneously. Swift mumbled his agreement next, but the glaring pause negated the words.

"I regret that you had to be called away from your families on Christmas Day," Wyatt allowed. "But keep in perspective the fact that another woman is missing today. We have no evidence and no leads. One of our own, Detective Cooper, has been threatened by this same perp. It's our job to protect Detective Cooper while stopping this bastard. And, if we're damned lucky, to bring his other two victims home alive."

Heads nodded in agreement.

"Guthrie, you and Cochran are dismissed."

Swift's eyes widened again as his comrades got the hell out of the office while the getting was good.

When the door had closed, Wyatt stood, rounded his desk, and sat down next to his deputy. "Swift, I didn't want to say this in front of the others. Out of respect for you." The younger man swallowed with difficulty.

"You're right," Wyatt said agreeably, "this is a free country. But Clay Cooper and the thugs he employs are trouble. Trouble that I will put an end to the first opportunity that arises.

"The uniform you wear represents a certain moral code, Swift. It took a long time to get folks in this county to believe that again. I won't have you or anyone else undoing that hard work. Whether you think this is a big deal or not, be warned, if you continue to fraternize with Clay Cooper's type, there will not be a place in this department for you come review time. Understood?"

"Yes, sir."

"Go home, Deputy Swift, and consider whether you want to work for me or for the Cooper family."

"Merry Christmas, Sheriff," Swift mumbled as he got to his feet.

"Same to you."

The door closed behind the dumbass. The idea that Clay had gotten information by any means infuriated Wyatt. But he had far bigger problems than that little prick right now.

Wyatt closed his eyes. Two missing women...no evidence.

Though he had no clue what this bastard's timeline was, Wyatt had a bad, bad feeling that time was running out...

...for Addy.

CHAPTER TWENTY

4720 Miller Road, 5:00 p.m.

Irene stared at the television screen, shock rippling along her nerve endings.

Another woman was missing.

Penny Arnold.

The pictures of the two victims were plastered across the screen. Both young. Wives. Mothers.

Blond.

Dear God.

In the statement to the press, the police had cautiously veered away from terms like "serial" and "murder." Since no bodies had been recovered it was still officially a potential kidnapping case.

If that poor Prescott woman had been murdered...

Irene clasped her hands together and sent another fervent prayer heavenward.

Too weak to hold the pose, her hands fell to her lap

and her gaze shifted to the framed photograph of her sweet daughter on the table next to her.

Adeline hadn't been able to meet her for lunch today since she'd received word that another victim had gone missing. She'd promised to make it up to Irene tomorrow.

Please, dear Lord, protect my daughter.

The images of Cherry Prescott and Penny Arnold appeared on the television screen once more. Irene's chest tightened as she studied each face. The nose and lips...the shape of the eyes. Blue eyes. She picked up the photo of her precious Addy and held it in the air so that it visually lined up with those on the screen.

Tears brimmed, blurring her eyes. "Sweet Jesus."

Irene's hand trembled. She hugged the photo to her chest. She had to do something. She couldn't pretend any longer that this would just go away.

Her hand still shaking, she reached for the phone. Tears spilled down her cheeks as she pressed the numbers. Her chest squeezed painfully yet somehow she summoned the necessary words. "I'd like to speak to *him.*"

She moistened her lips, tried to take a breath. It wasn't possible.

"Irene?"

A shudder rocked through her body.

"Something else has happened," she said with all the strength she possessed. Her lips quivered and she summoned her fleeing courage. "I'm coming over there. We have to talk, Cyrus. Something has to be done."

CHAPTER TWENTY-ONE

4718 Miller Road, 6:30 p.m.

Clay stamped up the steps and across the porch.

He'd been summoned.

Who the hell did he think he was, still ordering Clay around? His daddy was on his way out of this world and not a minute too soon for Clay.

The old bastard had gotten soft this last year. Fighting cancer had beaten him down. There had been a time when nobody messed with Cyrus Cooper. His very name had instilled fear in this whole damned county. But now he was nothing but a shriveled-up old man in a wheelchair.

If Clay was smart he'd put the old bastard out of his misery and be done with it.

But he had no desire to go to prison. Hell no.

Clay grinned as he stood outside the door to his daddy's house. Hell yeah, and he was too smart to end up the target of a DEA investigation like his stupid-ass brother

—God rest his soul—had been. And he damned sure didn't have no soft spots like his daddy.

Wasn't nothing ever going to own Clay that way.

No way in hell.

He jerked the door open and stalked inside.

"He's waiting for you," Everett announced, then gestured to the parlor.

Clay just stared at the man like he was an idiot or something. Of course his daddy was waiting for him. Where the hell else would he be?

No damned where.

Clay shoved the doors apart and stepped into the place where his father spent most all of his time when he wasn't in bed. "You called?" He didn't try to disguise the sarcasm in his tone. Soon, very soon, this shit would be over, and Clay couldn't wait.

The old man looked closer to death every day.

Thank the good Lord.

"Sit."

Clay banged his chest. "Do I look like a dog to you, old man?" What the hell? Sit? *Shit*.

"Clayton," Cyrus boomed, "sit *down*."

Clay rolled his eyes and collapsed into the closest chair. "What?"

"Have you been harassing Addy?" He glared at Clay as if that look alone would pull the truth out of his son. "I received a call suggesting you have."

"Depends upon your definition of harassing." Clay stretched his legs out and crossed his ankles. He didn't miss his daddy's glance at his healthy legs. *Yeah, look, old man. You're a cripple and I ain't.*

Cyrus smiled then. "You are quite the cocky fellow, aren't you, son?"

"Learned it from the best." Clay grinned. "You and my brother."

"And just look what it got your brother."

Fury shot through Clay. "It was that bitch's fault." He wanted her dead so bad he could taste it. She didn't deserve to be breathing when his brother lay under the cold ground in that damned cemetery.

Cyrus squared his shoulders, the only part of him that still worked worth a damn. "You will leave her alone. If you or any of your friends touch her, you will regret it for many years to come."

Yeah, yeah. The old bastard never failed to remind Clay that he still held the purse strings. "That's one thing you don't have to worry about," Clay assured him. "I'm not going to lay a hand on her. None of my friends will, either. I'll see to that personally."

"What about her tires?" Cyrus's gaze narrowed. "You told me you had nothing to do with that."

Clay shrugged. "I didn't. I ain't touching her or her shit."

His daddy studied him a long minute. He knew Clay was lying. But surprisingly, he let it go. "You are my only flesh and blood." He heaved a big breath. "You're all I have. But I will not watch you go down that same path your brother took."

"You mean the path you provided him the map for?"

Dead silence filled the air.

Clay was pretty sure he'd said too much. The old man was really pissed now. Clay could see it in his eyes. Shit. That was not good.

"Yes," Cyrus admitted.

The sadness that suddenly overwhelmed the old man's face was almost enough to make Clay regret his smartass remark. *Almost.*

"I was a different man then," Cyrus offered.

What the hell? What was this? Confessional time?

"I lost my oldest son and my only brother within the space of one year. That kind of loss changes a man."

Funny, Clay mused, he never mentioned missing his wife—the mother of his two sons. She'd died first, a couple years before Gage.

But Clay didn't have to ask why. He knew. His daddy had married the wrong girl.

Hell, probably wasn't the cancer killing him. It was more likely the regret.

A man just never got over some things. Apparently coveting was one of them.

"I don't want to lose you, too, Clayton," his daddy said, emotion shining in his eyes. "Whatever it is you're doing, just stop. That's all I'm asking."

This was too damned weird, but he couldn't deny the fact that the old man's words had gotten to him on some level. He wasn't completely heartless. Clay sat up, straightened his jacket. "You got nothing to worry about, Daddy. I told you, I'm not going to touch Addy. And just because it's what you want, I'll make certain that none of my buddies do, either."

"That's all I ask," Cyrus said wearily.

Clay stood, walked over to his pitiful old man, and gave him a little hug. It was the least he could do. "Merry Christmas."

If Clay was real lucky, this would be the last time he'd ever have to say that shit again.

By this time next year, he'd be planting that old bastard next to Gage.

And then Clay would show folks around here that Cooper law was still the only one that mattered.

IT ENDS WITH HER

7:30 p.m.

Clay barreled down the gravel drive, headed back to town. He had plans.

"Screw that old man!"

That old bitch, he thought, glancing west toward where her farm sat beyond his daddy's, was whispering shit in his daddy's ears. Clay knew exactly where his daddy was getting his information. All Clay could say was that she'd better watch what she said and did or she'd find herself asleep one night with the house burning down around her. She and her daughter were just alike. So damn self-righteous. Thought they were a cut above Clay and his daddy.

Clay grunted a laugh. It would be nice as hell to have both those bitches out of the way.

"No need to be greedy, Clayton, old boy." He grinned. One out of the way would be close enough.

Very soon he would have complete control. All the money, the land. And the whole county would look up to him then. He would have the power.

Wouldn't nobody dare to tell him what to do. Or even look at him the wrong way.

Hell no.

He turned onto the main road and headed to Pascagoula. The boys were waiting for him. They were going to party the night away. All the beer and girls they could handle. That was his Christmas present to his friends.

"Hell yeah!" He smirked. Lots of beer and girls.

Blue lights flickered in his rearview mirror.

"Shit." He glanced down at the speedometer. Hell, he wasn't even speeding. Well, maybe a little.

Didn't these bastards know it was Christmas? Annoyed as hell, he braked and pulled over to the side of the road. Depending on who it was, he could probably talk his way out of whatever had made them pull him over.

Stupid cops.

He glanced in his side mirror to get a look at who the cop was as he walked up to Clay's door. The headlights from the official vehicle glowed around him like a spotlight.

Henderson? What the hell? Clay powered the window down. "I wasn't speeding, Sheriff."

Henderson stared at him like he was ready to rip his head off and piss down his throat. "Get out of the truck, Clay."

"What?" This was ridiculous! "I wasn't speeding. I wasn't doing nothing."

"Get out," Henderson repeated.

Clay opened the door and slid out of the seat. He crossed his arms over his chest. "What now, Sheriff?"

"Get in the SUV." Henderson jerked his head toward his vehicle.

Clay held up his hands and waved them back and forth. "You ain't taking me nowhere until you tell me what the hell is going on." No way this guy had figured anything out. Even if he had...it had nothing to do with Clay.

"We're going to talk," Henderson explained. "And then you can get back in your piece-of-shit truck and drive away."

Clay swore under his breath. "Whatever you say, Sheriff." He walked back to the SUV but hesitated before climbing in. "Front seat or back?"

"Front."

Clay swung into the seat and closed the door.

Sheriff Henderson did the same. He didn't turn on the interior light. In fact, he'd turned the inside lights off completely. No glow from the dash at all. No prob. That big fat moon provided some light, which was good. Clay had no desire to sit here in the dark with some cop. Especially not dickhead Wyatt Henderson.

"I want you to think very carefully before you answer my questions, Clay."

More questions. Just great. "Do you need to read me my rights?"

"That's not necessary."

"I need a lawyer?"

Henderson turned his face toward him. "Have you done anything that might require the services of an attorney?"

Clay shook his head. "Don't think so." Not that he'd gotten caught doing anyway.

Henderson rested his arm along the back of the seat. "Here's the problem, Clay. There are some things going on that concern me."

"What things?" Clay stared at the back of his truck. He'd already be in town with his friends if this shithead hadn't stopped him.

When Henderson didn't answer, Clay opened his mouth to ask again but his head suddenly rammed into the dash. "What the hell?" Pain exploded in his forehead. "Jesus Christ!" He clutched at his face and turned to Henderson. "Are you out of your damned mind?"

The business end of Henderson's weapon was staring Clay right in the eyes. Fear charged into his throat, ensuring nothing witty came out of his mouth.

"Now you listen to me, you piece of shit," Henderson growled. "You go near her or her things again and I will see that you end up face down in the bayou."

"What the hell are you talking about?" Clay rubbed his forehead. "This is damned police brutality!"

Henderson shook his head. "No. You're wrong." He jammed the muzzle into Clay's temple, pinning his head between the gun and window of his door. "*This* is police brutality."

"You can't do this shit!" Clay hated like hell that he'd squealed the words. But hell, he was about ready to piss his pants. This bastard had gone crazy.

The muzzle bored more deeply into Clay's skull. "Who broke into her room at the Shady Oaks?"

"I don't know what you're talking about!" No way was he telling Henderson shit.

"That may be," the sheriff allowed, "but just in case, I want to leave you with something to think about."

Clay blinked. Prayed he wasn't about to get shot. *Shit.* He knew how cops could be. They could make it look like it was his fault.

The pressure suddenly eased on his skull.

Clay relaxed. *What the hell?*

The gun rammed between his legs. The muzzle shoved hard against his balls. All the air rushed out of his lungs. The whimper that echoed in the silence was his.

"Don't shoot!" he squeaked. Clay's balls tried to draw into his belly. His entire body shuddered. "I swear I didn't do nothing. I swear!"

"I'm going to take your word for that," Henderson said quietly. He increased the pressure of the muzzle.

Clay wailed like a goddamned girl.

"But," Henderson went on, "if you or any of your thug friends go anywhere near her, I will find you and then I'll blow your puny balls clean off. Do you understand me?"

Clay nodded, his head bobbing frantically. "Whatever you say, Sheriff. I swear to God, I won't go near her."

"And your friends?" The gun threatened to bust right through his scrotum.

"They won't go near her, either."

"Good."

Henderson drew his weapon back. Clay sucked in a shaky breath. His face was wet. Shit! Badass guys didn't cry like little girls!

"Now get out," Henderson ordered.

Body trembling, Clay snatched at the door, finally got it open. His feet hit the ground and his knees buckled. He'd barely gotten back to his feet and shoved the door closed when Henderson roared away.

"Asshole!" Clay stumbled to his truck. Somebody should've killed that son of a bitch long ago.

Muttering every foul word he knew, he climbed behind the wheel of his truck and took off.

Hell no, he wasn't touching that bitch. His daddy and Henderson didn't need to worry about him. Or his buddies.

Before going on into town, Clay drove to the place he'd been watching. He parked his truck. His balls had finally quit throbbing. He snaked his way through the woods until he reached that old, abandoned shack.

Clay smirked. Nope. He wasn't gonna have to lift a finger.

Dear old cousin Addy was on a short list.

And her name had just come up.

CHAPTER TWENTY-TWO

*Forrest General Hospital,
Hattiesburg, 8:00 p.m.*

She looked so innocent lying there.

Fury tightened his lips. *Bitch.* His gaze roved the white sheet, landing on her protruding belly. Disgust twisted in his gut.

He would not allow this.

His son would not suffer as he had.

More of that mounting fury exploded in his veins. It was Christmas and he couldn't even be with his son.

It was her fault.

But he had a plan. One that destiny had set into place centuries ago...then whispered in his ear just weeks ago. He relaxed. A smile spread across his face.

Soon. Very soon he would be with Danny.

Nothing could stop him now.

Everything was almost in place.

He touched his wife's hand. Soon her flesh would be cold and that damned princess growing in her belly would be dead.

Just like the others.

"Everything all right in here?"

His gaze shot to the door where the errant police officer now hovered.

Funny that he seemed interested in the patient's well-being now. The stupid cop hadn't appeared to notice when a virtual stranger walked into the room he was supposed to be watching. No, he'd been too distracted by a woman from another room.

Ridiculous. Worthless. A smart man would never allow his cock to override his brain. But, unfortunately, most all men fell victim to that traitorous organ from time to time.

Even him.

"I could use your assistance, Officer," he said in his gentlest tone. "This IV machine is acting up. I need to replace it," he gestured to the one he'd brought into the room with him, "but the cords are a tangled mess. I hate to have to call another nurse. We're shorthanded as it is tonight."

"Sure." The officer smiled. "I hope you got to spend some time with your family today. Christmas is a bad time to be on duty." The cop came around the bed. He chuckled. "Believe me, I know."

Smiling at the cop's words, he reached into his right pocket and wrapped his fingers around the hypodermic needle he'd prepared for just this sort of obstacle. The same one he'd used on the nurse in the pharmaceutical storeroom. The key to the success of any plan was preparation.

"Stand right here." He ushered the cop next to the bed. "Now hold her arm to ensure I don't pull anything loose. We wouldn't want to cause her any unnecessary discomfort."

He just wanted her to stop breathing.

"Okey-dokey." The stupid cop did exactly as he was told.

Keeping one eye on the cop, he placed his free hand on the IV pole and withdrew the hypo with the other. "Here we go."

The cop held on to the patient's arm with both hands.

Perfect. Gritting his teeth, he swung away from the IV and jammed the needle into the cop's shoulder and shoved the plunger downward.

The cop released his hold on the patient and spun around. He cried out at the burn in his veins. Tried to speak...but it was too late.

Potassium chloride worked very fast, stopping the heart as effectively as if he'd reached into the man's chest and ripped out the organ.

The cop crumpled to the floor.

He reared back to glance out the open door, checked the corridor. Now, he had to hurry. Time was not on his side. As soon as he'd injected the bitch the monitors would react. His escape plan was less than desirable. He'd watched for days and this was the only viable option.

This had to be done.

He reached into his left pocket and retrieved the second hypo. Carefully he inserted it into the tube of her IV. Perfect.

She moaned.

He froze.

One, two, three seconds he watched her. She lay still as stone. Must have been an involuntary response sound. The bitch was in a coma. He relaxed and returned to his work.

Her arm flopped.

She moaned. Louder.

Her eyes opened.

She flopped her arms again. Tried to roll toward the other side of the bed away from him, those hideous sounds gurgling from her throat.

The monitors screamed for attention as her heart's rhythm reacted to the fear.

Shit! He had to hurry!

He placed his thumb on the plunger, pushed. "Just die," he muttered.

"What're you doing there?"

The nurse didn't wait for his response. She dropped the patient chart she carried and rushed toward him.

He released the hypo. Hoped it would be enough. He jumped across the bed, bypassing the nurse. Then he rounded the foot of the bed.

He knocked down another nurse as he charged out the door. She scrambled up, screaming for help.

Would the small amount he'd injected prove sufficient? No way to be sure. He could hope.

As if to set his mind at ease, the code blue echoed through the hospital's intercom system.

Excellent. He mentally marked taking care of that bitch off his list of things to do.

Now he had to escape.

His son needed him.

And there was the business of the last princess.

CHAPTER TWENTY-THREE

*1708 Monroe Street,
Pascagoula, 9:00 p.m.*

Adeline tucked her cell phone into her back pocket and moved down the hall to join Wyatt in his living room. The chief had called her a third time. He wanted to send Detective Metcalf down to back her up. Metcalf had gotten his shield a couple months ago and she liked the guy. She wouldn't mind having him as a permanent partner.

But she didn't need backup down here. She watched the man pacing the living room. Wyatt wasn't going to let anyone close to her anyway.

That realization settled heavily against her chest.

What the hell was she doing allowing this to happen?

Those emotions she'd struggled with all day churned fiercely, way down deep inside her. She gritted her teeth, pushed the feelings aside. This investigation was unnervingly close to home to say the least. But she'd worked unnerving plenty of times.

It was being *here* with *him*. Every cell in her body was affected by him. By being *here*. From the day she had left Mississippi, she had disowned this place. Home wasn't home anymore. She'd worked hard to make Huntsville, Alabama, home. And she had succeeded...until about twenty-four hours ago when all the walls she'd built between her and here—between her and *him*—had come crashing down.

The choices she'd made, out of necessity at the time, now seemed all wrong. Misguided and hasty. Second thoughts weren't supposed to haunt a person nine years later.

Yet, she stood here now, staring at the single most relevant part of her life back then and she understood that she couldn't pretend there wasn't still something there. Couldn't ignore the hold he still had on some part of her.

She had loved him with every fiber of her being—with all that had made her who she was.

How had she imagined for an instant—even in the throes of passion—that she could have sex with this man and treat the incident like any other one-nighter?

Not possible.

If they hadn't stopped...

But they had. She squared her slumped shoulders. From this point forward their every interaction had to be about the case. No more dancing too close to the flame.

"That your chief again?"

Adeline pushed aside the troubling thoughts. "Yeah. He agreed that I should stay as long as necessary." Not entirely true. He'd actually wanted her back in Huntsville and Metcalf working this investigation. At the very least he'd wanted Metcalf with her. She'd nixed the former idea right off the bat. Then she'd had to do some serious talking to hold her ground on the latter.

In the end she'd gotten her way. Second thoughts attempted to steal her certainty on the choice.

Why was she doing this to herself? She never doubted her decisions. This man, she stared at the gorgeous hunk of male in front of her, this place...did *this* to her.

Wyatt nodded. "I guess that's good."

He guessed. "What the hell does that mean?" She threw her hands up in frustration. Being the subject of everyone's concern was getting damned old. Her mother had called five times. Her chief three. She was a big girl. With a big gun that she knew how to use.

Mainly, she was pissed at herself for being so damned wishy-washy.

"It means," he moved toward her, putting her senses on guard, "that I care about what happens to you and this investigation is getting intense. Whoever this bastard is, he wants you. Have you forgotten?"

"Now that's just stupid." She sliced her hands through the air. "Enough, Wyatt." Fury pumped up her confidence. "I'm a highly trained major crimes detective. I know what I'm doing and I can take care of myself. This coddling either stops now or I'm out that door." She stabbed her finger in the direction of his front door. "I'll stay at my mom's before I'll stand for this. You got it?" And that was saying something, by God.

He braced his hands on his hips. "Loud and clear." He shrugged. "I'll back off. Give you the breathing room you need."

But his eyes said otherwise. That was the thing. Wyatt had always worn his feelings right there where anyone who knew him well enough could read exactly what was on his mind. He wasn't going to back off any more than this freak who addressed her as "princess" intended to.

"You're lying. You won't do any such shit. You'll hover around me like a mother hen and try to—" She shook her head. "Forget it. I don't want to talk about this anymore." She glared at him. "Consider yourself warned, though. I'm done tiptoeing around this bullshit. You treat me like you would any other detective or I'm done working with you."

Uncertainty seeped into her bones. Okay. She'd put it out there on the table. Couldn't take it back. Brutal, honest. She hiked her chin. And she damned well meant what she said. For the most part anyway.

His expression cleared of emotion. "Understood."

That was easier than she'd expected. This time there was no indecision glimmering in his eyes. "So." She stretched her neck, right then left. "Where are we on the briefing with the folks in Wiggins?"

"Tomorrow. Ten o'clock. We'll rendezvous at my office with Womack and Sullenger. Detective Lonnie Ferguson from Hattiesburg PD will be joining us. He's been working the Prescott case from his end."

That was the first she'd heard about the Hattiesburg detective. "Okay. We can use all the heads on this we can get." Mainly because they didn't have one damned thing and those women were going to be dead before the investigation got a break. Not to mention that the bastard wanted her next. She repressed a shudder. Let him come. She wasn't going to make it easy. Then again, just maybe becoming a victim was the only way to get the break they needed.

She sure as hell wouldn't share the idea with Wyatt.

Adeline pulled at her tee. "I need to find some clothes."

With nothing open on Christmas, she had no choice but to wear this same getup tomorrow.

"I could call Emma White and have her open her shop."

Adeline laughed. "Emma finally got her shop?" Owning a boutique was all Emma White had ever talked about in high school. Damn, she'd gotten her wish.

"Yeah." Wyatt lifted one shoulder and let it fall. "She married some rich guy from Biloxi, then got divorced a year later. Apparently the settlement gave her the stake she needed to make it happen."

Not an easy thing to do in small-town nowhere. "Good for her." Adeline hitched her thumb toward the hall. "I think I'm gonna take a shower and hit the sack." She gave her head a shake. "I don't want to bother anybody on Christmas night. I'll just make use of your in-house laundry service." Maybe she'd give old Emma a buzz tomorrow afternoon. Though they hadn't exactly been friends in school, at least Emma hadn't been one of Adeline's mortal enemies.

"Sure." He stared at the floor a moment.

What now? If he started that whole "we need to talk" thing again she was going to scream.

"I caught the news a few minutes ago," he said, meeting her eyes once more. "It's supposed to rain tonight."

Adeline clenched her jaw. Banished the too familiar anxiety that climbed into her throat. "I'll be fine."

She gave him her back and headed for the hall bath. The dreams didn't come every time it rained.

In fact, until the other night she hadn't had that damned dream in a couple of months.

So what if she did tonight? It was just a dream.

CHAPTER TWENTY-FOUR

Sunday, December 26, 12:05 a.m.

Wyatt jerked awake.

He flopped onto his back and listened. Nothing but the rain beating against the roof.

Catching the time on the clock, he frowned. He couldn't have been asleep more than an hour. Addy had taken her shower and closed herself up in the guest-room. The light hadn't gone out for another thirty minutes or so.

He'd finally given up his vigil and hit the sack. Sleep had dragged him under in record time. Exhaustion would do that to a guy.

He frowned. Sat up. Listened hard. A muffled sound brushed his senses a second time. Somebody talking?

What the hell?

He kicked the cover back and got up, grabbing his service revolver from the bedside table as he went. Keeping his movements as quiet as possible, he eased to the door.

Addy's light was out. The light in the hall bath cut a dim path across the door to her room. A constant tick-tock whispered from the old clock hanging on the living room wall. Otherwise the house was quiet.

Maybe he'd heard the neighbor's cat yowling.

There it was again.

Definitely not a cat. Someone talking—no, not talking. Shouting.

He covered the distance between his room and hers in three long strides and threw open the door. The light filtering from the hall settled over the tousled sheets of her empty bed.

"Dammit!"

As he raced through the house he thought of all the things he should have done to prevent this. Like cuffing her to the bed. Or to him.

The front door stood wide open.

Resisting the impulse to burst out the door into an unknown situation, he moved to the window, drew the curtain back just enough to take a covert look outside.

"What the hell?"

Addy stood in the middle of the yard, her arms hanging at her sides, her weapon in her right hand. She was alone. No unfamiliar vehicles on the street.

He let the curtain drop and stormed to the door. What the hell was she doing? Didn't she get that standing out there in the dark all alone was a bad, bad idea?

As he burst into the pouring rain, she lifted her face to the dark sky. "This," she shouted, "is bullshit. It's just rain." The last was scarcely a whisper.

"Addy."

She whirled toward him, the weapon in her hand, thankfully, remaining pointed at the ground. In hindsight, he should have approached this a little differently.

"What're you doing?" The jersey he'd given her last night to sleep in was sopping wet and plastered to her body, hung practically to her knees. Her long hair was soaked.

Her lips trembled, she flattened them to stifle the reaction. She jutted out that stubborn jaw and hiked her chin. "Making a point."

Though it was about fifty degrees out, with the rain it was damned cold. "Come inside." He reached out, offered his hand to her.

She stared at his hand then at him. Without another word she walked around him and into the house.

He blew out a breath and looked up at the sky. What the hell was he going to do with her? He scanned the dark street and the shadows at the edge of his yard. Anything could have happened to her while he slept.

Water slid down his bare chest. He'd tried hard to do this her way. To stay off her toes. Just a couple of hours ago he'd promised to give her a wide berth. And then she pulled this kind of crap.

Shaking his head, he turned and walked back into the house. He locked the door and then followed her damp trail on the wood floor all the way to the hall bath. She'd dragged a couple of towels from the linen closet.

She tossed one at him. "Sorry I woke you up."

He scrubbed the terry cloth over his wet hair. "Not half as sorry as I am that you set foot out that door *alone*. You're not making this easy, Addy."

She didn't bother debating his statement. Her fingers worked the towel over her hair, squeezing those long blond tresses. His gaze dropped to where the jersey clung to her hips, then traveled up to her breasts. His throat thickened.

His gaze collided with hers in the mirror. "You," she pointed at his chest, "are dripping."

He looked down. Yep. Drops of water slithered down his skin and soaked into the waistband of his sweatpants. He scrubbed the towel over his chest and arms, then lifted his attention back to her reflection. "I'm not dripping half as much as you are."

Water trickled from the hem of the jersey and splattered on the tile floor around her feet.

She looked down and laughed. "Shit. I'm making a hell of a mess."

A laugh rumbled from his chest. "Just a little bit."

Her eyes met his once more. "I had the dream."

"Oh yeah?" He'd figured as much. Knots formed in his gut, clenched with the misery he saw in those blue eyes.

She nodded. "It was different this time. I could hear voices. My dad...I guess...and another voice. A man or boy. Sounded young."

"Your dad?" Maybe being back here was playing havoc with her emotions. What the hell was he thinking? There was no maybe about it. They were both on edge. Raw-nerved.

"He kept saying *"here's daddy's little princess."* Her gaze searched his. "He never called me 'princess.' I was his angel. Daddy called me his angel."

Princess. Wyatt's insides twisted with the worry that didn't completely fade even when he slept. "It's the case," he assured her, "that's all. Your subconscious is scrambling the past with the present."

She inclined her head, seemed to think about something before saying more. "And the voice was wrong. Not my dad's." She shook her head. "I didn't recognize it."

"How about I make some coffee? Warm us up?"

She ignored his question, seemed lost in her thoughts. "The boy—the other voice—that was truly bizarre."

"How so?"

"He kept saying, *just die...just die.*"

Those precise words hadn't been in any of the letters sent by the perp. Wyatt dropped his towel on the floor and swiped his feet, then ushered it across the tile in her direction. "Slide that under your feet so you don't slip. Tile's slick as hell when it's wet." He backed up a step, mostly to put some distance between them. This was, he felt fairly certain, one of those moments when she needed her space. "I'll make the coffee." The dream had really rattled her. But it wasn't just the dream. It was that and this case.

Addy wanted to present this situation as just another investigation, but it was deeply personal. This perp had picked her out, just as he had Prescott and Arnold. And he was coming for Addy. It was only a matter of time. That had to be getting to her.

It was sure as hell getting to him. He wasn't backing out of the cramped bathroom and into the hall because he thought she needed space...he needed it. He had to get his head on straight before she noticed and definitely before he said or did something he would regret.

"Wyatt."

He hesitated. "Yeah?"

"Can I sleep with you tonight?"

The urge to scoop her into his arms and carry her to his bed then and there hit him hard. "Sure."

He could handle having her sleep in his bed. It would be a little awkward, but he would manage.

Who the hell was he kidding? On a difficulty scale of one to ten...this was a definite twenty.

If he survived it would be a miracle.

CHAPTER TWENTY-FIVE

6:40 a.m.

Adeline moaned softly. The sound roused her from that sweet zone somewhere between asleep and awake. Something heavy lay across her back. She told her eyes to open but they refused. *This* felt so good. Warm and familiar. Her breasts were crushed against that firm warmth.

Her body tingled. She pressed her pelvis into something big and hard. Oh, now this was a good dream. She tilted her hips again. Sighed. *Felt real good.*

The weight on her back shifted.

Her eyes opened wide.

It was dark.

The smell of rain and warm flesh filled her nostrils. Her hand moved...glided along a muscled arm. *Wyatt.*

She raised her head, analyzed the situation.

She froze.

Her body was draped over his like a sheet.

If she moved—even breathed—he would wake up and...

His arm, heavy on her back, tightened around her.

She closed her eyes and bit down on her bottom lip. This was...not good.

All she had to do was ease out of his—

"Addy."

Her name was nothing more than a breath on his lips. She shivered at the sound. Desire detonated in every damned mutinous cell.

"Morning," she muttered.

His body tensed as his own realization dawned.

She told herself to say something or to just move. Couldn't.

His fingers tangled in her hair.

She gasped.

He drew her face down to his...their lips so close she could feel his warm breath on her face.

"Say the word," he murmured, "and I'll stop but I have to do this."

He lifted his head just enough to ensure their lips met. The kiss was slow, slow, slow. She told herself to pull away. To say the word. To do anything but...

Melt against him like butter on hot toast.

Not gonna happen.

Images of him standing in the rain...rivulets of water sliding down his chest as he reached out to her...the way those sweatpants hung low on his lean hips kept flashing in her brain. The feel of that powerful body under her now...all of it was just too much to resist.

She banished the warning voice...pushed away the propriety vying for her attention. Right now she wanted to feel...all of him.

He tugged her jersey upward. She reared back and

pulled it the rest of the way off then tossed it to the floor. His mouth found hers once more. Those lips...God, she had missed his lips. Full and firm and always hungry for more. He left a trail of kisses along her jaw, down her throat. Her body responded to his every touch.

She wanted him. All of him.

Now.

They made love, lost themselves in the sensations.

Later, spent, she lay against him. His arms felt so good around her. Safe.

Home.

The word echoed inside her. She tensed.

As if sensing the change in her, he rolled her onto her back. Cradled her face in his hands and kissed her hard. Not slow and sweet like before. This was desperate, turbulent.

When he finally drew back, he murmured, "I've missed you, Addy."

The words sent confusion and fear roaring through her.

She wasn't supposed to feel this anymore.

She wasn't supposed to be here.

How long would it take this time to exorcise Wyatt Henderson?

You're next.

Then again, if the perp had his way, she wouldn't have to worry about the future at all.

CHAPTER TWENTY-SIX

Jackson County Sheriff's Office
3104 Magnolia Street, 10:00 a.m.

Wyatt turned the floor over to Detective Sullenger to recap for the benefit of Detective Ferguson of Hattiesburg PD and Detective Cummings from Wiggins.

"The two victims share a few characteristics," Sullenger began. "Both in their thirties, blond hair, blue eyes. Petite, though Arnold is a couple inches taller than Prescott. Other than being career-oriented women, that's where the similarities end."

"Detective Cooper," Wyatt added, "fits that somewhat ambiguous profile and, according to the messages she has received from the perp, she is his current focus."

At the other end of the table, Addy met Wyatt's gaze but quickly looked away. He was pretty sure she'd purposely chosen to sit as far away from him as possible. What they'd shared this morning only appeared to have put more distance between them. As soon as they'd rolled out of bed, she'd mentally taken several giant steps back.

Something they would both have to deal with eventually whether she wanted to or not.

"And that's it?" Detective Cummings said, obviously frustrated. "Two women are missing and there's no evidence. No nothing. Two crime scenes, a dozen cops and techs, and this is it?"

The two letters sent by the perp to Arnold had been discovered in a drawer in her bedroom. There was no way to know when or how she had received them. Her husband hadn't seen the letters. Forensics had confirmed the letters were a match to both the ones Prescott had received as well as those sent to Addy.

Those knots of dread he'd been ignoring clenched hard in Wyatt's gut. How could they have two victims and not a single shred of usable evidence?

Womack nodded. "Unfortunately." He picked up one of the numerous documents he'd brought to the conference table. "According to the cell carrier report your office faxed over, the call Penny Arnold received early yesterday morning came from the pay phone at a convenience store on Highway 29 just outside Wiggins."

"That's right." Cummings slid a pair of reading glasses into place and looked over a report from the file in front of him. "As far as we can tell there's not a single connection between the two vics. Arnold's husband is certain his wife didn't know Prescott. He wasn't even aware Prescott was missing." Cummings lifted his gaze to those seated around the table once more. "His wife had been out of town, and with watching the kids, the laundry and meals, he said he'd had no time to catch up on the news."

"Was Penny afraid of the water?"

Wyatt's attention shot down the table to Addy. He

hadn't brought that up. He'd hoped to discuss that privately with Cummings, but the man hadn't arrived until the rest of the group was already assembled.

Cummings drew his eyebrows together in a frown. "That hasn't come up in the interviews." He looked from Addy to Wyatt. "Is that relevant somehow?"

"Cherry Prescott," Ferguson put in, "only a few weeks before her disappearance related certain fears to her closest friends. Fears she hadn't experienced in the past. Drowning was one of them."

True to the family's requests, Ferguson had veered away from specifics. They were way past protecting anyone's image at this point. Wyatt clarified, "She'd started having dreams of drowning her daughter. We've considered the possibility that she disappeared in some sort of desperate attempt to protect her child."

Cummings looked totally bewildered now. "You're saying there's some chance she wasn't a victim? That she just ran off? What about the letters?"

"That is absolutely not what we're saying." Ferguson blasted the point. "We don't believe that any more than you believe Ms. Arnold stayed in Phoenix an extra day to carry on an illicit affair. Even if there was some question, the letters undeniably connect the disappearances."

"In light of Arnold's disappearance," Wyatt intervened, "and the continued threat to Detective Cooper, the possibility that Prescott disappeared of her own accord is no longer a viable scenario."

"It was never," Ferguson pressed, "a viable scenario." Wyatt conceded to the detective's assertion with a nod. This case made maintaining objectivity next to impossible. His gaze settled on Addy once more. No one understood that better than him.

"I don't see the relevance then," Cummings tossed out.

"What does Prescott's fear of drowning have to do with anything?"

Addy pushed back her chair and got up. She rounded the table and snatched the pack of cigarettes from Womack's shirt pocket on her way out the door.

"Carry on, Detective Sullenger." Wyatt got up. He didn't need to hear the rest of what they *didn't* have. "I'll be back in a moment."

"Here," Womack called after him.

Wyatt turned back to the table. His deputy pitched him a cigarette lighter. "She might need this."

The frustrated voices in the conference room followed him down the corridor. All present were sick with the idea that there was not a single piece of evidence that provided any hint whatsoever to the perp or his motive. Not a damned thing to lead them anywhere.

How the hell were they supposed to stop this guy if they couldn't find a damned link between the victims much less to him? A pained laugh erupted from his chest. Hell, they even knew the identity of the next victim and they still couldn't do shit except wait for the bastard to act.

Wyatt passed through the lobby, disgusted with the cheery Christmas decorations. There wasn't a damned thing to be happy or festive about. He couldn't remember having such a screwed-up holiday...not since the first one after she left.

Then again, as bad as this one was, at least she was here.

His chest tightened at the idea that she would be leaving again. There was nothing he could say or do to stop her.

She had a life six and a half hours north of here.

The distance felt like another universe away...for him it was exactly that.

IT ENDS WITH HER

Addy stood on the sidewalk, the unlit cigarette dangling from her lips.

He moved up beside her and offered the lighter. "Womack said you might need this."

She shook her head. "I don't want to smoke it. I just want to feel it in my mouth."

Nine years ago Addy had smoked. He'd been surprised that she didn't now but asking about her decision to quit was out of the question. She'd made it loud and clear that she didn't want to talk about the past or her current personal life. He seriously doubted this morning had changed her mind.

He tucked the lighter into the pocket of his jeans. "You okay?"

She cut him with a dagger-sharp glare. "Are you out of your mind?" She snatched the cigarette out of her mouth and waved it in the air. "Some asshole is abducting women without leaving the first clue. He could be anybody. Anywhere!" Her arms went up then dropped to her sides in a gesture of resignation. "We don't know the first thing about him. The links between the victims are anorexic at best. The perp's evidently getting off on playing this princess game. And he claims I'm next. Hell no, I'm not okay, Wyatt. That's the dumbest damned question I've ever been asked."

He tried another tactic. "So you're scared."

She sent another of those cutting looks. "I'm not scared!" She pawed at his pocket. "Gimme that damned lighter."

Sliding two fingers into his pocket, he fished out the lighter and handed it to her.

She lit the tip of the cigarette, sucked in a long, deep drag of smoke. "I am not afraid." Her voice croaked with the harsh chemicals filtering through her lungs. "I'm just frustrated that I can't catch this bastard and bring those women home before he kills them." She turned her face up to Wyatt's. "Honestly," she searched his eyes, "I wish he would make a play for me. At least then I could do something besides nothing."

"That's it." Fury mushroomed in his chest. "You should not be working this case." He moved his head firmly side to side. "I must've been out of my mind to let you in this deep in the first place."

"Like you could've stopped me." She tossed the cigarette to the pavement. "Those women will be dead very soon if they're not already."

One dead princess . . .

"I'm aware of that." The rage drained away, leaving a sense of helplessness that no lawman ever wanted to feel.

"I'm the only connection, remember?" she said, reminding him of his own words. "Letting him take me may be the only way we can break this case."

"No way."

She went toe to toe with him. "See." Accusation flared in her eyes. "This isn't supposed to be personal, Wyatt. This is an official investigation. I'm not a civilian. Going undercover to nail a perp is a routine operation."

"There's a hell of a difference between going undercover and being nabbed by a man who in all likelihood is some sort of psycho. We have absolutely no reason to believe the vics are still alive. No way of knowing if either of them lived past the moment of attack. What the hell good could you do for the case if you're dead, too?"

"You need to watch more TV." She pushed past him, then paused at the door. "I'm putting you on notice." Her determined gaze backed up her words. "We had sex this morning. It changes nothing about the dynamics of this investigation. Don't even think about going there." She jerked the door open but hesitated again, glancing back at him once more. "Whatever this princess thing is, it ends with me."

Then she walked out, slammed the door behind her.

What the hell was he going to do with her?

CHAPTER TWENTY-SEVEN

Adeline squared her shoulders and reentered the conference room. She moved to the seat she'd vacated but didn't sit down. Instead, she surveyed the law enforcement personnel around the table. Wyatt waltzed in and Sullenger's face beamed. Adeline resisted the urge to roll her eyes.

"Here's the deal," Adeline began. "I don't swim. I don't do water sports of any kind. No boats. No nothing. I have nightmares about drowning." She fixed her attention on Ferguson. "Cherry Prescott had recently started having nightmares about drowning her daughter." Before the man could rationalize or dismiss that fact, Adeline pushed on. "She was so terrified of what she might do to her daughter that she refused to bathe her. I don't know what this means." Adeline turned her palms up. "I don't believe in psychic connections or any of that shit. But this is real." Her gaze bored into Ferguson's. "Trust me, the fear Cherry felt—if it was anything like mine—is damned real." Adeline shifted her gaze to Cummings. "Call the husband. Call her friends. Whoever you have to. Find out if Penny was afraid of the water. In the past or now. Whether we understand how it relates to this case or not, we need to know."

Silence thickened in the air for three seconds.

Womack shuffled his papers, cleared his throat. "We've had a few crank calls related to the disappearances."

Adeline's attention flew to him. "Explain."

"As you all know, we've taken hundreds of calls," Womack went on. "In the beginning some were useful. A couple of locals who saw Prescott in town the day she went missing. But, for the most part, they've been a waste of time. A blond woman might have been spotted but it wasn't Prescott. It happens anytime you have a high-profile case like this."

Making a rolling motion with her hand, Adeline urged him to get to the point. Since he'd brought the subject up, he must have a point.

"But late yesterday I got a weird one."

"Weird how?" Wyatt asked.

Adeline kept her gaze away from him. Each time she looked him in the eyes she understood one very important fact. She was a liar. This morning had changed everything. He'd gotten all the way inside her. . . physically, mentally. She had to focus on this case. If there was any chance Prescott and Arnold were still alive, Adeline had to do all within her power to find them. And to stop this psycho bastard.

"Well," Womack said, "we've had a few. Aliens took her. That sort of thing. But this one was different." The older detective's gaze settled on Adeline's. "This one claimed to be one of those psychics you don't believe in."

Anticipation and *fear* pounded from Adeline's every pore. He wouldn't have brought this up if there wasn't something bigger coming...something relevant. "What'd she have to say?" The tiny hairs on her body lifted as if on some level she sensed this was immensely important.

"The caller claimed the women were close to the water," Womack shook his head, "and that if we didn't find them soon they would be *under* the water."

Chills spilled across Adeline's skin. Her core temperature dropped significantly. "I want to talk to her. Bring her in. Today. Now."

Womack looked from her to Wyatt, who gave him a nod. "I'll get right on it."

A cell phone buzzed.

Half the people at the table checked their screens.

Detective Cummings stepped away from the group and took the call. The others gathered around the table resumed the discussion. Sullenger recited the steps that had been taken and the ongoing theme of finding nothing.

Adeline told herself to pay attention, but she couldn't shake Womack's words. Her phone vibrated against her waist. She ignored it. Probably her mom. Or worse, the chief.

…under the water.

She had to talk to this woman. As crazy as it sounded, her words were too eerily pertinent to ignore.

Psychic connection or no.

Cummings returned to the table. "That was one of Stone County's deputies." He settled into his chair, his face pale with whatever news he had learned. "You were right." He glanced at Adeline. "Her husband confirmed that Penny Arnold was terrified of water. She wouldn't even go with the family on outings if water was involved."

Shit. Adeline schooled her expression, beating down that uncharacteristic fear that kept gnawing at her. She didn't want the others to see the impact his words carried. The idea that both Prescott and Adeline had fears related to water could be chalked up to coincidence. But having yet another victim share that same trait, that was no coincidence.

This, as vague as it was, could be their first step toward a tangible link.

"There's more," Cummings related. "The reason the deputy called wasn't because of Arnold's fear of the water. I asked him that question only just now. He advised that the husband had mentioned her fear of water, but the deputy hadn't considered it to be relevant to the investigation, which is why that detail wasn't in his report." Cummings looked around the table, the gravity of what he had to say in his eyes. "We may actually have just gotten our first break. One of Arnold's colleagues remembered that she had been visited just over a week ago—right before she left for Phoenix—by Cherry Prescott."

Shock punched Adeline in the gut. Every face in the room wore that same reaction. "What was the purpose of the visit? Was Prescott interested in some real estate listing that Arnold represented?"

"The woman has no idea." Cummings collapsed against the back of his chair. "Prescott and Arnold met in her office, door closed. But," he added, "whatever they discussed, Arnold was visibly upset when the other woman left."

"There has to be something between these women that we're missing," Ferguson proclaimed. He turned to Adeline. "If you're the next victim, the answer lies with you."

His words bumped against Adeline's sternum. Her phone vibrated insistently. She grabbed it from its holster and checked the screen primarily so she could ignore Ferguson's scrutiny.

A text message.

Sender unknown.

Adeline tapped the key to download the message.

An image filled the screen.

Penny Arnold. Face all made up with too much makeup. Tiara perched on her head in exactly the same manner as the one Prescott had worn in the first photo.

Two dead princesses, one to go.

CHAPTER TWENTY-EIGHT

2:00 p.m.

Tawanda Faye Nichols was seventy-seven years old with the gray hair and gnarled fingers to prove it. She sat in the interview room, her hands clasped on the table and her head bowed over them. Her lips moved frantically in noiseless supplication of some sort.

"What the hell's she doing?" Adeline peered through the observation glass, her instincts on point.

"Praying, I imagine," Womack suggested. "She started doing that as soon as I picked her up." He sent Adeline a knowing look. "Lives in the worst shithole neighborhood over in Moss Point." He shook his head. "I know most of the cops over there and even I think they look the other way more often than not. I don't know how those folks survive."

Adeline chewed her lip. "By their wits. They've got nothing else."

"You ready?"

"Yeah." Adeline headed for the door. "Might as well see what the lady has to say."

Wyatt was mad as hell that he couldn't be in on this, but Hattiesburg's mayor as well as the brass here in Pascagoula had demanded a private conference with the man in charge. And that was the sheriff.

Womack held the door for Adeline to enter the interview room ahead of him. He'd spent a lot of time the year her father died trying to fill the void in Adeline's life. She hadn't appreciated his intent at the time. And she'd told him so. Part of her regretted that now. Besides Wyatt, he was the one person here who still appeared to care about her on some level. Or, at least, who respected her ability as a cop.

The caring about her part was not necessarily a good thing where Wyatt was concerned. She'd let this lingering thing between them get way out of control way too fast. She should have kept her distance.

Too late now.

"Afternoon, Ms. Nichols." Adeline pulled out a chair across the table from the elderly woman. "I'm Detective Cooper. I believe you've already met Deputy Womack."

Nichols's eyes opened and her lips stopped moving. She lifted her gaze to Adeline's and went wide-eyed as if she'd seen a ghost.

"Okay." Adeline placed the folder she'd brought into the room on the table and opened it. She positioned the two photos inside in front of Nichols. "Do you know either of these women, ma'am?"

Nichols picked up first one photo, then the other, examining each one at length. She placed the photos back on the table, one by one, and clasped her hands once more. "Only in my dreams."

Womack scooted his chair forward and rested his elbows on the table. "Ms. Nichols, when you called the hotline related to the abductions, you mentioned that you believed these women were being held near the water."

Fact was, Adeline didn't bother mentioning, most anywhere in the area was near water.

Nichols nodded emphatically. "That's right." She set her gaze on Adeline. "They gonna be under the water soon. You need to find them quick or it'll be too late."

Adeline cleared her throat, searched for the right way to go about this. As nonbelievers went, she was a total skeptic. "You had a dream, you say? That's how you know where the women are being held."

More of that ardent nodding. "But it don't happen when I'm asleep. Most of the time I'm awake. I guess it's more a vision than a dream."

Getting better all the time. "Can you describe, in detail, what you saw related to Cherry Prescott and Penny Arnold in your *vision?*"

"I was watching the news yesterday." She looked from Adeline to Womack and back. "Sitting in my chair minding my own business like I do most days. Don't pay to get in nobody else's business, if you know what I mean." She heaved a big breath. "Anyways, the news broke in to tell about the Arnold woman going missing."

She pursed her lips, appeared to carefully search her memory banks. "I was thinking what an awful thing this was. Poor woman. Her husband gave that heartfelt plea to whoever took her." Her pale blue eyes filmed over with emotion. "I wondered what the law was doing about this bad, bad thing. I know if she went missing in Moss Point nothing might get done. It's a pure shame." She eyed Adeline then Womack. "What y'all doing about this?"

"We're doing all we can, ma'am," Womack assured

her. "That's why we're talking to you. We're following all leads."

"That's when," Nichols went on, "the vision came. I could see them two. The ladies that's missing. They was all tied up and crying. But their crying sounded funny, like their mouths was full."

"So they were alive," Adeline clarified. Yeah, right. Like they could depend on this woman's vision to confirm the status of the victims.

Nichols looked to Adeline. "Oh, yes, ma'am. They still alive. But they won't be for long. I had a bad feeling about that part."

Adeline got that part. Beneath the table her foot wouldn't be still. Every time she halted its movement, it started right back up with that anxious bouncing. "Can you see anyone else? Or hear anyone speaking, besides the women crying?"

Nichols gave an eager nod. "A man. I can't see his face, though. Only his back. He don't have no hair." She narrowed her gaze. "I can see that real plain."

"The man who is holding the women is bald," Womack restated so there was no misunderstanding.

"Yes, sir. Bald as a baby's behind."

"Did you hear him speak or hear either one of the women speak?" Adeline didn't know why she bothered to ask the question. This was clearly bullshit. The longer she listened the more convinced she was that sheer desperation had driven her to have Womack haul this lady in for questioning.

You've discovered an all-time low, Adeline. As long as the boys back home don't hear about this...you might just live it down.

"Well, it's not exactly clear to me who's saying what," Nichols admitted. "The sobbing I know is coming from the women." She shook her head, her face pained. "Lots of sobbing. They're scared. Someone keeps saying something, but I can't tell if it's a woman or man." Her face pinched with fierce concentration as if she was trying to make sure she got this part right. "The voice keeps saying that the princesses have to die."

Adeline's spine stiffened. "What else did you see or hear?" That her voice quavered pissed her off. That all-time low had just dropped a few more pegs.

"At first," Nichols went on with her bizarre story, "I didn't understand what the voice meant. But then I remembered that they was wearing crowns. You know," she urged Adeline with her eyes," like a princess would wear. Them Miss America types. Both the women had crowns on their heads."

The bottom dropped out of Adeline's stomach. "What about their faces?" she prodded, her instincts screaming at her that this could be real. As damned ridiculous as that sounded.

This could be real.

"Pale. Eyes were red and swollen from crying." Nichols paused, cocked her head. "No." She shook her head. "Their faces wasn't all pale. They had big," she rubbed at her cheekbones, "red smudges on their cheeks. And black stuff, like mascara, smeared." She trailed her fingers down her cheeks. "Maybe from all that crying, I guess."

No way she could know this. Details of the photos Adeline had received had not been released to the public. But then, that information could have been leaked the same as the details about the letters had been.

Damn it all to hell.

"Ms. Nichols, do you or any of your family have any friends here at the sheriff's department? Or with the Moss Point police?"

Womack glared at Adeline. He understood where she was going with this question.

Nichols shook her head. "No. We don't get into town much. About once a month for supplies. And them Moss Point police ain't no friend to nobody."

"So no one shared this information with you," Adeline ventured. "You didn't hear about the makeup and crowns from someone who perhaps had heard this from someone in the department?"

Nichols's brow scrunched as her head wagged side to side. "No, ma'am. I told you, I dreamed this." She shrugged. "Saw it in a vision. Nobody didn't tell me nothing."

Adeline told her muscles to relax, focused on drawing in a decent breath. "Do you recall any details about where the women are being held?" This was a waste of time. The woman had to have been told these details. No way she'd dreamed all this. The whole idea was ridiculous.

"It's dark."

How original.

"A house, I think. Not a cave or nothing like that. They are walls around them."

"How long," Adeline decided to ask, "have you had these visions, Ms. Nichols?"

Her expression relaxed a little. "Since I was a child. My momma warned me not to ever tell nobody or they'd think I was crazy as a loon. So I never have until now."

How convenient.

"I never dreamed about no police case before," the woman added, her eyes widening again. "It upset me so I had to take some of my daddy's old remedy to sleep."

"Remedy?" Womack inquired.

The old lady leaned forward. "Moonshine. They still a

few quart jars in the cellar. I don't touch it except for times like when I can't sleep no other way."

Adeline turned to Womack. "Maybe we need a BAT."

Womack nodded. "Yeah."

Checking the woman's blood alcohol level might not be a bad idea.

"Well." Adeline stood. "If you think of anything else, Ms. Nichols, please give Deputy Womack a call."

Nichols stared at Adeline a long moment, her eyes seemingly unseeing. If possible, the atmosphere in the room got even weirder.

Adeline glanced at Womack and shrugged. "Moonshine."

"Ma'am," Womack offered, "is there anything else—"

Nichols jumped out of her chair and reached across the table, grabbing Adeline by the upper arms before she could turn and walk out the door. Adeline tried to peel her fingers loose, but the lady wasn't letting go.

Nichols shook Adeline hard. "You're next!" she warned, her expression wild with something resembling hysteria.

Adeline froze. Fear rammed into her sternum.

"You have to hurry," Nichols urged, leaning across the table toward Adeline. "They don't want to go into the water! Help them!" She peered deep into Adeline's eyes, panic in her voice. "You the only one who can. You're daddy's little angel."

Womack pulled the woman off.

Adeline stood there, shaking like a leaf.

What the hell?

"Go, Cooper," Womack urged. "I'll take care of this."

"You're next! You're next! You're next!"

The words followed Adeline out the door.

She scrubbed the back of her hand over her face. Her cheeks were damp.

She had to get out of here.

Adeline stopped in Wyatt's office and picked up her jacket and his keys. Her Bronco was at his house. She didn't give a shit what she drove. She just wanted out of here.

Sullenger called after her, but Adeline ignored her.

She couldn't breathe until she'd hit the street. Her heart thundered in her chest. This was insane. Absolutely over the top.

Tires squealing, she roared away from the curb.

She didn't know where the hell she was going. Somewhere to think.

Five minutes later she parked at the Greenwood Cemetery. The massive live oaks surrounding it were laden with Spanish moss. The cemetery was at least a century old. More of her Cooper ancestors than she cared to own were buried here.

She paused at Gage Cooper's grave and stared at the lavish granite headstone. "You piece of shit. Why the hell couldn't you stay that silly kid you were when we played together? Why'd you have to turn into such a scumbag?"

Adeline shook off the suffocating feeling of regret. He was dead because he'd made bad choices. It wasn't her fault. She glanced back down at the dates on the marker. Twenty-three damned years old.

"Idiot."

She trudged through the rows of tombstones jutting up from the ground, some leaning from age, others damaged after Katrina's ugly lashing. She reached the marker she was looking for and sat down on the cold, damp ground. The tree canopy in this section of the cemetery was so heavy that the ground had been protected to some degree from last night's rain. Not saturated or muddy, just a little damp.

Carlton Riley Cooper
Beloved husband and father

"I miss you, Daddy."

The whispered words curled around her, strengthened the emotions pressing against her heart. When her daddy had died, her life had turned upside down. Wyatt had accused her of having a death wish. She'd taken far too many risks on the job. Had her mother worried sick. Had Wyatt ready to kick her ass. And Womack looking over her shoulder.

Then Sheriff Scumbag Grider had assigned her to work with the DEA to carry out a big sting. She'd been thrilled beyond words. That had felt like her chance to do something big and to get back at her asshole cousin and uncle for getting away with breaking the law for so many years. Mainly, though, it had felt like a way to prove she was worthy of the high praise her daddy had always heaped on her.

"Why did you just ignore Cyrus?" she asked aloud. Her father had been a fine man. An upstanding citizen. A volunteer firefighter. He'd sacrificed his life to save others.

Yet he'd looked the other way when it came to Cyrus.

"I know he was your brother and all," she relented, "but you pretended not to know. That drove me nuts."

Adeline closed her eyes and let the fond memories flow. Her daddy had loved her so. And her mother. There was not a more devoted husband to be found. He'd been a good man, despite the genetic connection to the biggest asshole in the county.

She opened her eyes. What the hell difference did it make if he chose to love his brother in spite of his shortcomings? As big a hero as her father had been, he'd still been only human.

Adeline smiled. "Love you, Daddy." She kissed her fingers and pressed them to his headstone.

And really, that was all that mattered.

She pushed to her feet.

And went stone-still.

The hair on the back of her neck stood on end.

She palmed her weapon, scanned the gloomy cemetery.

Someone was watching her. She visually searched the tree line of the woods that backed up to the cemetery.

Let that son of a bitch come. She would blow his damned head off. She was definitely in the mood.

Her cell vibrated.

Circling cautiously to ensure no one sneaked up on her as she made her way back to the SUV, she gripped the weapon with both hands, ready to shoot anything that moved.

By the time she reached the SUV, she'd broken a sweat despite the cool temp.

Moving more quickly now, she checked the interior of the SUV, climbed in, and pressed the lock button. She started the vehicle, took one last look around, and pulled back out onto the road.

A glance in the rearview mirror confirmed that no one was behind her. Her hand landed on the gearshift to move into drive.

She stalled.

Slowly, her mind spinning, she pushed the gearshift back into park. The words written in the road film on the rear windshield blistered across her brain, automatically reversing their order from what her eyes saw in the mirror.

Adeline drew her weapon and shoved the door open.

She stormed to the back of the SUV, scanning the street...the woods...the cemetery as she went.

She stared at the words, fury exploding inside her.

Are you ready, princess?

Son of a bitch!

She stepped away from the vehicle, both hands on the weapon, ready to fire if she caught sight of the bastard.

"Who the hell are you?" she screamed as she turned all the way around.

The wind shifted the moss in the trees.

"Show yourself!"

She clenched her jaw against a glimmer of fear, stomped toward the cemetery entrance. "Afraid this princess will kick your ass?"

The furious words echoed around her, shattering the silence.

Dammit!

How the hell had he gotten that close?

Ready to tear through those woods after the bastard, she grabbed back some semblance of control. There was stupid and then there was *stupid*. Going after him alone would be *stupid*.

She marched back to the driver's side door and climbed behind the wheel. Shifted into drive and spun away.

Her cell vibrated again, snapping her out of the raging thoughts of decapitating the bastard. She took a breath and checked her cell. Wyatt.

Damn. He was going to be pissed.

Before she could call him back her cell vibrated. She hit the accept button and struggled for calm. "Cooper."

"Where in the hell are you?"

Don't tell him yet. He would hunt her down and bring her in. There was one more thing she needed to do.

Just be calm. He was worried. And she, well, she had just done another of those stupid things she did when life got out of control. She knew better than to take this kind of risk.

Another deep breath and she could talk. "I came to the cemetery to visit my father."

Until he'd finished yelling, she held the phone away from her ear. When he was done, she dared to put it back. "I have something I have to do before I come back to the office."

"Addy! You don't need to—"

"I'm going to see my mother," she said, shutting him up. "If you need me that's where I'll be."

She closed her phone and shoved it back into its holster. He wanted to protect her. It was his job. Not just his job. He still had feelings for her. She couldn't deny that any longer.

Memories from that morning rushed into her head, making her weak. Making her wish things were different.

Stop. This bastard was getting closer all the time. Escalating. No matter how hard Wyatt tried to protect her, this was going down.

There were things she had to do first.

Adeline needed to talk to her mother about the past. She couldn't do that with Wyatt anywhere near her.

It was time she and her mother cleared the air.

If this bastard got to her, Adeline didn't want any unfinished business between her and anyone she cared about.

That included having *the* talk with Wyatt.

Eventually.

CHAPTER TWENTY-NINE

4720 Miller Road, 3:38 p.m.

Adeline sat in the SUV and stared at the farmhouse that had been home to her the first twenty-one years of her life. Seemed she'd been doing a lot of contemplating lately. It was like taking a huge step back into a place that hadn't changed in the slightest. She had changed but everything here still felt the same. No matter how far she'd run, or where she'd run, the place and the people were still here. Waiting. Frozen in time and attitude as if her dramatic departure had changed nothing. As if her sacrifices hadn't mattered.

How was that possible?

Her gaze roved over the house she'd played in as a kid. Where she'd fought with her parents during those rebellious teenage years. The place where she'd felt safe when the rest of the world had seemed crazy.

All except for that once.

Nine years ago, after Gage's death, even this house hadn't felt like a haven. Granted, her mother had still been grieving her father's death. As had Adeline. Both their lives had been in utter turmoil. Nothing had felt right or real.

Except Wyatt.

And then he'd let her down, too.

Adeline shook off the bad memories. Sucked in a deep breath for courage and reminded her brain to stay out of the past.

There was enough crap going on right here in the present. No need to go digging up the past all at once. First, she had to talk to her mother. Get that out of the way.

She climbed out of the SUV and surveyed the condition of the house. Still in good shape. Her mother had stayed on top of the maintenance just as Adeline's father always had. Adeline had felt a little guilty over the years that she wasn't here to help out. Her mom had always insisted that she had everything under control. It was good to see that she hadn't been keeping anything from Adeline. Both of her parents had always been far too protective.

Came with the territory of being an only child.

The house wasn't nearly so imposing as the one Cyrus lived in just beyond the woods and fields to the east. As the oldest, Cyrus had inherited the family home. Adeline's father had renovated the only remaining tenant farmer's house. Carl hadn't been nearly so taken with appearances and material possessions. He'd never had any desire to prove he was better or wealthier than anyone else.

Too bad Cyrus hadn't taken a page from his younger brother's book on how to live right. Cyrus Cooper liked owning things and people. No matter the price, usually levied on anyone but him.

Funny how the good guys always went well before the bad ones. By rights, Adeline's father should be enjoying his golden years and that old bastard Cyrus should've been planted in that damned cemetery.

But life was rarely fair. Maybe that was why Adeline had decided to walk away. Walk, she supposed, was an understatement. Most around here called what she'd done "running."

Until now, she hadn't once cared what any of them thought. This sudden uncertainty about her past decisions she suffered now was more likely related to the case and the utter helplessness of being unable to do a damned thing. Two women were possibly dead, or would be soon, and she couldn't find one damned lead to follow.

And the bad guy just kept dashing it in her face. Getting closer and closer.

Prescott had visited Arnold. That had to mean something. Somewhere in her history, Adeline had to be connected to those two women.

Since her father was dead, that left only her mother to ask. It was a shot in the dark, but it was the only shot she had a clear window at making just now.

This wall that had erected itself between her and her mother over the past nine years had to come down. Her mother had assured Adeline over and over that she had made the right decision moving away and not coming back. Yet, her mother had refused to join her. Something had held her back. Maybe the need to be in this house close to the things and the life she had shared with her husband.

But it felt *disturbing*.

All these years Adeline had let it ride, not pushing the subject. She couldn't do that anymore.

She needed the whole truth.

Before climbing the steps, she assessed the sky. Not a cloud in sight, no more rain hopefully. A shiver went through her. Maybe she'd get a decent night's sleep tonight without having to resort to her old methods of consoling irrational fears from her childhood.

She'd scarcely crossed the porch when the door opened.

"Addy." Her mother looked her up and down, as she always did when her daughter arrived home after a day on the job as a cop. "Is something wrong?"

Her mother didn't have to state the obvious. Adeline was here—home—after nine years. She hadn't set foot on Cooper land in all that time until her recent visit to Cyrus. That she was here now would be startling for anyone who knew her. Still, it seemed strange that her mother would assume the worst. They had spoken by phone earlier in the day.

This case was making everyone edgy.

"Maybe," Adeline confessed. She shrugged. "Mainly, I need to ask you a few questions."

Something flickered in her mother's eyes before she stepped back and eased the door open wider. "Well, don't be so formal. Come on in."

A little puzzled by her mother's reaction, Adeline stepped across the threshold into the life she'd once known. Decades of memories bombarded her. Her father stepping through this same door and sweeping Adeline into his arms. The smell of chicken soup in the winter and fresh vegetables sautéing in the summer. And sweets baking in the oven. Adeline inhaled deeply. She could almost smell those chocolate chip cookies of her mother's.

"I was just having a cup of tea." Her mother smoothed a hand over her blouse. "I would have changed if I'd known you were coming. I've been baking all afternoon. Would you like some tea or cocoa?"

"Nah, I'm good." Adeline was too busy taking in the sights and smells. She'd thought she smelled cookies.

The house felt exactly the same. Cozy, clean, welcoming. Her mother had always kept a meticulous home. Same striped wallpaper in the entry hall. Same well-worn wood floor. Furnishings were the ones that had always been there. The lingering scent of baked goods in the air. It could have been ten years ago or twenty.

Her stomach rumbled. She had no idea when she'd eaten last.

"I made chocolate chip cookies." Irene smiled. "I know how you love them. I was going to bring a basket of goodies by the sheriff's office."

Since you didn't come by on Christmas, she didn't add. At some point Adeline needed to admit that she wasn't a very good daughter when it came to this sort of thing. She'd stopped going to mass when she turned eighteen. She hated going to church. The somber face of the priest. All the rituals. Just hadn't been her thing. Now that she thought about it, she'd spent a lot of time disappointing her parents.

"Maybe later," Adeline offered. Feeling guilty, she tacked on, "I do love them."

Smiling now, her mother led the way into the family room. A wave of nostalgia washed over Adeline as she took in the room. The Christmas tree stood in the corner near the front window. Same decorations her mother had always used, including a couple elementary school projects of Adeline's. A crooked star and a not so flattering snowman. The colors were a little faded now, washed out—kind of the way Adeline felt at the moment.

Despite the fact that Adeline hadn't been home in nine years and her father had been dead for ten, three timeworn velvet stockings hung from the mantel. Adeline walked over to the fireplace, briefly admired the familiar brickwork before turning her attention to the framed photographs lining the wood mantel. A smile tugged at her lips. Her daddy had been a handsome man. He'd gotten all the looks and Cyrus had inherited all the conniving, evil genes.

Irene had been quite the looker, as well. Still was. Some gray had invaded her dark hair, but otherwise she remained trim and youthful looking. Adeline turned to her mother who'd taken a seat in her favorite chair—the one in which her husband had spent his evenings watching the news for as long as Adeline could remember.

"You been watching the news?" Adeline asked as she settled onto the sofa. She rubbed her hand over the coarse, sturdy texture. Same sofa as when she'd been a hard-headed teenager. Her mother had been so proud the day it was delivered. The previous sofa had been pretty beat up from Adeline and her cousin's rowdy childhood antics.

Irene nodded, her expression somber. "Is there still nothing new on the case?" She reached for the delicate porcelain cup and saucer on the table next to her chair and sipped her tea.

Her mother always had hot tea in the afternoons. Two sugars and lemon. From a delicate white cup embellished with pink roses. The china had been in the family for as far back as Adeline remembered. Belonged to her grandmother if she recalled correctly. Unlike most who only used their china on special occasions, her mother used it every day.

"Nothing new. Really." This morning Adeline had filled her in on the latest. But the parts she'd learned this afternoon—those were the ones she wanted to discuss.

Except for the incident at the cemetery. *Not going there.* Telling Wyatt would be ordeal enough. "There are some small connections between the victims that, with the second abduction, are proving more significant than previously theorized."

Irene's fingers tightened on the fragile dishes. "What sort of connections? If you're allowed to say, of course," she qualified.

"Both victims are blond. The resemblance is noticeable but not inordinately noteworthy. Career oriented." She shrugged. "Like I said, nothing really significant." She didn't know why she even mentioned those details. Her mother was fully aware of what the victims looked like and who they were. With Penny Arnold's abduction, however, those points were, as she'd said, more relevant.

Irene nodded. "There are still no leads on who might be behind this awful nightmare?"

"Not a one." Adeline crossed one leg over the other. She resisted the urge to curl up at the end of the sofa the way she used to. Relaxing wasn't on her agenda. She had questions. Deciding on the proper avenue of approach was the snag. "There is this kind of strange link between me and the two victims. It may be nothing but we have to look into any and all possibilities."

The cup and saucer rattled. Irene set her tea aside. "This is something you learned today?"

Adeline nodded. Her instincts were humming. It wasn't unreasonable that her mother would be nervous about discussing the case. The ugliness had hit pretty close to home. The Prescott woman had disappeared only a few miles from here. Even so, there was something not quite right about her overall reaction. The way her back had stiffened and the fact that she didn't look Adeline directly in the eyes now.

"Yes." Adeline pushed to her feet. "Maybe I'll have one of those cookies after all." She wanted to watch her mother's body language and get a better grip on the situation before she said anything she might regret.

Irene chattered as she scurried around the kitchen before settling a plate on the counter then embellishing it with not one but three cookies. There was no way to miss the way her hands shook. The tension rippling through Adeline moved to the next level. This was so not right.

Maybe there was something going on in her mother's life that Adeline didn't know about. If she learned that Cyrus had been giving her trouble...

"You'll need milk."

Her mother's statement snapped Adeline from the troubling thoughts. "That'd be great." Relax. She'd come here for answers. No need to go making something out of nothing.

Irene reached for the fridge door and launched into more rambling about what some friend that Adeline couldn't remember had gotten herself for Christmas.

When the milk was poured and Adeline had selected the cookie with the most visible chocolate chips, she indulged in a bite and savored the decadent taste.

"Now." Irene had posted herself on the opposite side of the breakfast counter from her daughter. Her hands were clasped in front of her. "You were saying something about a connection."

"Yeah." Adeline sipped the cold milk. Tasted like old times. "Did I ever have a near-drowning experience?" She picked off another bite of cookie. "You know, in the tub or in a pool. Maybe a lake." She popped the sweet chunk into her mouth.

Her mother's brow furrowed in concentration. "Not that I recall." She shook her head. "I'm certain you didn't.

I would surely have remembered." She swiped the cookie crumbs from the counter into her hand and marched them to the trash as if another moment scattered on the counter would have created a tragedy of some sort.

Her mom had always been a little obsessive about cleaning.

"Why have I always been afraid of the water? Something had to have happened. Maybe I was with a friend's family."

"Oh, Adeline." Her mother waved her hands back and forth as if to dismiss the entire notion. "You know the reason for that." She pressed a palm to her chest. "I was always scared of the water. Never learned to swim and I guess my irrational fears rubbed off on you."

True. She placed the half-eaten cookie back on the plate. "Is there any chance at all that we knew Cherry Prescott's or Penny Arnold's family at some point? You know, when I was a little kid?" Neither family had lived in Pascagoula, but there were other possibilities. Church gatherings, Girl Scouts, school activities. It wasn't impossible.

Her mother blinked. Three times. Rapidly. Her face blanked. "Why would you ask that?"

Why would she ask why? Adeline swallowed back the hesitation. "We all three are afraid in one way or another of water. We're all three blond with blue eyes and have a number of other facial similarities." The implications of what she was saying loomed inside her head, made a breath next to impossible. "And some psycho is targeting us. Calling us 'princesses.' There is either a connection in our pasts that put us on his radar or this creep has made one hell of a big mistake."

That trapped-in-the-headlights expression claimed her mother's face. "I've...I've heard you say that those awful serial killers oftentimes pick women who look alike. Considering that, are these similarities really so unusual?"

Again, this was true, but…

Adeline's heart pounded harder, making her chest ache, with every statement her mother made. She was hiding something. There was no way on earth to deny that glaring fact.

"You're right," Adeline allowed. "The sticking point is the whole water thing. That's not exactly something I've broadcast over the years, and from what I've learned so far neither did the other two women involved in this case."

"I…I don't know what you want me to say, Addy." Her mother swiped at the counter again when there were no crumbs to swipe. She glanced around the kitchen as if looking for something else to do. Then she grabbed the dishtowel from the sink and rubbed her hands.

That bad, bad feeling that had taken root was wrapping round and round Adeline's throat and squeezing. For about five seconds, Adeline was at a loss for words. "I just want you to answer the question. Did we or did we not know the families of these victims at some point in the past?"

"Your question is preposterous. Why would you ask me such a thing?" Irene huffed. "I think you…you…" The color of frustration and no small amount of anger climbed her cheeks as she looked Adeline straight in the eyes. "I think it's not safe for you to be here. You should go back to Huntsville and let Wyatt do his job. Not only are you a target of this insane person, but you're thinking up all these ridiculous ideas."

Whoa. "You're overreacting to a simple question, Mother." Adeline backed off. This wasn't going to evolve into a battle. She hadn't come here for that. "But if discussing the case upsets you that much, we won't talk about it." Jesus Christ. It was a simple question.

"Good." Her mother picked up the plate Adeline had used and started toward the sink.

This conversation had officially gone from odd to totally bizarre. Did Adeline stay or go or apologize or what?

The plate crashed to the floor. Adeline jerked at the sound. Broken china and cookie remains lay scattered over the linoleum. Her mother stood, a step from the sink, her back ramrod straight, and turned to Adeline. That she didn't say something or rush to clean up the mess triggered an alarm that Adeline didn't want to acknowledge.

She opened her mouth to say something—anything—but couldn't come up with the right words, so she covered the two steps that separated them and crouched down to pick up the mess on the floor.

Her mother swayed.

"Mom, you okay?" Adeline shot to her feet. Barely caught her mother as she crumpled.

"Mom?"

Her mother's eyes were wide with pain and fear. She tried to speak...couldn't. The fingers of one hand clutched at her chest.

Shit. Shit. Shit. Adeline lowered her mother to the floor. "It's okay. I'm calling for help." Adeline reached for her cell.

Pounding on the front door echoed through the house. She ignored it. Keeping one eye on her mother, she gave the 911 operator the necessary information.

"Addy!"

Wyatt. He'd obviously opened the front door and stuck his head inside.

"Kitchen!" she shouted back.

Irene's eyes rolled back and her body tensed.

Adeline dropped the phone. Checked her mother's carotid pulse. Where the hell was her pulse?

Wyatt stamped into the room. "Why in the Sam Hill was the door unlocked?"

Adeline looked up at him, fear crushing her windpipe. "Help me.

CHAPTER THIRTY

Singing River Hospital, 6:37 p.m.

Adeline sat in the molded plastic chair in the deserted waiting room. The smell of pain and sickness had invaded her lungs. She felt cold. The stupid Christmas tree in the corner mocked her.

It was the day after Christmas and she'd done this to her mother. She truly was a bad daughter. A really bad daughter.

All these years she'd thought she had escaped the evil Cooper genes, but she'd been wrong.

Heart attack. Her mother had suffered a heart attack. Not a massive episode, the doctor had assured during the brief update Adeline had gotten half an hour ago, but enough to admit her mother for additional testing and further observation. Just in case.

As soon as Irene was settled Adeline could see her.

They'd run her out of the ER exam room because her presence seemed to distress the patient.

Bad, bad, bad. She was a bad daughter.

"This isn't your fault." Wyatt sat down next to her and shoved a cup of coffee her way.

"You weren't there."

"I didn't have to be." He gave up and set the coffee on a table next to a stack of out-of-date magazines. "You love your mother. Your mother loves you. Nothing you said or asked prompted this event. You have to know that."

Adeline felt numb, yet the sensation of devastation hovered around the edges of her consciousness. It was there. Coming, like a hurricane brewing offshore.

Her mother could've died. Still could. The doctor had admitted after relentless interrogation that part of the reason for the observation was because many times a second heart attack followed the first. It reminded Adeline of the aftershocks of an earthquake.

Only this wasn't someplace she'd never been or people she didn't know, this was her mother.

This was *her* fault.

"God." She braced her elbows on her knees and put her face in her hands. All of this was so damned wrong. Off somehow, and it just kept getting more and more twisted.

"Addy." Wyatt's big, warm hand settled on her back. "The doc said she's going to be fine. You have to believe that. And stop blaming yourself."

Adeline sat up, turned her face to his. "She's hiding something from me." She looked away, didn't want him to see the sting of tears in her eyes. She swallowed back the ones crowded in her throat. "There's something about the past and this case that she's not telling me. I saw it in her eyes…before." She blinked back the emotion that threatened to spill past her lashes. "Whatever it is...it's big."

Bigger than maybe Adeline wanted to know.

This case—coming back here—had ripped apart the fiber of her existence. And the split just kept getting wider and more jagged.

"Ms. Cooper?"

Adeline's attention swung to the double doors next to the admissions desk. Dr. Hubbard, the physician in charge of her mother's care, was coming toward Adeline.

She shot to her feet and rushed to meet him.

"You can see your mother now." He smiled, the expression more comforting than he could possibly comprehend. "She's been moved to the cardiac unit on the fourth floor. You may have a few moments with her and then she needs to rest. She's sedated so she may fall asleep on you."

"Thank you, Doctor."

She turned to Wyatt, relief so profound rushing through her body that her knees threatened to buckle. "She's gonna be okay."

He hugged her close and she wanted to cry all over again. Her heart ached, needed to feel this. To feel him.

Adeline pulled away. Exiled the powerful emotions. She needed to get a hold of herself. And to get to the fourth floor.

The journey from the ER waiting room to the main lobby and the bank of elevators beyond seemed to take forever. The delay for the elevator car to arrive was even worse. By the time they reached the fourth floor, Adeline felt ready to have a heart attack of her own. Her heart thumped so hard she could scarcely breathe. Her head spun with the lack of oxygen. And all the bizarre fragments of information that didn't fit together and yet went hand in hand.

Her mother's cubicle stood directly across from the nurse's station. There was no door, just a glass partition allowing visual access to the patient from the nurse's station. As much as it scared Adeline to see her mother in a place like this, she was glad for the close monitoring.

The nurse made Wyatt wait in the corridor since only one visitor at a time was allowed. He squeezed Adeline's hand, offering that support she needed so badly.

When Adeline approached the bed, Irene's eyes opened. "Addy."

Between the ultra-sterile environment, the collage of machines playing their out-of-sync symphony, and her mother's pale face, Adeline couldn't stop the tears. "You about scared me to death, lady." Her mother reached for her hand. Adeline's heart reacted to the too-cool feel of her skin. "I am so sorry, Mom. I didn't mean to upset you. This is all my fault. I shouldn't have—"

"This is not your fault."

Her voice sounded so weak. Adeline's gut clenched with fear and dread and worry, all at the same time. "I'm sorry anyway."

Irene peered down at their clasped hands. "I shouldn't have waited. I should have told you a long time ago." She licked her parched lips.

As much as Adeline wanted to ask what her mother meant, she reached for the ice chips on the table next to the bed instead. "Here." She placed a few in her mother's mouth. When Adeline offered more, her mother shook her head.

"I need you to listen to me."

"All right." Adeline leaned closer to ensure she didn't miss a word. Her mother's voice sounded weak and fragile. Nothing like the strong woman Adeline knew so well. It tore at her heart.

"There were three of you."

The statement ignited a new kind of fear deep in Adeline's chest. This moment—what she was about to hear, she instinctively understood—would change everything. "We don't have to talk about this, Mom. You should rest. I want you well." She defied the tears that crammed into her eyes once more. "I can't bear to see you like this."

"Three beautiful little girls." Irene's voice wobbled. "Your father wanted to take all three of you but there were others who desperately wanted children. I don't know who made the decisions on who went where. All I know is that your father and I got you. You were so beautiful. Only six months old. And perfect."

Adeline pinched her lips to prevent the multitude of questions to which she wanted to demand answers. She couldn't press her mother. *Just let her talk.*

"I believe Cherry Prescott and Penny Arnold are the other two—your *sisters.*"

What little oxygen Adeline had been able to draw into her lungs bolted. This wasn't possible. She couldn't be adopted. All the times she had wondered about why she didn't look a lot like her parents or cousins—the dreams about the water—the numerous pictures of her as a baby but none of her parents holding her until she was several months old. Those niggling facts that had haunted the rim of her existence her whole life came crashing down around her now.

"Ms. Prescott came to see me."

"What?" Adeline regretted how incredulous she sounded. She had to focus. Pay attention to what her mother was saying and work on figuring out the rest later. "When?"

Her mother's lips trembled. "The same day she went missing. She wanted to see you. Wanted to know where you lived. How to get in touch with you. Somehow she'd learned that she was adopted and had siblings. I told her I didn't know what she was talking about. That she had made a mistake." Tears streamed down her face. A sob hiccuped from her throat. "I lied to her."

Adeline banished the questions, the shock...the ache. "It's okay," she placated. "You did what you thought was right. Please don't cry. You don't need to get upset like this. We won't talk about this anymore right now." As much as Adeline wanted the truth she couldn't risk her mother's health. But, dear God—Prescott had come to her mother demanding the truth? At least now they had some insight as to what she had been doing in the Pascagoula area.

And Adeline was adopted. Her whole past was founded on secrets and...*lies*.

"I have to tell you the rest," Irene insisted. "I can hardly keep my eyes open, but you have to know. It may make the difference in how this turns out."

Adeline pushed away all thought but one—her mother's well-being. She glanced at the monitors. Her mother's blood pressure and heart rate had climbed since she'd come into the room. "Mom, you don't need to push yourself."

"Just listen to me," she urged. "The adoptions were sealed by the church." Irene exhaled a shuddering breath. "Somehow the Prescott woman learned the truth. Apparently, someone else did as well, but I don't know why they would do anything so awful as this."

More tears leaked from the corners of her eyes. Adeline gently swiped them away. Her fingers trembled in spite of her best efforts.

Her mother's gaze searched Adeline's, then grew distant as if she were looking back, remembering. "They're dead. I don't know why she had to do this now. After all these years. But she just kept saying that she had to know."

Adeline tensed. Was she talking about Prescott and Arnold? How could she know this? "Who's dead, Mother?"

"Your biological parents." Irene blinked, looked into Adeline's eyes once more. "I didn't want to tell you any of this." More of those tears spilled. "I didn't want you to know that you weren't my little girl."

"Mom," Adeline urged, "that's completely—"

Irene put her fingers to her daughter's lips, hushing her protests. "I realized I couldn't keep the truth from you any longer. Not with the situation getting worse and worse. It's been eating at me." Pain etched deep lines in Irene's face. "Was that woman taken because I didn't help her?"

Stunned all over again, Adeline dug way down deep and summoned her voice. If she sounded upset, her mother would only grow more agitated. "I'm certain none of this is your fault. You couldn't have guessed what some madman was up to."

"But if I'd told her the truth would this have happened?" Irene's head rocked slowly, wearily, from side to side against the pillow. "I should have told you everything a long time ago. I was a coward."

Adeline made a decision. There was no putting off certain aspects of this disturbing conversation. Not if her mother had information that could help the investigation. "You can help me now." She had to be careful. The last thing she wanted to do was overtax her mother. The pivotal piece of this puzzle lay in the past—her past. The one she'd had before her parents had adopted her. "You don't have to explain or to go into any detail," Adeline said. "We'll do that later, when you're better. Based on what you've told me, Prescott was digging into her past

—*our* past. If that's the case, all I need is a starting point. A name or place."

"Father Floyd Grayson." Irene's lips quivered. "The last I heard he had retired to an assisted living facility in Waveland. Tell him you need to know about the Solomon family, Quentin Solomon, and…and the tragedy."

Her mom's eyes drifted shut.

"Mom."

Irene's eyes blinked open once more.

Adeline squeezed her mother's hand and pressed a kiss to her cheek, then smiled with all the love bursting in her heart. "I will always be your little girl."

Irene nodded, the slightest dip of her chin, then closed her eyes once more.

Confusion rammed Adeline hard. Wait. She should have asked if her mother had told anyone else about this. Whoever had taken Prescott and Arnold had to be aware of their true past. "Mom," she whispered close to her mother's ear, "who else knows about the adoption?"

Surely her uncle Cyrus knew. Bastard. Was he involved in this?

"Ms. Cooper?"

Adeline started. Took a breath and straightened away from the bed as the nurse entered the cubicle. "Is she okay?"

The nurse nodded. "It's the sedative, ma'am. She needs to rest. I don't think she'll be coming around again for a while."

Adeline nodded. "Thank you."

She stood for a long time afterward, watching her mother sleep. Watching her breathe. She considered the glass wall that separated her mother's space from those in charge of her care. Adeline had no reason to doubt the competence of any of them. Yet, she was scared to death.

She had to go. Prescott and Arnold were out there. Maybe dead. Maybe alive. Those two women needed her to be strong. To find them. To stop this bastard...whoever the hell he was.

And now she actually had a direction to take.

Adeline kissed her mom's forehead and walked out into the corridor. Wyatt was speaking to one of the nurses. Adeline headed in that direction.

A big body T-boned her.

"Sorry." She looked up at the man who had backed into her. Big guy. The uniform indicated he worked for the hospital. The mop in his hand identified him as a janitor. The yellow plastic sign sitting on the damp tile in the middle of the corridor reminded her that it was late, after normal visiting hours, when stuff like this got done. Boy, if her reactions got any slower she would be a danger to herself and those around her. "Sorry," she repeated. "I didn't see you."

"No problem." He rubbed a hand over his shiny bald head and nodded toward the cubicle she'd exited. "Your mother?"

Adeline nodded. She fought another wave of emotion "Yeah. She had a heart attack." Which he likely knew already. This was the cardiac unit.

He glanced at the nurse's desk. "Don't worry. She couldn't be in better hands."

Adeline told herself he was right. She had to trust these people. "Thanks." She took one last look at her mom sleeping so peacefully. "I don't know what I'd do if anything happened to her."

The janitor gave her a sympathetic smile then went on about his mopping.

Adeline joined Wyatt at the station and left her cell number with the charge nurse. Grabbing her wavering composure with both hands, she met Wyatt's expectant gaze. "We have to go to Waveland."

She didn't give him time to ask questions. Adeline walked as fast as possible to the stairwell exit. She didn't have the patience for the elevator. She had to get out of here.

Wyatt didn't try to slow her or to demand an explanation. He followed, taking the stairs two at a time just as she did.

When she hit the parking lot, she sent him a sideways glance. "Take me to the nearest convenience store."

"Am I allowed to ask why?" He kept pace with her half run.

"I need a cigarette."

CHAPTER THIRTY-ONE

Waveland, Mississippi, 11:58 p.m.

The door had barely opened when Adeline spoke. "Father Grayson?"

Father Floyd Grayson peered over his eyeglasses at Adeline. "You two got any ID?"

Adeline displayed her credentials as did Wyatt. Grayson grunted, then sent her another speculative glare. "It took you look enough to get here."

"Yes, sir," she said. "I'm sorry. Remember, I told you we were driving over from Pascagoula?"

"Well, come on then. You're letting in the cold air."

Adeline glanced at Wyatt before going inside. So many confusing thoughts were whirling around in her head that it was a miracle she could still string together two words. Wyatt had pulled some major strings to get the information on the priest from the sheriff in Hancock County.

They followed the elderly gentleman into his cozy living room. Took the seats he offered.

The small home was exactly like all the others in the village. Postage-stamp-sized yard with a picket fence. Christmas wreath on the doors. Though the priest looked reasonably fit, Floyd Grayson was eighty-six years old and clearly this was well past his bedtime. When Adeline had spoken to him shortly after ten he had agreed, considering the urgency of the situation, to see her at this ungodly hour.

"You want to know about the Solomon tragedy."

Adeline tried to slow the adrenaline rushing through her body, couldn't slow the momentum. "Yes, sir. It's of the utmost urgency. Sheriff Henderson and I are working a case involving two missing women and we believe there may somehow be a connection to the Solomon family."

She was still reeling with the idea that she was adopted. Memories from her childhood kept flashing through her mind in some bizarre out-of-control fast-forward mode. Her father—she was his little angel. Her mother braiding her hair, taking her to school.

How could she not have come from those people?

There was no time for dealing with that now. Cherry Prescott and Penny Arnold were depending on her to find the facts and them.

Urgency or no, she understood, as the old priest sized her up, that he did not have to talk to her about the adoptions or the Solomon family. Even a warrant could not compel him to break his vow on the subject. Yet, he'd agreed to see her. That had to mean he was willing to talk.

"You're aware," he ventured, "that I'm not obliged to discuss with you the details of a private adoption or any other personal knowledge related to a current or former member of my church."

A mind reader, too. Before Adeline could launch another persuasive strategy, Wyatt said, "We're very much aware of the sensitivity of the situation, Father. Any assistance you can provide will be greatly appreciated and may," he urged, "help the two women—both wives and mothers—who are missing. We've exhausted every other avenue."

Grayson cocked an eyebrow. "I watch the news, Sheriff. That's why you're sitting in my living room right now. I hadn't made the connection between Ms. Prescott and Ms. Arnold. With the heinousness of crime mounting every day, sometimes it's easier not to look so closely and to simply pray for the world as a whole." He shifted his attention from Wyatt to Adeline. "But when I saw the two women's photos side by side on the news this morning, I began to consider the possibility that I knew them or I had when they were children."

Adeline eased to the edge of her seat. "If you're not certain, Father, tell us now. Time is too short to be chasing our tails."

"I did a little investigating of my own this afternoon." Grayson set his eyeglasses aside. "If I weren't certain of what I'm about to say," he scolded, "we wouldn't be having this conversation." He inspected her face with that too keen gaze. "In truth, I could have answered your questions on the phone. But I wanted to see you before I made my decision on just how fully to *cooperate*, as you call it."

"I feel confident your sheriff verified our credentials and relayed that verification to you before giving Sheriff Henderson your home phone number." Adeline didn't want to drag this out. She just wanted the man to get to the point. She had questions. He, apparently, had the answers.

"It wasn't about your credentials. It was about *you*."

She braced for the tsunami about to blast her emotions.

"You're the spitting image of your birth mother."

Adeline rode out the initial impact of his announcement, then pushed aside the emotions that had no place in this investigation. She'd been doing that all night. "Anything you recall about the family and the adoptions could prove useful. At this point we don't know how the fact that the victims are biological sisters ties into the abductions."

He studied her a moment more, his expression too knowing for her comfort. He was reading her like an open book. She supposed a lifetime of shepherding his flock had honed his insights into people to an uncommonly perceptive level.

"Quentin Solomon took an axe to his wife and then attempted to do the same to his children."

A shudder rocked through Adeline, every bit as jarring as when she'd read those words herself after a Google search on the name. It had taken some weeding out, considering the amount of time that had passed, but murder had a way of standing out amid the other subject lines. She'd printed the most detailed information while Wyatt contacted the sheriff here in Hancock County. The tragic story of the Solomon family had elicited images that haunted her even hours after learning of it.

"He'd been a good husband and father up to that point," the priest continued. "A good provider. Came to mass with his wife and children every week." Grayson turned his palms up. "No one could understand what made him snap like that. No financial troubles. No marital problems. Some would say the devil's doing. I would tend to agree."

"There was a fourth child." Adeline guided him toward

the specific information she needed. "A son. What happened to him? Was he adopted by a family, as well?"

"Another tragedy unto itself," Grayson explained without answering the question immediately. "The way I understand it, Tristan, he was ten at the time, hid his three sisters when the fight between his mother and father turned violent. When his father couldn't get his hands on the smaller children, his rage escalated and he tried to kill Tristan. There was a frightening scuffle and Quentin fell on the axe, killing himself instead of his son."

Jesus Christ. "What happened to Tristan?" Adeline asked again. That was the one part of the puzzle she didn't have. The newspapers had pretty much explained the facts in the homicide case, but nothing about what became of the children. His whereabouts were crucial to their next move.

"The doctors believed that the sheer horror of the event pushed him over a mental edge," Grayson explained. "His mind just locked down. He spoke to no one after that night. Not a word. I went to visit him as often as I could for a number of years, but then he refused my visits. The boy was completely mentally devastated." Grayson held up a hand when Adeline would have asked her next question. "But he did recover eventually. He was transferred to an adult supervised living facility when he was twenty-one. He remained there for five additional years where he began occupational therapy. He learned a life skill and later merged into society. I believe that was about twelve years ago. Where he went from there has never been released to anyone other than myself. It's my belief that he wanted a complete break from the past. Perhaps that was the only way he could cope."

"Did he change his name?" she asked when the priest fell silent. "Is he still in Mississippi?"

Father Grayson clasped his hands in his lap. "This is the part that gets sticky for me."

His position was easy to understand. Prescott and Arnold were missing and in clear and present danger; discussing their lives was an easier decision to make in light of that unquestionable urgency. But the boy—man—wasn't involved or in any danger, to their knowledge.

"Yes, his name was changed to protect him from the horror of his past. Just as yours was changed." Grayson searched Adeline's eyes a moment longer. "With all that he's already been through, I'm not sure that I can in good conscience facilitate your interference in his life."

Adeline put a hand on Wyatt's arm when he would have spoken. "Father Grayson, I don't need to talk to Tristan. I just want to ensure he isn't in any danger. If he's at home, living his life, and hasn't been contacted in any manner by our perpetrator, then there's absolutely no reason for us to talk to him. Having a member of law enforcement in his community check in with him in a very casual manner would suffice. The problem is, for all we know, he could be missing already. He could be in imminent danger."

Grayson saw through her strategy in a split second. "Or he could be your *perpetrator*."

"That's also a possibility," she confessed. "We just need to confirm his whereabouts. Verify he's safe and that nothing is amiss. If he isn't involved in this, he has nothing to worry about. There would be no need to disturb his life."

The old priest leaned forward, braced his forearms on his knees, and looked directly into her eyes. "You do understand, Detective Cooper, that this is your brother and sisters you're talking about. You may have been an infant when you were separated, but you share the same DNA.

There are memories of your time together, whether you can call them to mind or not, imprinted on your spirit. These are not just strangers. You speak so matter-of-factly, I'm not sure the reality of this situation has fully hit you yet."

She slammed a mental door on the emotions his words stirred. "Do you know his name and where he lives now?" She needed that information. Whatever it took, she had to find the one other person with a connection to the victims in this case. Her instincts were usually on target.

The seconds counted off, one trauma-filled instant at a time, before the old man finally spoke again. "When the tragedy happened, we scrambled to help. Our primary concern was the children. There were no grandparents, no aunts and uncles. Only the church and the friends of the Solomon family there. Several of the church hierarchy gathered and discussed the best course of action. We didn't want the children to go into the state system, not when we had fine families, some of which had not been blessed with children, among us."

Adeline let the matter of the brother go for a moment, was mesmerized by the story. *Her story.*

"The decision was made to send each child to a different home and that, as part of the agreement, the children would not be told before the age of twenty-five about the heinous tragedy. We felt this would allow the children to have a normal life without the taint of that horror haunting them. Beyond that age, the decision was solely up to the adoptive parents. You," he pressed Adeline with his gaze, "were our top priority. Your safety and happiness."

For a long moment Adeline simply sat there. She couldn't break from the trance. The images his words evoked kept flashing in front of her eyes and evolving. Three tiny girls whisked away from a horrific murder scene. Crying and clutching each other. Men in robes gathered in a small room, deciding their fate. This was like a bad movie.

"He lives in Laurel," Grayson said, dragging her from the disturbing thoughts. "His name is Daniel Jamison."

Adeline pushed to her feet, her legs rubbery beneath her. "Thank you, Father Grayson. You've been a tremendous help." She tried to summon an appreciative smile, couldn't do it.

Next to her, Wyatt reached out and shook the priest's hand. "I'll keep Sheriff Billings briefed on the situation so that he may keep you informed."

"Father Grayson." His name was out of her mouth before she'd fully made the decision to ask the question. But there it was. "How did you and the church hierarchy make your decision as to which families took the children, or did you only have three families in need?"

He searched her eyes for a time, then smiled. "There were many, many things to consider. In the end, we did what was best for all involved."

She nodded. Tried to recall the times she'd sat in church next to her parents. God, that had been a long time ago.

"Tread carefully," Grayson said to Adeline. "There is much more than you appear to realize at stake."

"I will." She did manage a tight smile then. "Between Sheriff Billings and the news, I'm certain you'll know if I don't proceed with caution."

"Whether I do or not," Grayson countered. "God sees all that you do, Detective Cooper. *He* will know."

CHAPTER THIRTY-TWO

Laurel
Monday, December 27, 3:50 a.m.

"Addy." Wyatt hated to wake her. She'd struggled to be so strong the last few hours. She was totally exhausted, physically and emotionally.

She roused, straightened. "Where are we?"

"Laurel city limits." Sheriff Henley had agreed to meet them at her office. Henley didn't do any explaining on the phone, but her tone had spoken volumes about the situation. Not good. Something big had already gone down here in Laurel and it was no doubt connected to this investigation.

"Man, I need coffee." Addy pulled her hair free of the ponytail and finger-combed it before putting it right back into the twisty rubber holder.

The ponytail was part of her standard operating procedure. The hair went back before her weapon slid into her holster after she dressed each morning.

If this night hadn't been so screwed up, he might have been able to work up the initiative to smile just thinking about all her little habits. "Coffee it is." He put finding an open drive-through on his mental radar.

That Adeline lapsed immediately into silence told him that waking had summoned the events of the previous ten or twelve hours. Life altering. Emotion shattering. Damn, this was hard on her.

"I should check on my mom."

"I called about half an hour ago," he said, slowing her fingers on the keypad of her cell. "She's still resting. Her vitals are stable."

Addy put her cell away. "Thanks."

The streetlights allowed him to see the dark circles under her eyes. The resigned set of her lips bothered him the most. She was dealing with the issues as best she could with a missing persons' investigation and a threat to her own safety on her plate.

Not just persons—her sisters.

The reality of what Addy had learned tonight blew him away all over again. How had Carl and Irene kept this kind of secret? He'd sure as hell never heard anything about Addy being adopted. A sign up ahead drew his attention from the troubling musings.

"Here we go." He pushed the blinker stem and prepared to make a right into the Dunkin' Donuts drive-through. He ordered two large coffees and proceeded to the pickup window. He paid up and passed her the first cup.

"Thank God." Addy cradled the cup in both hands and inhaled its fragrant aroma.

Wyatt set his in the cup holder. As he rolled back out onto the street, Addy carefully removed the lid and blew until she dared to take a sip. She expressed more of those appreciative sounds. That made him smile.

A few blocks later he parked in the lot at the Jones County Sheriff's Department and shut off the engine. "You ready?" He picked up his cup, took a much-needed swallow.

Adeline turned to him. "I've tried and tried to recall a moment when I should have known." She shook her head. "But there isn't one. The family photo albums have pictures of me going all the way back to infancy." She shrugged. "I mean, I looked like an infant. Maybe I was already six months old," she amended. "The only oddities were my blue eyes and blond hair and the fact that most of my baby pictures were of me alone. No photos of one or the other of my parents holding me while I was really small."

She shrugged, the movement screaming of just how tired she was. "No one in the family, none of our friends, ever had a slip of the tongue. How could none of them have known? Or been so careful that it never came up accidentally? I guess that's what makes the whole situation so unbelievable. It's too clean...too perfectly executed. You see this shit in the movies, but this is real."

Wyatt wished Irene had come forward and privately given him the information about the Prescott woman. He wasn't entirely sure it would have made any difference, but it would have provided another angle to investigate. Then he could have prepared Addy for this. On some level he understood why Irene hadn't. His gaze lingered on Addy. There were some things a person just didn't want to lose.

Get your head on straight, Wyatt.

"I suppose," he offered, "we'll understand how this all happened eventually."

"I suppose." She didn't sound convinced. "Sheriff Henley's waiting for us." She reached for her door.

Wyatt did the same. He hopped out of his SUV and started around it. At the rear bumper he stalled. From the moment Addy had come home, he'd been entirely focused on her and this investigation. He'd let everything else slide. Hadn't paid any attention to the routine things like the fact that his SUV needed a good wash.

He'd promised himself he wouldn't let this happen. And look at him, he'd spent scarcely three days in her presence and already she'd become the center of his universe. He considered the grime veiling his vehicle and shook his head. This was going to be like nine years ago all over—

The thought derailed as his gaze zeroed in on the rear windshield. "What the hell is this?" The well-lit parking lot allowed him to read the words scrawled across the skim of road grunge.

"Oh. Yeah." Addy wandered back to where he stood. "I forgot to tell you about that."

If Henley hadn't been waiting for their arrival, Wyatt felt confident he would have raked Addy over the coals right there in the parking lot when she told him about the incident at the cemetery. But Henley was waiting and Addy had been through enough for one day.

He didn't even bother rubbing in the fact that he'd warned her that going anywhere alone wasn't a good idea.

She knew.

Instead, he settled a hand at the small of her back and guided her to the front entrance. Fear of what could have happened ripped at his insides. It was a flat-out miracle she was here with him right now instead of out there somewhere with this psycho.

Sheriff Vicki Henley waited for them in the small lobby. "Come on in." She looked almost as weary as Wyatt felt. "I see you already have coffee, so let's go to my office and I'll bring you up to speed."

Henley was a petite woman but her bearing was strong and confident; she looked to be about fifty. He doubted there was a deputy in her department, female or male, who didn't walk the line for this by-the-book lady. Though Wyatt had never had the pleasure of coordinating an investigation with her, he knew her reputation.

When he and Addy had taken seats in front of Henley's desk, she launched right into the briefing. "I don't know how much you already know about Daniel Jamison, but whatever you've heard, everything has changed. We have a situation."

Wyatt had a feeling they should have checked the state database or at least Googled the man before coming. But Henley had insisted he come to her office ASAP. Three hours of hard driving had gotten them here. And it sounded very much like things were about to get exponentially more complicated.

Just what they needed.

"At this point," Wyatt explained, "we know nothing at all about Jamison. I made the call to you and we drove straight here."

Henley nodded. "It's all bad. One of my deputies is dead and a nurse at Forrest General was also killed by this man earlier today."

"Does Jamison have a history of violence?" This question came from Addy.

"No. That's the weird part." Henley opened a folder on her desk. "Ten days ago we received a domestic disturbance call through the 911 dispatch for the Jamison residence. The place is off Highway 29, basically in the middle of nowhere. The address was wrong in the system.

My two deputies had a hell of a time finding it. They showed up at the residence forty-five minutes after the initial call. Apparently Jamison either saw the vehicles turn into his drive or figured out his wife had made the call. He was nowhere to be found, but he hadn't been gone long."

"The wife?" Addy inquired, her voice somber.

"Nearly dead." Henley shook her head. "During the struggle he rammed her head through a set of French doors. There was bruising on her throat. We figure he thought he'd killed her. For whatever reason he just didn't choke her long enough." The lady sheriff shrugged. "Or maybe he just didn't care. He'd intended for her to be dead in the end. The bastard had been in the process of burying her in the basement when my men arrived on the scene and he cut and ran."

Wyatt kept a watch on Addy from the corner of his eye. This horror just kept piling up. "But she's alive?"

"She's hanging on." Henley stared at the file on her desk. "We believe he'd been planning to kill her for several days. The floor of the basement is rock. He'd removed enough to prepare a grave. My guess is he intended to bury her, then replace the rocks and suggest that she had gone missing."

"Anyone else in the family have any ideas on the reason he did this?" Addy rubbed at her forehead as if a headache had begun there.

"The wife's mother and father have never cared too much for Jamison," Henley related. "But he'd eventually grown on them. He'd been married to their daughter for ten years. Good job with the postal service. No financial troubles. No marital problems that anyone was aware of. The couple has a son, Danny. He's with his grandparents."

"The boy was unharmed?" Wyatt hoped like hell that was the case.

Henley nodded. "My deputies found him hiding in the closet under the stairs. According to his grandparents he's smart as a whip. Has been reading since he was four years old. An exceptionally bright student. But if he saw or heard anything, he isn't talking."

Addy's gaze collided with Wyatt's. This story just continued to get worse.

"Lydia, the wife," Henley went on, "had advised her mother that there was some tension related to her pregnancy. She was terrified of telling her husband that she'd learned the baby was a girl."

"She's pregnant." Addy's face paled.

"About seven months," Henley confirmed. "It's a miracle, but the baby seems to be okay. If we can keep the mother alive, that'll truly be a miracle."

Wyatt's cop instincts were roaring. "Did the wife's parents mention anything else that the daughter related regarding this tension in her marriage?"

"Jamison didn't want any more children. She'd already defied him once and ended up having a miscarriage. Fell down those same basement stairs. We don't know yet if he had anything to do with that. The wife never mentioned to her parents that she suspected anything along those lines." Henley slid the file she'd opened across the desk in their direction. "Two days after he almost killed her, the wife's parents hired a private investigator to find out if their initial suspicions about him had been correct."

As Wyatt and Addy reviewed the findings, much of which they had already heard from Father Grayson, Henley continued. "He spent almost eleven years in a mental institution, then another four and a half in a supervised living situation. His biological father killed his wife and would have killed the children, ironically, if Jamison hadn't stopped him."

Wyatt didn't mention that they already knew that part. There was no need to bring Father Grayson into this investigation—at least not at this point. "Was he taking any medications? Antipsychotics?"

Henley laughed but the sound held no humor. "When he and Lydia married he stopped taking his mood stabilizers as well as the medication for the bipolar diagnosis. Apparently, they interfered with the sex life."

"You said he worked for the postal service," Addy noted. "They do background investigations on their employees. How did a guy with his medical history get the job?"

"According to his supervisor," Henley explained, "his record came back as clean as a whistle. Nothing about his medical condition popped up. Evidently this guy knows how to work the system. That's not all," she added, "he worked at the supervised living facility as a nurse's assistant the last year he was a resident there."

Wyatt wasn't sure where she was going with that point but judging by the fury in her eyes he was about to find out.

"That's how he got into his wife's room at the hospital so easily."

"He made another attempt on her life?" Wyatt understood now. Henley had mentioned that a nurse and a police officer were dead.

Henley nodded, the movement visibly weary. "He dressed like a nurse's assistant, conducted himself as one. He killed a nurse to access the drugs. Then killed one of my deputies with the same drug he partially unloaded in his wife's IV. Potassium chloride. Stops the heart. It was too late for my deputy, but the code staff managed to resuscitate her. I'm here to tell you, that woman does not intend to go down without a fight."

God have mercy. When would this end? "I take it he wasn't apprehended." Wyatt felt fairly certain of the answer before he asked.

"He got away." Henley's lips flattened with fury. "But we'll get him."

"I'd like to see any photos you have of Daniel Jamison."

Wyatt glanced at Addy. This man was her brother. As horrific as he found the whole thing, she had to be reeling. He kept forgetting that nightmarish fact.

Henley shuffled through the file, tapped an eight-by-ten photo of a man, his wife, and son. "That's him."

Addy's hand shook as she picked up the photo and stared at it. Not only was her brother in that photo, but a nephew. Wyatt's gut twisted.

"The wife," Henley nodded to the photo, "I don't know if she suspected her husband really intended to hurt her or not, but she's one smart cookie. When she made the 911 call, instead of hanging up when she heard her husband coming back into the room, she left the line open and slid the receiver under the sofa so he wouldn't see it. The dispatcher couldn't make out all that was said and we've listened to the tape twenty times. Most of the verbal exchanges are inaudible. But there's one statement that's loud and clear. It's his voice, the in-laws have already identified it. So, if he gets his wish and his wife dies, he can't show up claiming to have been kidnapped and say it was an intruder. It's *him.*"

"Can we hear the tape?" Addy had dropped her hands into her lap, clasped them together so tightly her fingers were white.

Wyatt wished he could take her hands in his and at least try to console her just a little.

"Of course." Henley reached into a desk drawer and removed a handheld recording device. "By the way, when he entered the hospital and killed a nurse and one of my men," Henley met Wyatt's gaze, then Addy's, unadulterated rage in her own, "he had changed his appearance. He wore glasses and he'd shaved his head."

"Jamison is bald?" Addy echoed, her eyes suddenly wide with fear.

"According to the nurse who survived his attack and two other members of the hospital staff," Henley explained, "his head was as smooth as a baby's butt."

Addy turned to him. "Put Womack on my mother's room," she demanded, her expression, her voice, frantic. "Now!"

Wyatt reached into his pocket for his phone. "You think he knows your mother is in the hospital and might show up?"

Her face went even paler. "He's already been there. I saw him. He was mopping the floor. He bumped into me..." Her breath hitched. "He asked me if she—Irene—was my mother."

Wyatt made the call. Addy didn't stop twisting her fingers together until he'd closed his phone and confirmed that it was done. "He's filling in hospital security on our concerns en route. If Jamison is there or shows up, he's not going to get near your mother."

Addy breathed an audible sigh of relief. She turned back to Sheriff Henley. "Can we hear the call now?"

Henley pushed play on the recorder.

A new tension simmered through Wyatt as he watched the kaleidoscope of changing reactions play out on Addy's face. She flinched at the crashes and screams. The inaudible rants and snarls by Daniel Jamison had her leaning forward in an attempt to make out the words. His intent was unmistakable. He wanted his wife dead.

"Here it comes," Henley warned.

The screams and the sobs abruptly stopped.

A moment of taut silence, then...

"*There will be no princess in this house!*"

CHAPTER THIRTY-THREE

5:40 a.m.

Adeline stood in the yard in front of Daniel Jamison's house. The place where he and his family had lived before he tried to kill his pregnant wife.

Bald as a baby's behind. Ms. Nichols's words kept echoing amid Adeline's other churning thoughts.

Daniel Jamison—known in a former life as Tristan Solomon—was her brother.

And all this time she'd thought her biggest DNA glitch was Cyrus Cooper and his shitty sons.

She'd been wrong.

The windows of the old turn-of-the-century bungalow were dark. Like the soul of the man who lived here. His wife was hanging on by a thread, her unborn daughter's fate dependent to some degree on her mother's continued survival.

There will be no princess in this house!

Adeline whirled around, her gaze seeking and finding Wyatt where he stood a few feet away. "You know what this means?"

"That old Ms. Nichols was right."

Adeline nodded, not surprised that he was thinking along the same lines as she. "She knew he was bald. She knew about the princess thing." Adeline turned back to the house, shivered as the nasty vibes washed over her. "He's holding them in an old house or shack near water."

Not once in her career as a cop had she ever put any stock in a so-called psychic's claims. But this was real. Nichols had nailed too many details.

Dawn had started its slow winter climb above the treetops. The whole place was creepy. Deep in the woods. Jamison had settled his little family well away from town or any neighbors. The property had been searched already and no dead bodies, human or otherwise, had been discovered. Inside they'd found nothing to indicate he'd been looking into Prescott's, Arnold's, or Adeline's lives. Not a single piece of evidence.

What had she expected? This guy was meticulous. He'd spent years in that institution. Plenty of time to formulate a perfect plan.

But why now? More than ten years after his release? Had the news that his wife was growing a princess in her womb been enough to push him over the edge at which his existence apparently hovered?

Sheriff Henley had jumped in with both feet as soon as Wyatt had explained the situation in Jackson County. Henley, too, was certain Jamison was their man. Both his wife and son had been assigned a security detail. That hadn't stopped him from getting to his wife in the hospital. The wife had since been moved to ICU where security measures were stronger.

Between his grandparents and two assigned deputies, the boy was in good hands.

Adeline had a nephew.

Too much to absorb. She shook it off. Now was not the time to deal with those emotions. Or the fact that her mother had withheld important information related to an ongoing case. All of that would have to wait.

Whether Prescott and Arnold were still alive or not, they had to be found. Daniel Jamison had to be stopped.

Adeline wanted those women to be alive. She didn't want to fail them.

Just something else she would have to deal with eventually. She had two sisters. *Two*. No way was she going to count Jamison as a brother. Clearly he was a psycho just like his damned daddy.

Her daddy.

No. Adeline shook her head. Carl Cooper was her father. And Irene was her mother. No one else counted.

She settled her attention back on the house. "I'm going inside."

"Henley said the property had been released," Wyatt commented, moving up beside her, "but I'm not sure going in is a good idea. On a personal level."

Adeline shot him a look. "Get real, Wyatt. You know how I am. I need to feel the vibe of the place." Those she was getting out here in the yard were seriously creepy. Lots of pent-up rage. Intense secrecy.

Jamison wasn't the only one who'd been keeping secrets.

"We should have asked Henley for access. Gotten a key," Wyatt suggested.

"Come on." She headed for the porch. "Chances are there's at least one window unlocked. We probably won't even need a key."

"Breaking and entering, Detective Cooper," he reminded. "Just because we represent the law doesn't mean we're above the law."

"Yeah, yeah. So arrest me."

The windows in front were locked. In back, too. Damn it. Front and back doors were secure. The credit card thing didn't work. She had strong-armed Wyatt into trying when she'd failed to get the job done.

Wait. Adeline turned to Wyatt. "She was found in the basement. That's what Henley said, right?" A house this old likely had an exterior entrance that wasn't a typical walk-through door. Hope resurrected.

She hustled around to the back once more. The ground-level double doors were almost completely concealed by a thicket of shrubbery. She parted the dense greenery. Dawn's gray gloom provided sufficient light to see that there was a big-ass lock secured to the doors.

"Well, shit."

Wyatt crouched down to get a closer look. When he'd completed his assessment, he glanced up at her. "I think I can handle that."

"You carry bolt cutters in your SUV?" she called after him as he jogged toward the corner of the house.

"You'll see," he called back.

That was the problem. She'd already seen too much. Her biological father was literally an axe murderer. Her brother, too. How screwed up was that?

She should call her old partner. Braddock would laugh his ass off and give her kudos for coming up with such a great joke. But it wasn't a joke.

And Adeline wasn't laughing.

Wyatt hustled back to where she waited. She got to her feet. He'd brought a flashlight. Good. She frowned when she recognized the tool in his hand. "So you don't carry bolt cutters but you carry a hammer?"

He adjusted his hold on the tool. "Carrying a hammer makes getting into places considerably easier when the need arises." He tapped the hammer at a nonexistent target. "One tap, the glass breaks."

"And you were warning me about breaking and entering?"

"Never without reasonable cause," he clarified.

"Whatever." She bracketed her hands on her hips. "So what're you going to do, beat the doors in?" That could prove time-consuming.

"The doors are wood," he said, "the lock is attached to the doors with screws. Nails and screws can be pried out of wood if one is persistent."

She hadn't thought of that. "Good to know." She stepped back and let him have at it.

He passed the flashlight to her and set to the task. Ten minutes later she admitted that he'd been right about one thing, persistence was essential.

A little more splintering and groaning and the brackets holding the lock on the doors burst free. He pulled them open. "And there we go."

"I'm impressed, Wyatt."

He shoved the hammer between his belt and the waist of his trousers. "I'll go first."

Fine with her. She passed the flashlight back to him. It was dark as all get-out down there.

The basement smelled like dirt. Wyatt roved the flashlight's beam around the room until he located a light switch. A bare bulb in the overhead fixture glowed, filling the fairly large area with dim light.

Adeline blinked to focus. Shelves lined the walls. Lots of stuff and dust. Her attention settled on the pile of rocks at the far end of the basement floor. A hole, about six feet in length, maybe two feet wide, had been dug where the rocks had once rested. She walked over to the makeshift grave and squatted for a closer inspection.

The shovel he'd used had likely been tagged into evidence. The smaller piles of dirt inside the hole were probably from the shovelfuls he'd tossed in atop his unconscious wife.

What kind of piece of shit did this?

CHAPTER THIRTY-FOUR

Wyatt surveyed the last of the shelves lining the wall. Nothing that shouted psycho. Just the usual tools and boxes of last year's holiday decorations. He turned to see what Addy was up to. What he saw took him aback.

"Addy, I'm sorry." He shook his head as he walked over to the grave Jamison had dug for his wife. "That's just too weird."

From her reclining position in the grave, she shot him an I-couldn't-care-less-what-you-think look. "Imagine, Wyatt. If she roused at all while he was covering her, she would look up into the face of the man she'd married—the father of her children. When she'd first started to suspect things weren't right, imagine going to sleep next to him every night."

Adeline reached up. Wyatt took her hand and assisted her climb out of the grave. Brushing the dirt off her backside, he considered giving her cute ass a swipe but she took care of it before he could put thought into action.

She moved over to the stairs. Walked slowly up, then backed down. She examined each tread with her fingers on the second trip up. "Henley said she fell down the basement stairs." Adeline stopped about a third of the way from the top. "Here we go." She patted the tread. "This one's been replaced. It's a lot newer than the others."

"Doesn't mean he did it," Wyatt reminded. "This is an old house. Could have just had a bad board that he replaced after her fall."

She studied the rest of the treads, then shook her head. "I don't think so. The treads aren't that old." She descended once more and ducked around behind the staircase. "Bring your flashlight under here."

Wyatt joined her beneath the primitive stairs.

"Check the bottom of each tread, from one stringer to the other."

Starting at the top, Wyatt moved the flashlight's beam from left to right over each tread.

"Right there." Addy pointed to the bottom side of the one that had been replaced.

The tread was just over his head, but not so far that he couldn't reach up and touch the bottom of it.

"Check that out." Addy pointed to where the tread sat atop the stringer on the right.

Wyatt focused the light's beam there. He stood on tiptoes, reached up, and touched the markings on the stringer. The wood was marred as if something had rubbed against it repeatedly. Addy was right.

"He sawed the tread from the bottom until there was only a microscopically thin layer of wood on top," she surmised. "The first time his wife stepped on that tread, that thin layer gave way, sending her headlong to the rock floor."

Wyatt shook off the brutal images. "I'll be sure to pass this along to Henley. The forensics folks weren't likely looking for anything related to a prior fall."

He checked the time on his cell. "We should get going. We can make the necessary calls en route." Hattiesburg and Wiggins needed to be updated on Jamison. They finally had a break in the case. Whether it helped find Cherry Prescott and Penny Arnold alive was yet to be seen, but it was something.

"I want to walk through the house." Adeline rounded the staircase and headed upward. "Just once."

"Sure." They had already broken the law, what was a few more minutes?

Wyatt watched her move from room to room, touching things, studying others. She considered the Christmas tree at length, fingered an ornament that looked like something the son had made at school. Wyatt's heart thumped harder and harder. How had he allowed these last nine years to get past him without making her listen? Without trying harder to get her back?

He'd pretended not to miss her that much. That he was too busy to care about a real social life. Just because he was thirty-two didn't mean he needed to be married with kids or even dating steadily.

But he'd been lying to himself.

The one thing he had needed had been gone.

The worst part was she would be leaving again.

How would he ever live with losing her twice?

Wyatt's phone vibrated, yanking him from the painful thoughts. He pulled it from his pocket. "Henderson."

"Wyatt, you and Addy need to get back here."

The tension in Womack's voice chilled Wyatt's blood. He turned away from where Addy was checking out a family photo album. "What's going on?"

"It's Irene . . ."

Wyatt's heart surged into his throat.

"The bastard got to her just minutes before security

could get into place. The doctors were already working on her when I reached the hospital. Wyatt...Jesus Christ. They tried everything they could."

Womack's voice quavered on the last. Wyatt tried to push the words he needed to say past his lips. Couldn't.

"Goddammit, Wyatt," Womack sobbed, breaking down. "She's dead. Addy's mother is dead."

CHAPTER THIRTY-FIVE

It was daylight. Cherry could see the dim rays of light attempting to invade the cracks in the walls. Her body ached from being in one position too long. Her wrists and ankles burned where the ropes cut into them. She was cold. So cold. She just wanted to go home.

Please, God, let them find us today.

She'd prayed for days. Over and over. But no one had come. Each morning when she woke bowls of water and oatmeal sat within her reach. At first she'd refused to touch either. Then, desperation had taken over and she'd gobbled from the bowls like a starving dog.

Yesterday or maybe the day before Penny had been dragged into this awful place with her.

Cherry couldn't estimate how long she had been here. A week? Maybe.

Penny had cried at first. Her wails had been nearly unbearable. Finally, she had fallen asleep again. That was the only relief Cherry had gotten from the pitiful sounds. Penny lay sprawled on the floor, her shackles twisting her arms and legs at an odd angle.

Cherry prayed he wouldn't come back today. Maybe he would be hit by a car or would have a heart attack. Glee gathered in her chest. She and Penny might die here if they weren't found, but at least he wouldn't have the satisfaction of torturing them anymore. Or killing them.

And he was going to kill them as soon as the last princess had joined them.

Cherry closed her eyes and sobbed softly. She wanted to hold her children. To kiss her husband. There were so many things she wanted to say to them before she died.

So many, many things unsaid...undone.

She should never have tracked *him* down. She had started this horror.

The nightmares had pushed her to do it. Once the nightmares had begun, she'd started to remember things. Little snippets of a life that wasn't the one she'd always thought was hers. A woman with blond hair and blue eyes rocking her, singing to her. A smaller girl, maybe two years old, sucking her thumb and holding on to Cherry's hand. An infant in a crib in her and the other little girl's room. She'd remembered the pink girly wallpaper. Toys, especially a stuffed bear.

Then she was under the water.

Hot tears burned her cheeks. Something or someone was holding her beneath the surface. Eventually the images in the nightmares started to change, became Cherry and her sweet daughter. In the awful dreams, she would hold her precious baby beneath the water, ignoring the child's frantic struggles. Her baby's eyes would widen and then her little mouth would open and the battle was over.

Desperation had pushed Cherry to find answers. She hadn't told her husband, but she'd driven all the way to Jackson and spoken to a psychologist—using a different name of course. Skeletons in one's closet were bad for political careers. The psychologist had told her that the sort of memories she was experiencing were likely real. Repressed by some childhood trauma. Was it possible that she had been adopted? Had some traumatic event blocked those memories until now?

That was when Cherry had started her search. She was an attorney, she'd known the places to go and the buttons to push to find what she was looking for. She'd quickly discovered that she had in fact been adopted. She'd learned her real name and the names of her siblings. But not their new names—the ones they'd been given, as she had, in their new lives. She'd struggled with the need to question her parents, but she couldn't bring herself to drag them into the misery overtaking her existence. So she'd kept quiet and kept digging.

No one from the Dioceses would give her the priest's name who had handled the adoptions. They had pretended the information had been lost years ago. But she had known they were keeping their secret.

Since her brother had been the oldest at the time, she began her search with him. Reason dictated that he would be the most likely to remember what really happened. Cherry had gone to the reporter who'd followed the Solomon case the closest thirty years ago. He'd been in a nursing home. Macular degeneration had stolen his sight. Complications from diabetes had stolen his legs. She'd told him she was a writer and wanted to do a true crime novel on the case. The enticing scent of a story still alive somewhere in that shell of a body, he'd given her everything he remembered, including the fact that the boy had gone to the Healing Institute in Jackson.

Finding her brother from there had been a breeze.

Along the way she'd discovered that Sarah Solomon was now Penny Arnold and Tessa Solomon was Adeline Cooper. She'd printed pictures from the Internet of both women. Of the two, locating information on Penny had been the simplest. Though her adopted parents were now deceased, as a real estate agent Penny maintained a significant presence on the Web. Adeline had been a different story. All the information Cherry had found on her was around nine years old. But her adopted mother had still been alive.

Cherry had been so damned clever. No one had suspected for a moment that she was involved in a clandestine investigation into her murky past. As painful and confusing as all she'd found had been, she hadn't shared even a hint of it with her parents or her husband. She'd told herself at the time that it was the only way to protect them. Hurting them had been the last thing on her mind.

What a fool she'd been. Her most monumental mistake had been going to Daniel Jamison first. She'd taken the photos of their sisters she'd gotten from the Internet. She'd so hoped to gain some insight into what had happened to them as children. And to see if he had the nightmares, too. He'd refused to talk to her. Had ordered her off his property. She'd left him the photos, including one of her, in hopes that he would have a change of heart.

A couple weeks later, when she'd worked up the nerve, she'd gone to Penny. The reception hadn't been much better there. She hadn't believed Cherry. No matter that she'd shown her the proof. But Cherry had seen the fear in her eyes when she'd asked about the nightmares. *Are you afraid of water or do you have bad dreams about water?* Like Daniel, Penny had promptly ordered Cherry to stay away from her.

Eventually Cherry had again summoned her courage

IT ENDS WITH HER

and attempted to find her other sister. Adeline's mother had repeated that pattern. She'd denied everything. Refused to give Cherry any information about where Adeline was now. Disgusted at that point, Cherry had prepared to go home. She'd climbed into her car, tears pouring from her eyes, her nerves frayed.

And *he* had been in the backseat. He'd forced her to drive to a remote location. He'd injected her with something that rendered her unconscious. When she'd awakened, she had been in this despicable place.

Cherry shuddered, let the hot tears gush. At least her baby was safe now. Cherry couldn't harm her baby now.

She was here with poor Penny.

They couldn't hope to break free. Their wrists were tethered to their ankles by a length of chain, then the chain was attached to a support beam that held up the roof of the old shack.

Cherry had tried so hard to get free, her wrists and ankles bled from the metal abrading her skin.

Defeat sucked the last of the hope from her.

They were going to die. He'd said so.

Maybe they should die. Maybe they had inherited their biological father's compulsion to murder. Daniel had ranted on and on about his wife and how she would die. Cherry had suffered the dreams of killing her own baby girl. Just maybe they all should have died thirty years ago.

But she didn't want to die. She wanted her life back.

No one was going to find them. Fate had caught up to them after three decades. They would die.

The only delay to that promised end was Adeline Cooper.

Daniel had boasted that to their families they were already dead, but the final departure from this earth would come when all the princesses were together. Then they would march to their true destinies.

He would take the three of them to the river and send them to heaven.

Adeline would be here soon, he'd promised.

Cherry closed her eyes and placed another urgent plea in the hands of her Lord. *Don't let him catch Adeline...*

CHAPTER THIRTY-SIX

Pascagoula, 7:45 a.m.

Clay's cell phone chirped. Since he was driving and alone, he allowed the call to come in over the car's speakers. "Yo."

"This has gone too far."

Well, if it wasn't his favorite cop. "You should've thought about that before you tampered with evidence." Clay resisted the urge to laugh. Didn't this cop understand how things worked? "Besides, it's almost over. No need to wimp out now."

"This kind of shit wasn't supposed to happen!"

Clay rolled his eyes. The dude was seriously freaking out. "What can I say?" Clay wasn't letting anything get in the way of his plan. It wasn't his fault Irene Cooper had been murdered. As far as he was concerned, the old biddy had gotten what she deserved. "Life's a bitch sometimes. You," he warned, "just better keep your cool. You spill your guts, and that little incident of evidence-tampering could make you an accessory."

"I didn't tamper with evidence...not technically," the nervous shit muttered. "The idiot up in Laurel was the one who tampered with evidence. Hell," he started shouting again," it wasn't even evidence...as far as we knew then. But you knew! You knew something was going on days ago. I don't know how, but somehow you're responsible!"

"Whatever." Clay wasn't worried about it. No one could connect him to any of this. His cop accomplice couldn't say the same. And if this fool or the one up in Laurel dared to turn on Clay, then they would pay the consequences. "You got nothing to do with this now. I'm in control. So just back off."

"Her mother's dead!" he practically screamed. "No one was supposed to die, you stupid little asshole! *No one was supposed to die.*"

Clay maneuvered his truck into the parking lot of the pancake house and slammed into park. "Chill! Damn! I had nothing to do with that. I told you what I'm doing is just a joke. My chance to mess with Addy's head after what she did to my brother. Don't blame me if you dumb bastards can't do your jobs and find that crazy son of a bitch who's going around abducting and killing people." When the idiot on the other end of the line started ranting again, Clay ended the conversation with, "Stop bugging me and do your job or something."

He severed the connection. Idiot.

That was the problem with people. They thought they could roll with the big boys. Ask for help, then when it came time to pay the price they turned into whining wimps.

When would they learn the most basic principle of all: you dance, you gotta pay the fiddler?

Clay wasn't letting nobody take advantage of him. He was way smarter than his older brother had been, God rest his soul. Clay wasn't just smarter, he was more determined. He was going to get the job done.

And then his damned old daddy might respect him the way he'd respected Gage.

He hadn't exactly lied to the dumb shit on the phone. This was a joke, in a roundabout way. It wasn't Clay's fault that things had turned deadly. He didn't have a crystal ball and he wasn't responsible for what other folks did. His plan was simple. There was just one last thing Clay had to do and then it would all be over as far as he was concerned. Would've been over already if that damned Wyatt hadn't kept Addy stuck to him like glue.

But Clay had a plan for that, too.

A smile cut across his face. "Bye, bye, princess."

CHAPTER THIRTY-SEVEN

Singing River Hospital, 9:05 a.m.

They had moved her mother to a private room in anticipation of Adeline's arrival. She appreciated not having to go to the morgue to do this.

Adeline's lips quivered.

Her mother was dead.

"You want me to go in there with you?"

She peered up at the man standing next to her. The sadness in his eyes tore at her already broken heart. Wyatt had always loved her mother. Had checked on her often, Irene had told Adeline so. This was hard for him, too.

Dragging in a breath for courage, Adeline shook her head. "I need to do this in private."

Wyatt pulled her into his arms, held her tight to his chest. "I understand." The softly spoken words reverberated against her temple. "I'll be right out here if you need me."

"Okay." She pulled away from his strong arms and faced the door that stood between her and her mother's *body*.

Her mother had always been there for her. No matter what happened and no matter how far Adeline had run. She had been able to count on her mother when and if she needed her.

How could she be gone?

Adeline reached out and opened the door. Her hand shook. She wanted to back away. To deny this awful truth. No. She would not be a coward. Her mother deserved every ounce of courage Adeline could muster. The son of a bitch who'd done this had to be stopped. Adeline wanted his ass so bad it hurt. She would make him pay.

Stepping into the room, she closed the door behind her and leaned against it. Before attempting to move toward the bed, she took a good long look.

Her mother looked peaceful. The sheet was folded down at her shoulders, wasn't covering her face. Somehow she found comfort in that insignificant detail.

Potassium chloride. The bastard had killed her mother using the same technique he'd used in Laurel on the cop. Same one he'd tried to use to kill his wife, but the smaller dosage had allowed his wife to pull back from the edge.

They hadn't been able to pull Irene back. Maybe because of the recent heart attack. Maybe because of her age. She hadn't responded to the attempts to resuscitate her.

Now she was gone. And the bastard who'd did this had just walked away. The hospital's CCTV had shown him walking out an exit and then walking across the parking lot to God only knew where…just as he'd done in Laurel.

Adeline banished the thoughts as she pushed away from the door and walked to the bed. Tears blurred her vision and she swiped them away with the back of her hand.

"I'm sorry, Mom." Adeline's face crumpled with the agony flooding her. "I should have figured this out before now. I shouldn't have been so stupid."

She reached beneath the sheet and took her mother's cold hand in hers. An aching sob expanded in her throat. This wasn't fair. It just wasn't fair.

"Anyway." Adeline cleared her throat. "He won't get away with hurting you like this. I'll stop him. I promise."

The idea that her mother might have survived this attack if she hadn't had that heart attack—if Adeline hadn't stressed her out—had more of those hot tears streaming down her cheeks.

She'd always been a bad daughter. Her parents had deserved far better.

Adeline shouldn't have left nine years ago. She should have told Cyrus to go screw himself and stayed right here with her mother.

Selfish. That was what Adeline had been. She'd been a selfish, indifferent daughter and now her mother was dead because of her.

I will get you, you bastard. Wherever Daniel Jamison went, whatever he did, Adeline would find and stop him.

Leaning down, she kissed her mother's forehead. "I love you." She bit back more of the tears, steadied her voice. "No one else could have been a better mother. I will always be your little girl. Yours and daddy's."

She fingered the edge of the sheet, told herself to go ahead and cover her mother's face. It was time. There was nothing more Adeline could do here. Nothing else to say.

Getting the bastard who'd done this was all that mattered now.

Raised voices outside the room drew Adeline's attention to the door. Hope pushed aside some of the pain in her chest. Maybe they'd found that son of a bitch. She stormed across the room and jerked the door open.

Wyatt stood between the door and Cyrus.

Adeline looked past Wyatt, the agony inside her instantly morphing into white-hot fury. "What do you want?" Wyatt stepped fully aside, allowing Cyrus to feel the full brunt of her glare.

Cyrus hiked up his chin and glared right back at her. "I want to see her."

"I told him to leave," Wyatt explained. "I can call security."

Unable to shift her gaze from Cyrus's, she could have sworn that for a single moment she'd seen misery in those beady brown eyes. Whatever she'd thought she saw, it cleared in one blink and was immediately replaced by the condescension she'd always associated with the man.

"Addy," Cyrus said sternly, though his voice trembled ever so slightly, "I have the right to see her. Call security if you'd like, but I will not leave without seeing her."

His man Everett hovered a few feet away. Adeline braced for war. No way was she letting this old bastard anywhere near her mother.

She opened her mouth to say as much but swallowed back the words. Her mother wouldn't approve of her acting this way. Cyrus Cooper, bastard though he was, was still family.

"All right." Adeline backed into the room, opened the door wider to facilitate the wheelchair's entrance. When Wyatt sent her a questioning look she just shook her head. This was something she couldn't exactly explain.

Adeline closed the door and moved to the side of the bed opposite Cyrus's position. He stared at Irene for a long moment then redirected his attention to Adeline. "Are they any closer to finding the animal who did this?"

A moment was required for her to set aside the years of animosity she'd felt for this man. She was doing this for her mother. "Yes," she finally said. "We know who he is now. We'll get him." Her attention settled on her mother once more. "Soon. I won't stop until I find him."

"When you find him," Cyrus said, drawing her contemplation back to him, "I want you to kill him."

There was something in his eyes. An agony that nearly matched Adeline's. He was dead serious. "I'm..." She swallowed with difficulty, her emotions vacillating between disgust and empathy. "I'm a cop, old man. Not an assassin." She resisted the urge to reassure him about her objective. She had every intention of killing the bastard. In the line of duty, of course.

"Not just one shot," Cyrus cautioned, as if she hadn't spoken at all. "Keep shooting until there's no question he's dead."

Bewildered by the strange tension vibrating between them, Adeline dragged her focus away from Cyrus and back to her mother. She smoothed her hand over her hair. She wasn't giving the old bastard the satisfaction of seeing in her eyes that she would like nothing better than the opportunity to carry out his suggestion. That was wrong. It wasn't a suggestion, it was an order. The kind he'd been giving his whole life. The same kind that people around here had been jumping through hoops to follow.

"She loved you more than anything in this world," he said quietly.

Adeline didn't need him to tell her that. "But she stayed here when I begged her to join me in Huntsville." She knew damned well her mother had loved her despite the frustrating decision. Mainly Adeline just wanted to defy anything he said.

Cyrus didn't speak again for a while, just stared at Irene as if by sheer force of will he could change this reality. Even Cooper law couldn't resurrect the dead.

"That was my doing."

More of the disgust she always felt in his presence settled in Adeline's stomach. "What does that mean?"

"It's a long story," Cyrus said, his voice weak, distant. "And complicated. You wouldn't understand."

What the hell? Adeline had tolerated about as many secrets and lies as any one person could be expected to stomach. It was past time for the whole truth. "What the hell are you talking about?"

Cyrus met her glare with an uncharacteristic softness. "Your mother and father dated for two years before they married."

"I knew that." Adeline had no idea what he was getting at. She was tired. The pain had settled into a dull ache. She had no patience for listening to a pointless story. Particularly from this man. "What does that have to do with anything?"

"Your father and I…" The old bastard sighed. "We sort of competed for Irene's affections. We both loved her."

Oh, yeah, right. "My mother would never love you," she countered, allowing him to feel every ounce of disdain his claim elicited. No way was she going to listen to this kind of crap. She shouldn't have let him in here. The ache in her chest protested with another harsh wave of pain. She'd done this for her mother…arguing with him was wrong under the circumstances. Just hear him out. She gave him her attention once more. "Why are you telling me any of this? It's irrelevant."

Incredibly, Cyrus nodded as if he agreed with her

assertion. "I longed for her to choose me, but she loved your father. And I wasn't about to try and take that from him. He'd suffered so much his entire life. I just wanted him to be happy."

The polio. Adeline blinked, remembering. Her father had suffered with polio as a child. He'd been a fine, strong man when Adeline was growing up but his childhood and teen years had been very different. She remembered hearing her mother say that Cyrus had always looked out for his little brother, especially while they were growing up. Adeline had never known that side of her uncle. Didn't really believe it existed even now.

"I accepted your mother's decision, but I..." Cyrus's gaze rested on Irene then. "I never stopped loving her."

Shock rolled through Adeline. Jesus Christ. She'd had no idea. Something else her mother had never told her. Adeline couldn't imagine the old bastard really loving anyone, except his own evil spawn. But now that she thought about it, she'd never seen Cyrus look at his own wife the way he had Irene.

"My God," Adeline muttered. How could she have missed so much? Had she been that self-centered? Maybe she just hadn't wanted to see.

"Shortly after your father and mother married, Irene discovered she was expecting their first child."

The news rocked Adeline back on her heels all over again. She needed body armor here; the bullets just kept coming. "I thought—"

"Irene lost that child." Cyrus's tone had turned dull and listless. "She was about four months along and your father was away on business. She had an appointment with the obstetrician and I offered to take her. I was driving too fast the way I always did and there was an accident. Your mother wasn't visibly injured. She seemed fine."

Her mother had told Adeline that Cyrus had been in an accident and that was the reason he'd ended up on crutches and then in a wheelchair. Only Irene had left out the part about being in the car with him.

"You said," Adeline prodded, "that Mother wasn't visibly injured. What happened to the baby?" She hadn't heard anything about a miscarriage either. As far as Adeline had known, she'd been the one and only child. The one and only pregnancy. Of course that had proven wrong.

Just another indication of how little she actually knew about her parents.

"You know they didn't have the tests back then that they have now," Cyrus explained. "At least not around here. There was damage they didn't catch. Later that night she had to be rushed to the hospital, right here in Singing River. By then the internal hemorrhaging was so severe, it's a miracle she survived at all. She was airlifted to Hattiesburg for emergency surgery. The only way to save her life at that point was a total hysterectomy."

"Oh my God." Adeline turned to where her mother lay, studied the sweet face that had hidden so much pain. Why hadn't her mother ever told Adeline any of this?

I didn't want you to know that you weren't my little girl.

More of that misery twisted Adeline's insides.

The door opened and Wyatt stuck his head into the room. "Everything okay in here?"

Adeline wanted to run into his arms. To feel his heart beating against her breast. But right now she had to do the right thing...she had to hear her mother's story. "Give us another minute."

Wyatt held her gaze a moment then drew back, pulling the door closed once more.

When she settled her attention on Cyrus, he continued. "Both your mother and father were devastated." That same monotone that sounded nothing at all like the old bastard she knew echoed softly in the room. "I took full responsibility." His shoulders sagged wearily. "It was my fault. Your mother couldn't deal with any of it. She wouldn't even talk about it. She left the hospital with your great-aunt Joan. Went straight to Cincinnati. Your father couldn't talk her into coming home. He'd lost his child and, from every appearance, was about to lose his wife. He tried not to hold it against me, but I saw it in his eyes. He wanted to hate me...but he couldn't."

Adeline could only stare at the man she'd thought she knew. But like everything else about her past, she hadn't known half the story. "My father didn't possess the capacity to hate." That she knew for a certainty.

Cyrus moved his head in agreement. "I didn't deserve his compassion. I hated myself enough for the both of us. Your father was worried sick about your mother. Months passed. Joan told him that Irene stayed in bed all the time. Wouldn't talk to anyone, not even Joan. We were losing her."

We? Adeline couldn't deny that Cyrus's feelings for her mother appeared real enough. Jesus. Adeline swiped at her eyes, ordered herself not to cry again. She'd had no idea about his feelings or about how her mother had suffered as a young woman. None at all. How could she have not recognized how complicated her mother's life had been? Not paying attention, that was how. Adeline had only been worried about herself and her career.

"I realized I had to do something," Cyrus said. "I went to the church and spoke to the priest." He shook his head. "I hadn't set foot inside those doors in years. But your mother and father were faithful members. I explained the dire situation." He drew in a deep breath. "Two weeks later I received a call."

Tremors worked their way along Adeline's limbs. "From the church?"

Cyrus gave a nod of confirmation. "Your father and I met with a priest named Grayson. That same night we drove all the way to Cincinnati. It was three or four o'clock in the morning when we arrived at Joan's." Cyrus's expression reflected his unwillingness to apologize for his actions, then or now. "We brought you to her and suddenly she was alive again. The light returned to her eyes." A sad smile haunted his lips. "She came back to us. We brought the two of you home that very day. Everyone thought your mother had gone to Cincinnati and had the baby. No one ever knew any differently. You were such a tiny thing, by the time your parents started to show you off, no one seemed to notice you were older than we claimed."

Why hadn't Grayson told Adeline that part? Emotions she couldn't label churned inside her. The idea that she had in fact been whisked away in the middle of the night shook her. Another realization hit hard on the heels of that one. No matter how sweetly Cyrus painted this story, the bottom line would be the same. "How much did I cost you?" The roiling emotions coalesced into one—anger.

"That information is between me and the church." Cyrus met her angry gaze with lead in his own.

Try as she might, Adeline couldn't hold on to the anger. She felt dazed. This was...difficult to take in. Like everything else she'd learned the past few days. "Wait." Another question jarred her. "Where did the baby pictures of me come from?" If she was six months old when her biological parents were murdered...how had her mom and dad gotten those photos?

"The priest gave them to us. He'd gone through the

Solomon photo albums, since there was no family to pass them onto, and collected the photos of each child—alone—and sent those to the new parents."

"This is…" Adeline couldn't find the words to adequately quantify or encapsulate these incredible facts. She put her hands palms up in front of her. "Unbelievable."

At least now she knew how Prescott's family had photos of Cherry as a baby despite the fact that she'd been four when she came to them. Adeline imagined that if Prescott survived this, she—like them all—would need some serious therapy. Evidently, she'd totally repressed any recall of her own early childhood until her own daughter had turned four. Now that Adeline thought about it, this was the reason Prescott's family had moved to Hattiesburg when she was four. And Arnold's had moved to Wiggins when she was two. That was part of the deal, they had to extract themselves from their former lives to some degree to limit the questions. But what about extended family?

Adeline pushed aside the mounting questions. All those issues could be sorted out another time. Not that they really mattered. What mattered was finding those women—her sisters—alive.

And stopping the man who had done this. She stared down at her mother. She was gone. Nothing Adeline did or thought or said would bring her back. The agony swelled in her chest once more.

"I did what I had to do to save my family," Cyrus said, that commanding tone he generally used back in full force. "I make no apologies for that."

Adeline arrowed him an incredulous look. "What do you want me to do, old man?" she demanded. "Give you a medal?"

"I expect you to do what needs to be done." Fury tightened his face. "Kill the bastard who did this."

Adeline sliced her hand through the air, cutting him off. Did he think she was a fool? That he could come in here spouting this fairy tale and have her suddenly seeing him in a different light? The idea of all the time she'd lost with her mother because of him abruptly bobbed to the surface of all the other churning emotions. "You know, if you loved my mother and father so much—paid whatever the price for me—why the hell did you threaten my life nine years ago?"

That made no sense at all. The bastard had run her clean out of Mississippi. He'd never treated her with anything but disdain. Was she just supposed to buy this damned story?

"To protect you," Cyrus admitted, though he looked away as he did. "Gage was my son. I loved him no matter who and what he was. I knew that none of his or Sheriff Grider's supporters would sit back and allow you to get away with the part you played in his death. As long as you were here, your life was in danger, and I couldn't protect you from the fallout."

Adeline wasn't going to waste her breath arguing with him about her so-called part in Gage's death. Nor could she swallow his too pat answer. "You hated me." She let him see the frankness in her eyes. "And, I always got the distinct impression that my mother hated you as much as I did."

Pain, fierce and genuine, flickered in his eyes, taking Adeline aback yet again. "She despised me most of the time, but she always came to me for help. That was enough for me."

Then Adeline understood why her mother would never move to Huntsville. "That's how you kept her here."

"I couldn't bear the idea of her moving away."

"So you made her stay. That was the price for your so-called protection of me." That cold reality slid through Adeline's muscles, settled in her bones. This selfish piece of shit had blackmailed her mother into staying put.

Adeline had to get out of here. She didn't want to be in this room with him any longer. She bent down and kissed her mother's cheek. "Love you," she murmured. Then she raised up and said to Cyrus, "Get out." She didn't want him alone in this room with her mother.

He held her gaze a moment before rolling his chair back from the bed and moving toward the door. She went around him and opened it wide. Hatred seared through her veins. Nothing he'd said had changed how she felt. He was a selfish bastard.

Those beady brown eyes locked with hers one last time. "You remember what I said, Addy. You do it for your mother."

She bit her lips together to prevent telling him to go to hell. She would find Jamison all right and she would see that he got what he deserved.

But it wouldn't have anything to do with her uncle or anything he had to say.

When Everett had ushered Cyrus away, Adeline took one last look at her mother then walked out of the room and let the door close behind her.

The only thing she could do for her mother now was to see that justice was served.

"Let's go," she said to Wyatt. "We need to get a new search started." The old woman, Nichols, had insisted that Prescott and Arnold were being held in a building near the water. Around here that could be most anywhere, but they had to start somewhere.

"Addy." Wyatt stopped her, a hand on her arm, when she would have headed for the elevators.

She saw the worry in his eyes. "Don't say it, Wyatt. Don't say anything. Let's just find this bastard."

He hesitated but then nodded.

Her mind spun with possibilities as they started for the elevators. "We need to know how this thing started." Since their identities had been protected and Grayson hadn't spoken to anyone related to this investigation, the answer could very well lie with the steps Prescott had taken to find the truth. They needed to determine who else Prescott may have spoken to here or elsewhere. Since she'd disappeared in the area and Adeline's mother hadn't given Prescott what she wanted, had someone else? Or had Jamison followed her here?

Who had started this thing? Prescott or Jamison? Bottom line, they needed to know who else might be involved in this somehow. Someone Prescott or Jamison had spoken to. Detectives Ferguson and Cummings were questioning Prescott's parents again, considering what they'd learned in the past twenty-four hours. Arnold's parents were deceased. But someone somewhere had to know something.

Since they'd had no luck finding Jamison or the victims from the perspective of how, when, and where they had gone missing, the goal was to continue looking, of course, but also to reconstruct the steps taken by each known player and see where the map led. To find the spot where their paths intersected.

"Just so you know," Wyatt said, "whatever steps we take, I'm not letting you out of my sight for a second."

"I know how to take care of myself, Wyatt." Her mother was dead, yes. Adeline felt vulnerable, yes. But she wasn't going to tolerate him starting that whole protective bullshit again. "I've had training, not to mention a decade of experience, that Prescott and Arnold don't have. I figure that's why Jamison is taking his time coming after me. He has to plan the event just right. And when he strikes, I'll be ready."

Wyatt started to argue—

"Ms. Cooper!"

Adeline turned back to the nurse's station. "Yes?"

The nurse motioned for Adeline to return to the desk. Was she supposed to sign something?

Her mother was dead. More of that overwhelming misery rose inside her.

Adeline turned, her movements on autopilot, and headed back to the nurse's station. Wyatt stayed close behind her. A man stood at the counter, he glanced back once. Young. Not bald. Not Jamison. Adeline shook off the paranoia. Jamison wasn't here. He'd already done the worst he could here. He would be watching Adeline, that was a certainty, but not this openly.

"Yes?" Adeline glanced from the nurse who'd called her name to the young man still loitering at the counter and back to the nurse.

"This was delivered for you." The nurse gestured to the huge bouquet of flowers on the counter.

"I was told to bring the flowers here," the young man explained. He shrugged. "I figured you were a patient." Anticipation detonated deep in Adeline's veins. She reached for the envelope, picked it up by the very top corner and looked at the name written there.

Adeline Cooper.

What the hell?

While she considered the envelope, Wyatt started questioning the delivery guy.

A tinge of fear diluted the pounding adrenaline. "I need latex gloves," Adeline said to anyone listening.

The nurse immediately collected a pair and passed them to Adeline. The delivery guy was sweating bullets, insisting he had no idea who ordered the flowers. It had been done by phone. All he did was write the message as ordered by the customer and hang around to see that they were delivered to Adeline Cooper. Was he under arrest? he wanted to know.

Ignoring the freaked-out guy, Adeline carefully extracted the single white card from the envelope. The printed letters were not the usual MO since the perp had called in the order, but the words screamed out at her.

It's time, princess.

CHAPTER THIRTY-EIGHT

Jackson County Sheriff's Office
3104 Magnolia Street, 10:30 a.m.

The briefing had gone on too long. Adeline couldn't sit here much longer. Cummings and Ferguson were sending some of their troops to assist with the search. Half an hour from now they would divide up into groups and begin. Couldn't happen fast enough for Adeline.

Wyatt had attempted to get her to eat. She couldn't. She just needed to focus on the investigation. To find Jamison. And make him pay.

"Detective Cooper."

Adeline jerked to attention, scanned the faces around the table.

"I want you to know," Detective Ferguson said via the teleconferencing system, "how deeply sorry I am for your loss. I'm certain it's very difficult for you to continue assisting with this investigation."

Cummings chimed in with a similar sentiment. Adeline managed a nod. "Thank you."

The silence that followed closed around her, suffocating her. "I..." She stood, sending her chair sliding backward. "I need to..." She skirted the long conference table and rushed for the door. In the corridor she made a mad dash for Wyatt's office. She needed to be alone for just a moment.

The breakdown was coming and she couldn't stop it. To allow anyone to witness it...she couldn't do that. She couldn't allow anyone to doubt her ability to continue being part of this investigation.

The secretary didn't try and stop her as she twisted the knob and pushed inside Wyatt's office. Adeline let the door close and sagged against it.

Her whole life, the one thing she'd been relatively certain of was who she was. Even when the bullshit had gone down over Gage's death, she hadn't once questioned herself as an officer of the law or as a woman.

She looked at her hands, turned them palms up and studied the lines there, then the veins beneath the pale skin of the backs of her wrists. She had no Cooper blood in her veins. She hadn't gotten the blond hair and blue eyes from her great aunt on her mother's side.

Her mother was dead. *Murdered.*

Because of *her.*

Adeline hugged her arms around herself. She had no one. She was alone.

Wyatt's image swam before her eyes.

No...he...they were over. Too much time had passed. He had a life. So did she. A life she would return to as soon as this was over.

She would go back to Huntsville and get her promotion. Her life would resume.

Her life? What a joke. How could she just pretend that nothing had changed?

Her mother was dead!

Adeline didn't even know who she was anymore.

She pushed away from the door. Grabbed her courage with both hands. "Adeline Maureen Cooper." She was from Pascagoula, Mississippi, where she had at least one shithook for a cousin and an old bastard of an uncle.

All that Cyrus had said whipped around inside her.

He had nothing to do with who she was. She was Irene and Carl Cooper's daughter. A good cop...if not a good daughter.

Stop. Letting herself go down that road would only hinder what she had to do. She would be okay. As soon as she took care of Jamison. Made him pay for what he'd done. A sob twisted inside her. She would be okay.

"Damn it." She refused to cry again. "Suck it up, Cooper."

Her mouth tightened with the anger lingering around the edges of the pain. She had a job to do here. Her mother was dead. She deserved to have her death avenged. Adeline did not have the luxury of time for this poor-me crap. She was a major crimes detective. She had a killer to catch.

The urge to run all the way back to Huntsville overwhelmed her for several seconds. She could put all this behind her there. Forget these people...this place. This insanity.

Once the case was closed, she reiterated. Then, going back would make life a hell of a lot easier.

She didn't have to look back in this direction...ever.

Just when she thought she could pull it together, her heart pounded so hard it hurt. The facts she had learned in the past twenty-four hours crashed in on her. How could she not have known any of this? She was a cop, for Christ's sake. Not once had she suspected that her parents had been less than honest with her. Left out this one huge important detail.

Adeline Cooper wasn't who she thought she was.

Those moments in her mother's kitchen when she'd collapsed in Adeline's arms elbowed their way into her thoughts. She'd been so afraid. The ride to the hospital in that ambulance. Then waiting for word. If her mother had died—Adeline had been absolutely positive she couldn't have handled that. Cop or no. She was strong, but she wasn't that damned strong.

I didn't want you to know that you weren't my little girl.

The tears escaped, slid down her cheeks.

And then that bastard Jamison had killed her. Now Adeline had no choice but to handle it.

Her mother was dead.

"Goddammit." She staggered back, collapsed against the wall next to the door and slowly slid to the floor.

She just wanted her mother to be well and at home, where she had always been. Her whole life Adeline had been able to count on coming home to find her there.

Until she had selfishly walked away from everything. No, not walked—run...she'd run as fast as she could. Why the hell had she let that old bastard send her running? She'd pretended not to give a shit. Had even pretended the decision had been hers and had nothing to do with Cyrus's edict.

Lies. All of it. She'd lied to herself and everyone she cared about. How could she hold her parents' decision of nondisclosure against them when she was just as guilty of holding so very much back?

How could she return to her life in Huntsville knowing all that she knew?

But then, what the hell did she do when this was finished?

Go someplace new?

Running would damned sure be a hell of a lot easier than dealing with all *this*. Someplace where no one knew her. Where none of this history could find her.

But she wasn't twenty-one anymore. Shaking off the dust and heading for new territory would change nothing.

This was her life. Who she was.

No matter where she ran, she couldn't escape herself.

All this time she'd thought she had done just that, but she'd been fooling herself.

More lies...more pretending...

The runaway cop—sounded like the perfect theme for a movie.

The door opened.

She glanced up as Wyatt crouched down next to her. "Addy." He searched her face. "You should stay here while we get things started out there. Take a break. Let the rest of us deal with this search."

Was he out of his mind? She struggled to her feet. "No way in hell. I'm fine. Let's go." She straightened her jacket. What was wrong with these people?

"You are not fine."

She closed her eyes, tried to stop the sound of his voice from reverberating in her ears.

"Addy?"

She glared at him. "The truth is, I may never be fine again. But that's not going to stop me from finding this son of a bitch."

"You're exhausted," he said gently. "You're upset. You have every right to be."

"Look, Dr. Phil," she glared at him, "give me five

damned minutes and I'll be good to go." All she had to do was wash her face and take a few more deep breaths.

"If you insist," he relented, his frustration showing. "But, like I told you before, I'm not letting you out of my sight," he said flatly, those hazel eyes hard with determination. "You stay right where I can see you twenty-four/seven until this is over. After what happened in that cemetery, I'd think you would be down with that."

"And what happened to my mother?" He needn't forget that part. If Adeline had been on her toes she would have sensed the danger before it happened. She'd fallen down on the job as a cop and as a daughter.

"Yes," he confessed.

She folded her arms over her chest. "And if I don't agree to those terms, what do you plan to do about that, Sheriff Henderson?" This was ridiculous. How could she do the job if she had to be right under his thumb every second?

"Put you in protective custody as a person of interest to this case."

Impotent laughter bubbled into her throat. "You are seriously cracked if you think I'd let you get away with that shit. Remember, I know as much about the law as you, hotshot." Anger had completely taken over all those weaker emotions now. Even she realized she wasn't reacting rationally.

"Try me."

She took a mental step back. He was serious. The fury in his tone as he'd uttered those two little words warned that he would not back off. Allowing him to control her every move was out of the question.

"I'm out of here." She started around him, but he reached out, closed his fingers around her arm.

"If anything happened to you," he stared into her eyes, "I don't think I could bear it."

A fist rapped against the door. "Sheriff Henderson?" The secretary. "The others are waiting for you."

Wyatt's gaze held hers as if there was more he wanted to say. There was certainly more she should say, but she didn't dare.

As much as Adeline wanted to, she wasn't entirely sure she could trust him not to let her down again.

He certainly couldn't trust her not to run again.

The only thing they could both count on was that they were damned good cops.

For now, getting the job done—for her mother, for the missing women—would have to be enough.

CHAPTER THIRTY-NINE

5:42 p.m.

Wyatt removed his cap and swiped the sweat from his brow. The fifty-five degrees felt like ninety. The teams had filed out nearly six hours ago to search their designated grids.

Womack, Sullenger, and Addy were on Wyatt's team but they'd gotten a later start than the others. Addy had insisted on bringing Nichols to the location.

Wyatt couldn't deny the woman had sensed some of the details about the killer, but he wasn't so sure how far to follow that lead. And daylight was wasting.

He'd kept a close eye on Addy. He could hardly believe her mother was dead. Even more unbelievable was the idea that he'd allowed her to be a part of this search.

Admittedly, as long as she was focused on the investigation, she didn't dwell on all the insanity.

But there was no way to avoid the issues. She was in

denial now. He couldn't let her fall apart without being close by to back her up.

The way he'd failed to do nine years ago.

Wyatt shook off the painful thoughts. He couldn't afford to be distracted.

Nichols turned all the way around, her eyes wide, her big wool coat swallowing just about all of her but those eyes. "He came this way." She pointed to the water and nodded with complete certainty. Then she stilled. Her head started to wag back and forth. "He didn't bring them here." Her gaze settled on Addy. "But he was here..." She gave her head another good shake. "Don't know why, but he came here for something. Or maybe he passed this way going where he was going."

"A lot of these waterways intersect," Womack suggested. "He may have used a canoe, moved about that way with his victims."

Wyatt heaved a disgusted breath. "Yeah. We'll keep searching until dark." Scarcely a few minutes more. There was nothing else to do at this point. "Tomorrow we'll take another sector and do the same. We'll just keep doing it until we find them."

Pain tightened in Addy's face. She offered her arm to the older woman. "Come on, Ms. Nichols, I'll walk you back to the command post. From there one of the deputies will give you a ride home."

Wyatt started to argue, but Sullenger jumped in. "I'll go with you, Detective Cooper." She smiled at Wyatt. "Better to move about in pairs, right, sir?"

Addy rolled her eyes but didn't argue.

Wyatt checked in with the team leaders. He knew damned well that if any of them had made a discovery he would have known about it within seconds. Still, it was something to do until Addy was back at his side. He'd sworn he wasn't letting her out of his sight. But they weren't that far from the temporary command post and Sullenger was with her, both were armed. If he didn't give her some breathing room, she would revolt.

He shook his head. So far they hadn't found a damned thing and Nichols had just insisted the women weren't anywhere near here. Of course, she could be wrong. But she'd been right about a hell of a lot so far.

Damn it.

What the hell was wrong with him? One minute he thought the woman being involved was a waste of time, the next he'd done an about-face.

He seemed to be doing a lot of that lately. Wyatt shoved his phone back into the holster on his belt. If this thing hadn't happened, Addy likely would never have come back home. Selfishly, he was glad she was back. But every minute that this crazed bastard was on the loose, her life was threatened.

Damn it. He felt helpless. Just plain damned helpless.

"This guy's a true psycho, don't you think?" Womack asked. "What he did to his wife is unthinkable."

"Yeah." Wyatt had read about the children of killers and how sometimes they ended up following that same path, but he'd never worked a case where the perp fell into that category. Well, there were the Cooper boys, Gage and Clay. But, to his knowledge, neither one had resorted to murder. If Cyrus had ever committed a homicide, he'd kept it under wraps. No way to be certain with a man like that.

Womack scanned the woods all around them; the trees and underbrush grew right up to the riverbank. "I'm scared to death we're going to be too late for those women." He settled his attention on Wyatt. "No harm in a man admitting fear, especially in a situation like this."

"None at all," Wyatt agreed. "We hope for the best and brace for the worst. Then we do all we can." *It may already be too late.* Wyatt exiled that truth.

Every county from here to just north of Laurel and all the way west to Picayune was looking for those women and the damned man who had taken them. He couldn't be that good.

Wyatt turned to stare in the direction Addy had gone with Nichols and Sullenger. He shouldn't have let her out of his sight. How many times had he said that and gone on to let her have her way? He started in the direction of the command post. Womack called out to him, but Wyatt just kept walking.

He had to get to Addy and this time she wasn't getting more than two feet from him.

CHAPTER FORTY

"Thanks for your help, Ms. Nichols." Adeline assisted her into the back of the county cruiser.

"You be careful now," the lady urged. She searched Adeline's face. "He's watching you real close. Almost as close as he's watching his boy."

Adeline resisted the urge to look over her shoulder. "Don't worry about me, ma'am. I'm watching for him."

Ms. Nichols grabbed her hand before Adeline could close the door. "Stay away from your kin, Detective. You can't trust none of 'em."

Adeline promised she would as she extracted her hand from the old lady's surprisingly strong grip. She closed the door and banged the top of the car with the flat of her hand to give the deputy the go-ahead to get moving.

Nichols had picked up on the fact that the man they were looking for was her biological brother. And that he had a son. No way to ignore she had some sort of gift.

The whole thing gave Adeline the willies.

At least she'd kept her mind occupied and off her mother. Images of her lying in that hospital bed ached through Adeline. It was so hard to believe her mother was gone. Forever.

"That old woman is one strange lady," Sullenger commented as she watched the cruiser roll down the dirt road, leaving a faint cloud of dust in its wake.

Adeline blinked the images away. "Very strange."

Her attention settled on Sullenger. She really was attractive, despite the long nose. Seemed like a good deputy. Had Sullenger and Wyatt dated? Or just flirted at the office? Her gaze narrowed on Sullenger. *Jealousy never looks good on anyone*. That was what her mother would say. A renewed ache deep in her chest took her breath.

"So." Sullenger started back in the direction they'd come. "Will you be staying long once this investigation is wrapped up?" She shook her head. "And, after the funeral? I'm really sorry about your mother, Detective."

Yep, the girl was getting the lay of the land. Sizing up the challenge the competition represented. The sympathy was just something she tacked on for appearances' sake. "Thanks."

"You've got a lot on your mind," Sullenger suggested, answering her own question. "The funeral. Taking care of your mother's place. You'll probably be around for a while."

"I don't think my chief would be too happy," Adeline admitted, "if I hung around too long." But the woman was right. Adeline had a lot to take care of...none of which she wanted to think about right now. God, she hadn't even considered that reality.

Sullenger made an agreeable sound. "Sheriff Henderson probably won't be too happy about you going."

"He's a big boy, he'll get over it."

"He never stopped loving you." Sullenger stopped and faced Adeline. "You do know that, don't you?"

If she'd slapped Adeline in the face she wouldn't have been more surprised. "Do you always nose around in folks' personal business?" Adeline folded her arms over her chest and met the woman's brazen stare. No point beating around the bush.

The deputy hiked her shoulders, then let them fall. "Only when it affects me."

Adeline's gaze narrowed a second time. "If you and Henderson have something going on, you don't need to worry about me." Adeline started forward again. "When this is done and *things* are taken care of, I'm out of here." The question of whether she would stay or go had never been a real issue. Had she inadvertently given the impression she might stay?

"We don't exactly have anything going on," Sullenger confessed as she trailed behind Adeline, *"yet."*

With everything else that was happening, the pure jealousy that roiled inside Adeline pissed her off. She had no right feeling jealous. She had way bigger problems than Wyatt Henderson. They'd had sex, yes. But they were both adults and it hadn't meant anything real. Had it? Of course not. "You got no competition with me, Deputy."

"Ha."

Adeline shot the smart-mouthed deputy a look.

"Every woman who's given him a second look has to compete with you."

"Well now." Adeline kicked aside the ridiculous feeling of victory that attempted to roar through her. "Maybe the right one just hasn't come along."

"Is he why you're still single?"

Now she'd stepped on Adeline's toes. She laughed it off. "I'm married to my shield, Sullenger. It's what I do and that's all I need."

"Funny," the deputy commented, "that's what he says."

CHAPTER FORTY-ONE

Laurel, 6:05 p.m.

His daddy had told him to wait until five o'clock.

Danny had followed his daddy's instructions. Every one of them. Just like he said in the note.

Danny didn't know how his daddy had done it because his grandparents wouldn't let his daddy come to their house anymore. But after Danny got home from visiting his mom at the hospital last night, his grandma had tucked him into bed. When she'd left the room, he turned on his side and stuck his hand under the pillow the way he always did and there was the note. He'd switched on the light, saw it was from his daddy and smiled.

His daddy had written that at five o'clock today he was to make sure no one was watching him. Then Danny was to put on his coat, put the letter in his pocket with his gloves, and go into the upstairs bathroom, the one by the room where he slept. Over the bathtub there was a window. It was really little but Danny could fit through it. Being real careful that he didn't make any noise, he had slid the window open and climbed out onto the roof. Then he'd made sure he closed the window real tight. His daddy had written in his note that the police would be looking at the windows. Danny had to be sure he didn't forget that part. It was real important.

The roof was the one over the big old side porch. Climbing out onto the roof had been scary at first, but his daddy had told him not to be afraid. He was a big boy now and he could do anything his daddy told him.

This was the only way they could be together again.

Danny had to inch all the way to the part of the porch that connected to the garage roof. Soon as he was on the garage roof, he lay flat on his belly and wiggled his way toward the farthest end from the driveway. The next part was the hardest, scariest part. He had to climb down.

The ladder was there, just like his daddy had said in the letter. Slowly sliding his body off the edge of the roof, he climbed down one rung at a time. Turned out it wasn't too hard, either.

Peeking around the corner of the garage, Danny made sure no one was looking for him on this side of the house. His daddy had said to be sure the searchers had moved toward the woods first. Danny could hear them calling his name in the woods beyond the backyard.

He hurried over to the garbage cans his grandparents kept lined up at the side of the garage, climbed up onto the smallest one—the one his grandfather used for sticks and stuff he picked up in the yard. Then he opened the lid of the big one next to it. It didn't smell very good in there but his daddy had promised he would be fine.

Danny scrambled into the can and pulled the lid closed. It was really, really dark. He closed his eyes and thought of that Christmas song he liked so much. Danny couldn't remember ever being so scared, but he had to do what his daddy told him. They were going to get his mommy out of the hospital and then they would go home to get his Christmas presents. The ones his grandparents wouldn't take him to get.

His daddy promised that what the police and his grandparents were saying was all lies. They just wanted to take Danny away from his daddy. They wanted to turn Danny's mom against his dad. All they cared about was getting his mom and the new baby. They didn't even care about Danny. Seemed like his daddy was right about that. His grandparents had been pretty mean to him. They made him stay in his room a lot. Wouldn't let him watch television. He hadn't had any fun at all since he came here.

He wanted to go home.

What they were doing to his daddy was bad. His grandma and grandpa shouldn't be doing something so bad.

Danny didn't like the police. They looked at him funny.

Well, he was gonna do just what his daddy said and then he wouldn't have to worry about the police anymore. He would be with his mommy and daddy far away from here. His daddy had promised that, too.

Danny wondered, as he huddled in his stinky hiding place, if that was what his daddy had meant when he'd said the princess wouldn't take his place.

He was pretty sure he hadn't seen a princess around here. But he might not have understood what his daddy meant. Maybe he meant the girl baby his mommy had in her tummy. If his grandparents wanted the girl and didn't want Danny, that might be what his daddy meant.

It was getting colder, but Danny didn't care. His coat and gloves would keep him warm enough in this stinky old trash can. He felt bad that his grandma was probably crying since they couldn't find him. But she shouldn't have been mean to his daddy. That wasn't nice.

Danny closed his eyes and sang Christmas songs in his head. Tonight he would get the presents his mom and Santa had brought him. Santa hadn't come to his grandparents' house. His daddy explained in his letter that Santa's presents were waiting for Danny at home. He couldn't wait to open his presents and to see his mom.

Everything would be okay then. His daddy never told him lies. He always told Danny the truth.

All Danny had to do was be very still and not say a word.

When it got dark enough the police would stop looking for him. Then his daddy would come get him.

Jingle bell...jingle bell...jingle bell rock.

He wished he remembered the rest of the words.

CHAPTER FORTY-TWO

4718 Miller Road,
Pascagoula, 8:42 p.m.

Cyrus stared at what he had found in his son's room.

His heart ached. Clay was his only child now. He couldn't bear to lose him.

Cyrus closed his eyes to hold back the uncharacteristic tears. Irene was dead. Clay was all he had left in this world.

How much was one man supposed to endure?

Somehow, he had to stop this without revealing his son's part in any of it. Clay could not go to prison. He'd made far too many enemies to survive in that shithole.

Cyrus opened his eyes and stared at the evidence he had discovered. As much as he loved his son, this had gone too far.

Irene was dead. The light of his life had been extinguished. But there was one thing he could do for his Irene. He could ensure that his son left Addy alone. Irene had loved her daughter so. She would want Cyrus to protect Addy.

He would not fail.

Cyrus had to stop this travesty before it was too late.

The front door slammed.

Clay was home.

Rather than bother with the elevator down to the first floor to meet him, Cyrus waited for his son in his room. Clay would grab a few beers from the refrigerator and then he would come here. After a shower and change of clothes he would go out again. To take care of business.

The business Cyrus had built. Bitter bile rose in his throat. A part of him understood that he was as much responsible for Gage's death as the man who'd fired the weapon. Cyrus banished that truth. This day and time a man had to do what a man had to do.

Irene had held that necessity against him. But she hadn't understood that after the accident, he'd been forced to resort to other means for maintaining his wealth. His medical bills had eaten through most of what he'd inherited.

And his very generous donation to the church had put their names at the top of the adoption list. That part she should have appreciated enough not to care where the money had come from. Cyrus had known that on some level she did, but she'd never said as much.

A Cooper always found a way to survive. No matter which side of the law it landed him on. His great-great-granddaddy had operated numerous bootlegging operations.

In times of need, it was what it was.

Survival of the fittest…of the most clever.

He would sorely miss his Irene. Just as he still missed his sweet brother. No Cooper before him had possessed the heart his younger brother had been born with. Perhaps God had ensured that Carl received Cyrus's measure in addition to his own. A sort of balance to keep things interesting.

Clay stormed through the open door. "What the hell you doing in here, old man?" He turned his bottle of beer up and emptied half of it down his throat.

So young. So full of himself. He would be lucky to survive the stupidity of youth.

Cyrus gestured to the items he had spread on the bed. "What is all this?"

Clay froze, the bottle inches from his thirsty lips.

"Are you the one responsible for this?" Again he gestured to the words clipped from magazines, the glue and paper. All of it sickened Cyrus. He thought of how much pain *this* had caused Irene. Fury tore through him.

"Look." Clay lowered the bottle, shrugged his shoulders. "It was a joke, okay? I heard about the letters that bitch was getting and I thought I'd mess with her head. I put one in her room and tore up some of her shit. That's all."

He was lying. Cyrus knew his son. He'd always been able to read the both of them. Gage hadn't been quite the liar that Clay was. He was too focused on business to bother with getting into other kinds of trouble. But Clay, dear Clay, had spent every moment since he was fifteen getting into some sort of mischief.

"I will not be able to protect you from this," Cyrus warned, "unless it stops now. Henderson is not like Grider. He will not be bought."

Clay expelled a disgusting belch. "Screw Henderson. I don't need your protection. I've got it all under control." He glared at his father. "I told you, it's just a joke. Don't get your panties in a wad. It's no big deal."

"Did you harm those women?" Cyrus demanded, the fury escalating inside him at his son's cocky attitude.

He'd asked these questions before and Clay had adamantly denied any part in this. Any knowledge whatsoever of these events. But Cyrus had found evidence to indicate otherwise. Clay wouldn't be playing him off so easily this time.

"Hell no!" Clay emptied the bottle in his right hand. "Are you senile? I told you I ain't got nothing to do with that. A friend of mine who's involved in the investigation told me about the letters and, like I said, I just wanted to mess with her head. Get a little revenge for what she did to Gage."

"If you were half as smart as you think you are, you would have destroyed the evidence of your *joke.*"

Clay tossed the empty bottle onto his bed and opened the other one. "You don't care what happens to me. You're only trying to protect her damned momma. I know the deal."

"Her mother is dead." The need to shake him whipped through Cyrus. God, if he could climb out of this chair...

"I don't know nothing about that, either." He downed half the second bottle.

"Do you really expect me to believe you know nothing?" Cyrus growled. Before his son could come up with a response, he warned, "You stay away from Addy the remainder of her stay here. No more games. Do you understand me?"

"Yeah, yeah. I understand perfectly. You don't have to worry, tonight is the end of this for me."

He pushed between Cyrus's wheelchair and his bed and started gathering the incriminating evidence.

"What does that mean?" Cyrus demanded, uncertainty niggling at him.

Clay twisted at the waist to look down at his father.

"Exactly what I said. I'm not playing no more. I had my fun. Now I'm done."

If only he could trust his son's word. Cyrus rolled to the door. There was one more thing he intended to say. "If I discover that you've been lying to me or that you had anything at all to do with Irene's death, I will cut off all support. There will be no forgiveness. This is your final warning." Perhaps the boy could benefit from eking out his own living. Or perhaps Cyrus would just put him out of his misery. Agony seized his insides once more. To some degree he now looked forward to his own death.

Without Irene...he wasn't sure this pathetic life would be worth living.

He was certain it would not be.

Clay strode right up to him and braced his hands on the arms of the mobile chair. He put his face in Cyrus's. "This is *your* final warning, old man. You keep giving me shit and you will end up at the bottom of those stairs. And then it'll all be mine and I won't have to answer to you about any damned thing."

Cyrus produced a taunting smile. "You don't have the guts to take a life, much less mine. You have no idea just what it takes to go that far."

Clay didn't flinch. He held Cyrus's gaze. "You sure about that?"

Cyrus's confidence in the matter drained away like the evening tide. Perhaps he didn't fully comprehend what his son was capable of. Time would tell, he supposed.

"Test me again," Cyrus cautioned, "and we will see who has the largest balls in this family."

CHAPTER FORTY-THREE

1708 Monroe Street, 10:05 p.m.

Adeline sat on Wyatt's sofa. She felt numb. Beyond exhausted. They had found nothing. Not one sign of the women or Jamison.

The bastard could have tucked Prescott and Arnold away almost anywhere. Hundreds of tiny shacks and cabins dotted the waterways. Hunters, drug smugglers, and the like built small, primitive shelters all the time. Many were abandoned and left to rot down.

It could take weeks to cover every square mile of land near the water. But Adeline was determined to keep searching until she found the women or their bodies.

She closed her eyes and dropped her head onto on the sofa back. God, she did not want them to be dead. Sheriff Henley had called. The boy, Danny, was missing. Defeat sucked at Adeline's determination. Would Jamison hide his son with the women…to watch him play out his crazy scheme?

The idea of a child being in harm's way made her sick to her stomach.

They had to find Jamison.

Adeline failed at blocking the thoughts of her mother that nudged their way into her consciousness. The funeral home would have picked up her body by now. They would be waiting for Adeline to make a decision on the arrangements.

She opened her eyes and sat up straight. She couldn't think about that. It was too fresh. Hurt too much.

Focus on the case. The women. The boy. Henley had no idea how Jamison had gotten into the home belonging to his in-laws, but he had to have gotten in. The boy had vanished. Even with the grandparents and a deputy keeping a diligent watch the bastard had managed to get to the kid.

At least there had been no casualties. The last time this psycho hadn't been quite so generous.

He'd killed Adeline's mother. She hadn't done a damned thing to hurt the son of a bitch. He'd done it to hurt Adeline. By God, she wouldn't rest until she had hurt him back.

"Bastard."

She thought of the flowers he'd had delivered to the hospital. The call to the flower shop had come from a phone booth right here in Pascagoula. He was close. But how had he known when she had arrived? They'd rushed back from Jones County. Jamison couldn't have known hers and Wyatt's movements.

Yet he had. He'd been watching. Somehow.

He's watching you real close. Almost as close as he's watching his boy.

You're next. It's time, princess.

Fury blasted through Adeline.

Bring it on, asshole. I will fucking end this.

"You need to get to bed."

She looked up at Wyatt. He stood over her, his protector mentality in full force. "Is that an invitation?"

"Addy." He lowered himself onto the coffee table in front of her, took her hands in his. "We're both beat. You're operating on nothing but adrenaline. Think about what you've been through today. You can't keep going like this."

She turned her face away from his. That was the last thing she wanted to think about. Even as she blanked her mind on the subject, the knife of reality sank deeper into her chest and twisted.

"Look," he said gently. "If we're going to be able to function in the morning when the search resumes, we need sleep." He jerked his head toward the hall. "Take a shower and hit the sack. I'll be right behind you."

She pulled her hands free of his. "I don't need you hovering over me. I'm a detective, not some little girl who needs watching over. How many times do we have to talk about this?" She didn't like this feeling of helplessness. The aloneness was even worse. His tactics were only driving those points home. She needed rest. That was true. She would be able to think more clearly if she got some sleep. Expectations for finding Prescott and Arnold alive had run out about ten hours ago, longer for Prescott.

Two dead princesses...one to go.

She closed her eyes, exiled the words. Adeline didn't want them to be dead. Their kids would be orphaned...just as each of them had been. Was that why the bastard had waited so long? So he could inflict the same sort of pain his father had?

Adeline was an orphan now...her mother was gone.

Fury tightened her lips. She would find those women and the kid. And she would make Jamison pay.

"Forget the shower," Wyatt urged, "take one in the morning. Get some sleep now. Please, Addy."

She didn't have the energy to debate the issue.

"Everything else can wait," he said softly. "Take a day to think about what you want to do about arrangements for your mom. You don't need to be in a hurry."

Her gaze collided with his. Why did he have to bring that up? "Sullenger told you what I said, didn't she?" Adeline should have known she would. Why the hell was she surprised?

Wyatt frowned but not before Adeline saw the truth in his eyes. Damn that little bitch. "Were you surprised?" Jesus Christ. She hadn't come back here to stay. If she hadn't intended to stay before her mother was murdered, why would she decide to now? "Christ, Wyatt, I came here for the case. When it's done...when everything's settled, I'm out of here."

Disappointment claimed his every feature. That he didn't bother arguing only made her angrier. "Say something!" She couldn't bear him just sitting there staring at her like that.

"I thought you might reconsider."

The softness of his voice, the sheer misery in his eyes, had the same effect as someone reaching inside her chest and twisting her heart. She couldn't pretend he hadn't gotten to her. Despite the fact that she'd promised herself she wouldn't let this happen—that she wouldn't trust him again. Wouldn't let him get close, here she sat, exactly in that place.

"Why would you think that?" She banished the little voice that shouted *liar, liar* inside her head. "Because we had sex? Get over it, Wyatt, it was sex. Just sex." *Liar, liar!* Adeline clenched her teeth, exiled the voice a second time.

"I know what I felt," he insisted, his own defenses in place now. His shoulders were tense, the muscle in his jaw throbbing with frustration.

Enough. "And I know what you did nine years ago. Whatever else there is between us," she reminded him, driving a dagger of her own into his heart, "that betrayal will always trump everything else. Great sex isn't going to change that."

"You never gave me a chance to explain," he countered. "Even an accused felon gets his day in court. Gets to tell his side of the story."

"Fine." She couldn't believe they were doing this now. What the hell difference did he expect his side of the story to make? "Spit it out, Wyatt." She flung her arms upward. "You've wanted to talk about this ever since I arrived. Go ahead. I'm just dying to hear what made you decide to leave me hanging."

He stood, moved around the coffee table to pace the room. Was he buying time? If he didn't have his story straight by now he should give it up.

Adeline told herself she was being unreasonable. She was tired. Hurt. Guilty. And too many other negatives to mention. She'd screwed everything up. Let her mom down, and now it was too late to make up for those mistakes. She didn't need this trip down memory lane. Even now that old familiar anger that simmered each time she thought about nine years ago heated deep in her gut.

Wyatt stopped, set his hands on his hips, and stared directly at her. "Cyrus had put the word out that if you stayed you were dead. Gage and Grider had too many allies to doubt that scenario. I was," he looked away a moment, seemed to struggle to collect himself, "scared to death you wouldn't listen to his warning." His gaze meshed with hers once more. "That you'd end up dead."

Outrage propelled her to her feet. "I wasn't going anywhere until I ensured that Grider got what was coming to him. He couldn't avoid charges with the DEA, but I knew he'd set me up. I was supposed to die that day—not Gage. I wanted him to pay for that decision. We *both* knew he'd set me up."

For Christ's sake, Wyatt was the one who'd heard rumors about the setup before the sting went down. Gage wanted Adeline off his back, and he'd worked a deal with Grider to get the job done during the DEA operation. Wyatt had even tried to talk her out of moving forward. She'd refused. He'd never understood that she could take care of herself.

The stare-off lasted a full ten seconds. "Grider wasn't going to escape punishment," Wyatt said at last. "What difference did it make if he got twenty-five years or life, at his age it was irrelevant. I just wanted you safe. The only way to ensure your safety was if you were gone."

"So you lied to the review committee." She let him see the old hurt in her eyes. "You let them believe that because we were lovers I expected you to back me up even though you claimed to know nothing. I remember every moment of it, like it was yesterday. You took the fifth and left me to face the powers that be. It wasn't pleasant, Wyatt. What it was, was wrong."

To her surprise, he nodded. "You're right. It was wrong." His words totally stunned her. She couldn't find the right way to respond before he started talking again.

"I told the review committee," he admitted, "that I didn't know what you were talking about. I wanted you mad enough to leave. The only way to accomplish that was to betray you—to make you hate me enough to walk away.

If I'd taken your side, you wouldn't have left. You would have stayed right here and told Cyrus to kiss your ass. The whole department was in turmoil and blaming you. You were sick of the dirty cops. You were still grieving the death of your father. You and your mother were on the outs. I knew I was the only thing keeping you here. So I did what I had to do to turn you against me. It was the only way to ensure you were away from here and safe."

Nine damned years! He'd let nine years go by with her thinking that he hadn't loved her enough to back her up. "You bastard." How could he have done such a thing? "You couldn't have explained this to me after the fact?" How could he have allowed her to suffer the loss of everything without telling her the truth? "You could have backed me up and then we would have left together."

He shook his head, his expression adamant. "If I'd backed you up, you wouldn't have left. You would've insisted on staying here and cleaning up Grider's mess. I know how you think, Addy. I had to make you angry enough to walk away. I needed you to hate me."

"Well," she glared at him with all the pain and rage that had been building for nine long years, "you succeeded." Why couldn't he see what he'd done? "You could have told me the truth after I left. At least then I wouldn't have had to live with those feelings all these years."

"As you'll recall," he pressed, his tone reflecting his own rising frustration, "I tried to talk to you. To explain." He shook his head. "But you wouldn't talk to me. I sent letters. Sent messages through your mother. I even showed up at your door once and you called your HPD friends to haul me away. You ignored everything. Finally, I gave up." He sighed, the sound weary with the old hurt. "It was enough for me just knowing you were safe. Keeping you safe is all that has ever mattered to me."

How could he do that? Just let her walk away thinking what she thought of him. "Well, that's just great. Thanks for clearing things up for me. I'm going to bed." He'd thrown everything away because he didn't think she was strong enough to take care of herself. Just proof positive that he'd never really known her at all.

She hesitated, turned back to him. "Just so you know, you worry for nothing. You threw *us* away for nothing." She bopped her chest with her fist. "First, I've told you a million times that I can take care of myself. I'm no princess. I'm a cop. A damned good one. Second, I wasn't afraid of Cyrus then and I'm not afraid of him or Jamison now. That bastard's not killing me. So back off, Wyatt, and let me take care of myself."

She stalked down the hall. She bypassed the guest-room and went straight to his bed. He could sleep in the guest-room or take the couch. His bed was by far the most comfortable.

The rumpled sheets were welcoming. They smelled like him. That shouldn't have given her any comfort, but it did. She burrowed into the pillows and forced her brain to shut off.

She didn't want to think. Her mother was gone and Wyatt was a fool. He'd thrown them away because he couldn't see the truth. Because he didn't respect her ability.

Vaguely she heard him come into the room. Heard the water go on in the shower of the en suite bath.

That was the sound that followed her to sleep.

Deeper and deeper she sank.

She tried to fight her way back to the surface, but

hands were clutching at her...pulling her down, down, down.

Adeline struggled against the hands...felt that familiar pressure settle on her chest.

No! She wanted to live. She didn't want to die.

Her lungs burned with the need to suck in air. She clenched her jaw. Held her breath.

The hands stopped clutching at her. But the weight remained on her chest, rendering her immobile. Helpless.

The water suddenly cleared. So clear she could see the moonlight shining down through it.

She turned her head to the right. Cherry Prescott lay beside her. Her eyes were closed and a tiara was tangled in her hair. Adeline shook her head. Almost opened her mouth to scream.

Help me! Please help me!

Her heart pounding, she turned to her left. Penny Arnold lay on that side of her. Eyes closed. Tiara twisted in her long blond hair.

Adeline flung out her arms. Tried to rise up. Couldn't. Finally her hands settled atop her head. She felt around. Her fingers curled around something metal. She pulled it free of her hair.

A tiara.

Adeline jerked upright.

Sweat dampened her skin. Her breath heaved in and out of her lungs. She coughed. Dark. Water running. She looked at the clock. Ten fifty-six. She'd been asleep, what? Four or five minutes?

Shit.

She threw back the covers Wyatt must have spread over her and got up. Her legs wobbled so she took a moment to regain her equilibrium.

Damned dreams.

The bathroom door was open. She peeked past it. Wyatt was in the shower. How the hell had only four or so minutes of sleep allowed that damned dream?

Her throat felt sand dry. She needed something to drink. Anything but water.

She shoved the hair that had fallen loose out of her face. Apparently she'd done some tossing and turning during that short dream. The images haunted her. Penny and Cherry lying beside her. Adeline shuddered.

In the kitchen, she poured a glass of orange juice and downed it.

Better.

Her cell vibrated. She stared down at her waist. Damn, she hadn't even taken off her utility belt. No wonder she felt achy. Even five minutes of sleep wearing all that gear poking and digging into her muscles was bad.

She pulled out her phone. A text message. She smiled. The only person who ever sent her text messages was Braddock. It would be a relief to hear from him. She frowned at the unknown number. Did he have a new cell number?

She opened the message.
She stopped breathing.

It's time, princess. Meet me
at the command post. Come alone
or they die.

For about two seconds Adeline considered walking in there and dragging Wyatt out of the shower. But if he came and this bastard spotted him the vics would die.

Was it possible they were even still alive?

She read the screen again.

Going alone was her only option. That Wyatt would go ape shit sent anger buzzing along her nerve endings. He didn't trust her to handle herself. Didn't have any faith in her ability. She was a good cop. It was way past time for him to notice.

Still, she wasn't stupid enough to do this alone. As much as she wanted to assure the safety of those two…going without backup would be the quickest way to get dead.

No problem. She would arrange backup. All she needed was a ten-minute head start. As long as Jamison thought she was alone, when reinforcements showed up, what could he do?

Die, because she was going to kill his sorry ass.

She checked her weapon, grabbed her jacket and the keys to her Bronco as well as Wyatt's SUV, and slipped out the front door. Wyatt would be pissed but he'd get over it. He needed to learn to trust her.

With a quick survey of the dark yard, she hurried to her Bronco. Hit the unlock button, hopped in, and locked the doors. She backed out of the driveway without turning on the headlights.

Maybe even a ten-minute head start was foolhardy, but if there was any chance at all those women and that child were alive, she had to go for it.

Half a block from Wyatt's house she turned on the headlights and put through a call to Deputy Womack.

"Yeah." From the sound of his voice, she'd gotten him out of bed.

"I got another message," she blurted. Her nerves were vibrating with anticipation. This could be it.

"Addy? Where the hell are you? Where's Wyatt?"

"Just listen to me, Womack. Come to Wyatt's house and get him. I took his keys. By the time you get here I'll be at the rendezvous point. I'll forward you the location by text in five minutes. So get up, buddy, it's going down."

"Addy, listen to me."

She hung up before he could attempt to talk her out of her decision. Focus was what she needed right now. Extreme focus.

A shiver rattled her bones as Nichols's last words echoed in her brain. *Stay away from your kin, Detective.*

Her kin, right. The bastard was nothing to her. Except a dead man. He wasn't getting away with what he'd done to her mother.

The farther out of town she got, the more her tension ratcheted up. She braked as she reached the turnoff to the dirt road leading to the command post they'd used today. As promised, she forwarded the text message to Womack's cell as well as Wyatt's.

She made the turn. A big-ass tree lay across the road.

She braked hard. "What the hell?"

They'd been down this road just a few hours ago. The entire search had started and then ended just a mile or so from here. There hadn't been any strong winds.

She rammed the Bronco into reverse. She'd been set up. "Shit!"

"Get out!"

She hit the brake at the same time she turned to see who had shouted the command.

Clay stood outside her door; a .357 Magnum revolver aimed at her head.

"Shut off the engine and get out."

She was going to kick the shit out of him. She rammed the gearshift into park, jerked the door open, and slid out of the seat. When her feet hit the ground her weapon was in her hand and pointed at his damned head.

"Drop the .357, you dumbass." She was definitely going to kill this prick. If he'd messed with this case, he would so regret it.

"You don't understand," he argued, his tone strained as if he were afraid or was nervous about something. "This is the only way I could get you away from Wyatt." He lowered his weapon. "I was scared shitless you'd drive off when you saw it was me if I didn't do it this way." He gestured to the tree. "I didn't know what else to do."

"Are you out of your damned mind?" He was dead all right. She bored the barrel into his forehead. He drew his chin down, squeezed his eyes shut. "I could kill your ass right now and no one would give one shit, you idiot."

He held up his hands surrender style. They actually shook. "No, Addy! Listen to me." He raised his eyes to meet hers, evidently afraid to move the rest of his head. "I know where they are. I swear to God, I know where those women are."

Adeline lessened the pressure on his forehead. Her instincts were screaming. "How would you know that when about fifty damned cops haven't been able to figure it out?"

"I'll tell you on the way." He pointed up the road. "My truck's parked up there. Let's just go before it's too late. I ain't going back there by myself. It's too damned creepy. He's got them all shackled up like…" He shook head. "I don't know. You just have to see it for yourself."

"We'll take the Bronco."

He bobbed his head up and down. "Whatever you say."

They climbed into her Bronco. She shoved into reverse. "Which way?"

"Down the road about four miles." He pointed west.

"There's a real narrow dirt road that's all overgrown. If you didn't know it was there, you'd miss it. You have to park there and walk the rest of the way. It's another mile or so back in the woods. An old hunting shack next to Singing River."

Adeline glanced at him, her suspicion growing. "That still doesn't tell me how you found it. Or why you didn't call the police."

He blew out an exaggerated breath. "All right. I did some business there once or twice."

Son of a bitch. "Drugs." She shook her head. Of course. Easy access to the water for importing and exporting.

"I went there this afternoon to check out the situation for a future transaction," he explained. "You know, to see if it was still safe to conduct business there. I freaked out when I saw...*them*."

"Why didn't you call someone then?" Could he be any more stupid? "You couldn't try to set them free?"

"I was afraid, okay? That psycho almost caught me there. I had to hide, then sneak my way out. After what he did to Aunt Irene, I wasn't taking no chances." He huddled in the seat as if he expected her to beat him.

The ache of loss pierced Adeline's senses. She pushed it away. "You should've come to us before now."

"I had to wait until I could talk to you away from Wyatt. He'd try to blame this on me and I ain't got shit to do with it."

Still suspicious, she demanded, "Why didn't you tell your daddy?" God knows that old bastard had taken care of every fix his sons had ever gotten into.

Another of those big puffs of breath. "I'm on thin ice with my daddy, okay? He's real pissed at me because I slit your tires. Like I said, I was afraid if Wyatt found out I had this information, he'd try to pin this shit on me." He wagged his head from side to side. "I might be a little hotheaded and irrational but I ain't no freak. This dude is a damned freak."

That they could agree on. She would kick his ass about the tires later.

"Let's just go," he urged. "I want this over with."

There was a condition coming. She could feel it.

"I'll show you where they are," he continued. "Then I'm getting the hell out of there. You tell Wyatt that bastard contacted you. The phone I used to text you was one of those throwaways. I pitched it in the river. Wyatt don't have to know I was involved in this at all."

"I'll have to think about that one." She reached for her cell.

"Wait," he wailed. "First, you see for yourself that I'm right then you call your people and I'm out of there, deal? I don't want to be nowhere around when you call him. I'll walk back to my truck. I don't care if it takes all night."

Adeline didn't like playing by anyone else's rules. Clay was a piece of shit, that was for sure. But he wasn't a killer. At least not yet.

"We'll play this your way for a few more minutes," she relented. "But if I get the first hint that you're bullshitting me or that anything at all is off I'm shooting your ass. Got it?"

Clay nodded. "Got it. Trust me, I want this freaky shit over."

Stay away from your kin, Detective. You can't trust him.

Adeline stole a glance at her cousin.

A lump of dread settled in her gut.

She knew better than to trust him...no matter the excuses he gave or the assurances he offered.

Her fingers tightened on the steering wheel.

But she couldn't ignore the possibility that he might be telling the truth. Or that Nichols had been talking about Jamison.

Either way, she hoped like hell she wasn't going to have to be responsible for the death of Cyrus's only other son.

And if she survived this, Wyatt was going to kill her.

The important thing here was saving Cherry Prescott and Penny Arnold and if Adeline was really lucky, Danny Jamison.

Maybe, just maybe, Wyatt would get it through his thick head that Adeline could take care of herself.

CHAPTER FORTY-FOUR

Laurel, 11:00 p.m.

It was past Danny's bedtime. He was sleepy. He rubbed his eyes. He never stayed up this late.

He wished his daddy would come back.

Danny cuddled up to the new puppy his daddy had given him. He'd opened all the presents his mom had hidden for him and the ones Santa had left.

Danny smiled. He'd got lots of good stuff. But the puppy was the best. He couldn't wait to show his puppy to his friends.

He frowned. He might not get to do that. His dad had said they would have to leave Laurel or the police would never stop bothering him. Danny's grandma and grandpa had poisoned their minds. He didn't know what that meant exactly except that it was bad. His daddy said Danny would make new friends.

Danny was glad to be back in his own bed. His daddy

had said no one would come looking for him here. But Danny had to stay in his room and he couldn't turn on any lights except his little flashlight. The windows were covered with blankets just to make sure no light got out if he forgot. The police might drive by or something.

There was food and water for the puppy. Food and water for Danny. And all the presents. His dad had even brought a bucket to the room and said that Danny should pee-pee in it. He wasn't to leave his room for anything.

Danny smiled again. That meant he didn't have to take a bath!

Wouldn't be for long, though. His daddy was coming for him before the sun was up in the morning, he'd said. They would pick up his mommy and then they would go far away. Danny got to pick the place.

He liked that.

His mommy would be glad to be out of the hospital. She still didn't talk, but his daddy said that she would talk as soon as all the lies stopped being whispered in her ears.

One thing was for sure, she would make Danny take a bath.

A loud creak made Danny's eyes get big. He made a sound in his mouth—the same kind he made when he watched a movie and something happened that he wasn't expecting.

He hugged his puppy tighter. It whimpered.

Danny sat up. Maybe his daddy had come back early.

He scooted out of bed and went to the door. His hand stilled on the knob. His daddy had said not to leave the room.

But if his daddy was here it would be okay.

Danny turned the knob and opened the door enough to stick his head out. He listened for the sound of his daddy coming up the stairs.

IT ENDS WITH HER

The house was quiet.

And dark.

Danny shivered. He didn't like being here alone.

His puppy jumped off the bed and ran over to him. Danny reached down to pick him up but he ran out the door.

"Puppy! Stop!" He still had to decide on a name for his puppy. "Come back!" The puppy just kept going.

Danny ran to his bed and got his flashlight. He couldn't let the puppy run around the house by himself. He might get into something.

"Puppy!" Danny could hear him yapping. He followed the sound down the stairs.

His daddy had made him keep his eyes closed when he brought him inside the house. He'd kept his eyes closed all the way to his room. That's where Santa had left his presents. The living room was a mess. Broken glass was on the floor. Stuff was turned upside down. What was that big red spot on the floor?

He remembered his daddy had ketchup on his face that night. Boy, he'd made a big mess. Danny's mom wouldn't like that. But they were moving anyway. Didn't matter. The next people who lived here could clean up the mess.

Danny found his puppy in the kitchen. "You silly puppy." He stepped in something wet. "Ooo. Bad puppy." His dad said he'd have to learn the puppy to go potty outside.

Danny picked up his puppy and turned to go back to his room. The beam of his flashlight landed on the door to the basement. It was open.

Was his daddy down there? Maybe he had come home.

Danny went to the door and peeked down the stairs. "Daddy?"

No answer. It was quiet down there.

"Daddy!"

The puppy scrambled out of his arms. Danny tried to grab him but he was tumbling down the stairs before Danny could catch him. He yelped and whimpered.

"Puppy!" He hurried down the stairs. If the puppy was hurt, what would he do?

He finally reached the bottom step and scooped up the whimpering puppy. "You're being a bad boy." His daddy said boy puppies were the best. The puppy snuggled against him, reached up, and licked his face. Danny giggled. Maybe he'd forgive him for being bad this time.

Danny started to go back up the stairs but something out of place made him look again. His daddy always kept the basement perfectly clean, just like his mommy kept the house. His daddy didn't like messes. He was probably mad he'd spilled all that ketchup.

Rocks were piled up.

Danny hugged his puppy tighter. "How did those get there, boy?"

Had someone been in their house while they were gone? Boy, his dad would be mad about this! Danny looked around some more, moving the beam of his flashlight over the basement floor. He made that scared sound in his mouth again. He walked closer to the pile of rocks, looked down at the big hole. He shined his flashlight around the whole thing.

It looked like...like a *grave*.

CHAPTER FORTY-FIVE

*1708 Monroe Street,
Pascagoula, 11:15 p.m.*

Wyatt stepped out of the shower. He'd stood under the hot water until it went cold. Damn, he felt better.

He scrubbed the towel over his body. His cell phone vibrated, trembled against the counter.

A call at this time of night was never good.

He picked up the phone. Womack's name was displayed on the screen. "Henderson."

"You need to let me in."

"What?" Womack was here? Shit. That definitely couldn't be good. "I just got out of the shower. Let me get some clothes—"

He froze in the doorway between the bathroom and his bedroom.

The bed was empty.

No Addy.

"Wyatt, open your door."

Fear abruptly released him. He rushed to the bed. Lifted the covers as if his eyes had betrayed him.

She wasn't there.

"Addy!" he shouted as he moved down the hall.

"Wyatt," Womack shouted in his ear. "She's not here. Open the damned door!"

Wyatt stalled halfway to the living room, his deputy's words filtering past the panic. "What do you mean, she's not here?"

"Wyatt, open the door. I'll explain everything."

He was at the door three seconds later. He unlocked it and jerked it open. "What the hell is going on?" he demanded. "Where's Addy?"

Damn it. She wasn't supposed to get out of his sight. She was likely pissed at him now that he'd admitted the motive for his decision nine years ago.

Womack looked him up and down. "You probably want to put some clothes on. Then we'll go find her."

Wyatt stalked back to his bedroom and tugged on his discarded jeans and shirt. He grabbed his socks and boots while he was at it. She was gone. Had she contacted Womack? How the hell had this happened?

He hurried back into the living room. "Where is she?" Womack had to know something, otherwise he wouldn't have showed up here like this.

"She called me about fifteen minutes ago. Said she got a message from the perp." He opened his phone and showed the forwarded message to Wyatt.

"Goddammit!" He went for his keys. They weren't on the table by the door where he normally kept them. "Did she take my SUV?"

"No, your SUV is out there. She wanted ten minutes head start," Womack explained. "She's already got that and more. We need to get going."

She'd sneaked out of here. Had taken his keys so he couldn't follow her until Womack arrived. What the hell was she thinking?

Where the hell was his spare set of keys?

"Wyatt," Womack urged, "let's go. I've already called Sullenger and Guthrie. They're meeting us at the rendezvous location."

This was real. Addy was out there somewhere. Wyatt had failed to keep a close enough watch on her.

Ten minutes later they were at the turnoff to the area where they had set up the command post earlier today to launch the search.

Sullenger's Civic was there. She and Guthrie, stood in the middle of the main road.

Womack eased to the side of the road. He'd been too damned quiet on the drive here.

Wyatt hadn't said much, either. Fear had put a chokehold on him and he couldn't shake it.

This bastard had killed three people, including Addy's mom, possibly more.

Wyatt needed Addy to be safe.

He was out of the car before Womack braked to a complete stop. "Where's Addy?" he demanded of the two deputies staring at him.

"She's not here." Sullenger was the first to answer. "No sign of her Bronco." She hitched a thumb up the road. "We did find a truck pulled off the road about thirty yards that way."

"It's Clay Cooper's truck," Guthrie explained. "I didn't have to run the plates. I know his vehicle."

Silence fell over the four of them. Wyatt told himself that the possibility of Adeline's being with Clay wasn't nearly so scary as the idea of her with Jamison. But something didn't feel right.

"Did anyone call old man Cooper to find out if his son was at home?"

Sullenger and Guthrie exchanged a look.

"What?" Wyatt demanded.

"He's not at home. Or any of his usual hangouts," Sullenger explained. "We called around as soon as we recognized the truck was his."

"Son of a bitch!" Wyatt braced his hands on his hips and turned all the way around in the road. There was nothing out here. Woods and water. They had searched most of this area already.

But she'd been here tonight...or at least she'd been headed here.

"We need to talk," Womack said to Wyatt.

Wyatt turned to Womack. Judging by the look on the man's face, things were going to get worse.

"Give us some space," Wyatt instructed the other two. Sullenger and Guthrie walked over to her Civic and leaned against it, looking less than comfortable.

"What the hell's going on, Womack?"

"It's my son." Womack blew out a heavy breath. "He got into some trouble with drugs." The deputy turned his face away as if he couldn't bear to look Wyatt in the eye now. "I'd already spent every dime I had in savings trying to get him rehabilitated."

Wyatt was aware that the man's son had been to rehab a couple of times, but he'd had no idea the trouble had started again. More importantly, why was he telling Wyatt this now?

Womack shrugged. "I was desperate to help him. Clay said he could help. He knew the thug my boy had gotten

IT ENDS WITH HER

involved with. Had some influence. He could make it right."

Tension coiled around Wyatt's chest. "What did it cost you?"

"For a long time, nothing." Womack met his gaze. "But he never failed to remind me that there would come a day when he would need a favor from me. And that if I didn't pay up when that time came, my boy would end up face down in a river somewhere. Clay said all he had to do was give the word and the trouble would be back at my door."

Wyatt couldn't speak. If he said a word, he would blast the man. He had to hear him out first. Keep him talking until he knew everything.

"When that crazy bastard tried to kill his wife, I got a call from one of my buddies up in Laurel."

"Are you talking about Jamison?" A band tightened around Wyatt's chest.

Womack nodded. "There was a picture found in Jamison's car. The kind you print off the Internet from articles you've Googled. Stuff like that."

"What picture?" Wyatt didn't recall hearing anything about any pictures.

"A picture of Addy."

Rage roared inside Wyatt. "And you kept this information from the investigation?" Keeping his hands at his waist and off Womack's throat took every ounce of willpower he possessed.

"There were dates written on the page. Address. Occupation. Indications that Addy was adopted. Stuff like that. Apparently Jamison had been researching Addy for some reason. But it wasn't relevant to the case or to what he'd done to his wife."

"What did you do with this information?" Wyatt

demanded, his jaw clenched so hard he could hardly utter the words.

"My buddy in Laurel recognized Addy and gave me a call. I convinced him that this was sensitive information and that maybe we should keep it between the two of us and that I would handle it. Like I said, it didn't appear to have anything to do with what the bastard had done to his wife."

Womack shrugged. "I figured Clay would be more than glad to get his hands on this information. I didn't see how it could hurt anything. Addy was long gone from here anyway. And Clay would like nothing better than to figure out a way to prove she wasn't a legitimate heir so he did all the inheriting. I'd heard him talk that shit before. I was convinced it couldn't hurt anything, but it could help...save my son. I'd give the info to Clay and my son would be off the hook."

Wyatt restrained the urge to beat the hell out of the guy. "But then Addy showed up here with info on the Prescott case," Wyatt suggested, his blood boiling in his veins. "That made you a little nervous, didn't it?"

Womack didn't answer at first. Just stood there looking like the dog he was. "Yeah, it made me start thinking, but there wasn't any connection. Seemed like a coincidence that she showed up not long after the photo was found in Laurel."

"Then Arnold went missing and you started to think maybe this wasn't a coincidence." The idea that a man with this many years in law enforcement would do such a thing sickened Wyatt. What the hell had he been thinking?

"It wasn't until you called from Jones County and confirmed Jamison was the one behind these abductions that I knew for sure. I begged Clay to let it go. To leave Addy alone," Womack admitted, then shook his head.

"Her momma's dead. And she don't need no more bullshit. But he wouldn't listen."

Wyatt stilled. "What do you mean, you told him to leave Addy alone?"

Womack plowed a hand through his hair. "He was the one who slashed her tires. He slashed her clothes and left that message on the motel room mirror." He gestured to the road. "Evidently, he's still got a plan to have his revenge."

Revenge. Jesus Christ. "Do you have any idea what he's planning to do?" Fear ignited deep in Wyatt's arteries.

Womack shook his head. "He just said it was a joke. A way to mess with her head and get his revenge for what she did to his brother. He swore it had nothing to do with the missing women. That's all he told me."

"I can't believe you're scared of that piece of shit." Wyatt shook his head. "That's pretty damned pathetic, *Deputy.*"

"When you have a son," Womack challenged, "you'll understand."

Wyatt wanted to kill him. "One more question, how did Clay know about the letters? The kind of paper? Glue? How did he learn those details?" Wyatt already knew the answer, he just wanted to hear the man say it out loud.

Womack looked away.

"Deputy Sullenger." Wyatt glared at Womack. "Read Deputy Womack his rights and put him in lockup."

Sullenger looked less than happy about the assignment but she said, "Yes, sir."

"Guthrie," Wyatt said to his other deputy, "I want you to get the whole department out of bed. I want everyone here in twenty minutes. Call Chief Parker and get his people here, too. We're going to find Addy and that piece-of-shit cousin of hers."

Guthrie pulled out his cell and started making calls. "Wyatt, wait," Womack said even as Sullenger took him by the arm. "I can help."

Wyatt was so pissed off and disgusted with the man he was lucky he hadn't beaten the crap out of him right here. "What the hell can you do?"

"I know a lot of Clay's friends and," he shrugged, "contacts. Let me check around and see if any of them have some ideas on where he might take Addy." Womack jerked his head in the direction of Clay's truck. "If he asked her to meet him here, they can't be that far from where he left his truck. Chances are, when he's finished with whatever the hell this is he's planning on coming back for it."

That was the first thing Wyatt should have considered. This was way too personal for him...he wasn't on his toes. And Addy needed him to do this right. "All right." To Sullenger he said, "Don't let him out of your sight."

Sullenger nodded.

Wyatt closed his eyes and prayed for Addy's safety. Whatever Clay was up to, surely he wouldn't kill her. He was a dirtbag, that was for certain. But Wyatt wasn't sure he was capable of killing anyone.

The old man, now that was a different story. He might just be capable of anything, despite the good deed he'd done for Addy's mother all those years ago.

Addy. His body ached with agony. Wyatt refused to even entertain the notion of losing her again.

Not again.

He would find her.

And when he did, he was going to give her a good shaking for scaring the hell out of him. And Clay, well, Clay was going to pay for a long time to come.

CHAPTER FORTY-SIX

11:50 p.m.

"If you're lost," Adeline threatened, "I swear to God I'll kick your ass."

"I know where I'm going," Clay groused.

She hadn't taken his weapon. If they came up on Jamison, they would both need firepower.

She hoped like hell that wasn't going to turn out to be a bad decision. Unfortunately, this whole night was leaning in that direction.

Her phone had buzzed a dozen times. Wyatt. When she determined whether or not Clay was telling the truth, she would give Wyatt their location, or at least the general direction they had taken. She sure as hell wasn't going to have him dragging all of the Jackson County Sheriff's Department out here if this was some bullshit Clay had trumped up. He didn't appear to be drunk. Stone-cold sober, the best she could tell. But she knew her cousin too well. This could be some sort of elaborate hoax designed to make her look bad or to scare the shit out of her. If that proved to be the case, maybe she would kill him.

"That's it." Clay pointed through the trees to a small shack maybe fifty yards ahead.

"You're sure?" The shack was dark. Moonlight filtered through the trees, making the outline visible in the near darkness. But she couldn't see shit else. Singing River whispered in the background, the sound much quieter than in the summer and fall.

"I'm positive. That's it," he urged.

Adeline considered the options. It was best to go in under the assumption that Jamison was inside. "You move wide around the back. I'll make my way to the front. Keep your eyes and ears open." She sent him a hard look. "And for God's sake, don't shoot anywhere near my position."

He nodded. "Got it."

This still felt wrong. But maybe it was the whole idea of working with Clay. The last time she'd been involved with a member of the Cooper clan, Gage had ended up dead.

Some part of her kept screaming *setup*!

If there was any chance Prescott and Arnold were in there, she was seeing this thing through.

Clay disappeared into the darkness. Adeline did the same. She hunkered low, moved through the saw grass and underbrush. She wasn't going to make being a target easy for either of those bastards. She cringed at the sounds Clay continued to make. Damn it. Did the guy not know how to move with any stealth?

Making scarcely a sound, she eased closer to the front of the shack. Anticipation seared in her blood, making her heart pump faster. There appeared to be a window on the side closest to her position, but it had been boarded shut.

When she'd reached the west side of the structure, she

moved in close, flattened against the rustic wall. She held her breath and listened. The cold night air stirred, rubbing the branches of trees together. The constant hum of the river filled the air with its melody beyond that. Clay muttered a curse, the sound carried in the darkness. Dumbass.

No sound inside the shack.

Keeping her back against the wall, she eased around to the front. The door didn't have a knob or lock. Just a loop of rope hooked over a wooden dowel protruding next to the opening.

Still no noise other than those nature made. She crept to the left side of the door, reached across it and unlooped the rope. She held her breath. Still not the slightest noise inside.

Using her left hand, she slid her flashlight from her back pocket. She slammed the butt of the flashlight into the door, sending it flying inward.

No reaction.

If this place was deserted, Clay Cooper was so screwed.

She rolled her body toward the edge of the door opening, roved the flashlight's beam over the interior.

The light pooled on a body.

Adeline froze...let the light linger there. Definitely female. Blond hair. Her pulse rate jumped into overdrive. Victim was breathing. But she hadn't moved.

She shifted the light to the left.

Eyes, wide with fear, reflected the light.

The woman whimpered as best she could with the gag stuffed into her mouth.

Blond. Adeline studied her face. Cherry Prescott.

And she was alive. Relief flooded Adeline.

With one last look around the area behind her, Adeline

moved into the shack. "I'm Detective Cooper," she announced. "I'm here to help you." Ignoring the desperate sounds Prescott made, Adeline checked the small room. The smell of feces and urine were overwhelming. Feeding bowls sat on the floor between the women. At least he hadn't left them here to starve.

Adeline, her weapon still palmed, moved to where Prescott huddled on the floor. "Don't be afraid. You're gonna be okay now," she said gently as she surveyed the woman for injury. Then she moved to Penny Arnold who had started to move about. "Ms. Arnold?" She scanned her for injury, as well. No visible injuries.

Arnold struggled to a sitting position and started sobbing.

Adeline inspected the shackles. Attached to a wooden support beam with a length of chain and a heavy-duty lock. She would need tools to get them loose. Or a key.

Time to call in reinforcements. Adeline knelt down, one knee on the floor, the other braced for rapid movement. She set her flashlight on the floor and pulled out her phone. She hit the call button. "I'm calling help," she assured the two women now staring at her.

Prescott started to whine frantically.

"Hold on," Adeline urged, "we're going to get you out of here."

The desperate sounds escalated. A creak splintered the air. Her weapon leveled, Adeline twisted at the waist to see if it was Clay.

Clay kicked her in the side of the head.

Addy lost her balance. Her phone flew from her hand and spun across the floor. She rolled to her back just as he moved over her. She kicked him in the crotch.

Clay howled.

She shot to her feet. Though he was still standing, he struggled to unfold his body.

"What the hell are you doing?" She rammed the weapon into the side of his head.

Clay laughed. "He's coming." He looked up at her, nodded knowingly. "He comes back every night about this time and you're going to be here waiting for him. The problem is, you're going to be dead already."

"Funny." She smirked. "I'm the one with the gun to your damned head."

Clay groaned, straightened up. His right arm came up, and the business end of the weapon he'd been hiding between his legs leveled on Adeline's chest.

"Well, well." She took a step away from him. "You sure you know how to use that thing?"

He swung the barrel toward Prescott. "How about I shoot her right now and we'll see who flinches."

"You're bluffing." Adeline's finger twitched with the urge to pull the trigger. She couldn't kill him. Goddamn it. Going down that road again was out of the question. But they had the proverbial Mexican standoff.

She could shoot him in the leg. Or maybe the dick.

He drew the hammer back. "Say good-bye to your big sister, Addy." Prescott tried to scream; the sound came out strangled and muffled. "Now give me your gun or I'm going to shoot that pathetic bitch."

Adeline placed her weapon on the floor and kicked it across the room. "You want it, you go get it." She wouldn't need her weapon to take care of this dumbass. All she needed was for him to put down his guard. Now that she was unarmed, he would.

Clay shifted the aim of his .357 to her. "In a minute. Now get over there on the floor with your sisters." He snickered. "I always knew you couldn't be one of us. Guess I was right."

"Whatever you say." Moving backward so she didn't have to turn her back on him, Adeline kept her hands up. "What do you think you're accomplishing here, Clay? You owe this guy something? Maybe he sucked your dick once?"

He laughed. "Have your fun while you can, Addy. This was all meant to be. I knew some psycho was watching you. The cops found your picture in his car. I just didn't know he had anything to do with this until I came out here to see if this place was still standing." He gestured to Prescott and Arnold. "Then I overheard your batty old momma telling my daddy about how someone had found out the truth about you being adopted. When you showed up, I knew this was my chance to see that you got what you deserved."

Adeline let the remark about her mother go, she would get him for that later. "Why don't you let Prescott and Arnold go? This is really between me and you, right?"

"No way." He shook his stupid head. "What I'm doing is getting you the hell out of my life for good. You're going to die tonight, cuz." He smiled. "That psycho brother of yours would never have gotten to you the way Henderson has been all over you. I just made his job a little simpler. Works out great for me, I get rid of you and nobody ever has to know I had anything to do with it. That keeps the old man off my back."

"Well, aren't you smart," Adeline mused. "I guess everyone's been wrong about you. You aren't the stupid brother."

His lips twisted. "At least I won't be dead. It's so sad," he mocked. "The police will finally find the three of you and you'll all be dead. Too bad, too sad."

Adeline wondered briefly where the boy was as she eased over a little more. She hoped if he wasn't here that meant he was safe. When she'd positioned herself in front of the women, she asked, "You've got me where you want me, Clay. I guess you can go." Time to use a little reverse psychology. "You wouldn't want to risk getting caught here if Wyatt shows up. You know it'll only be a matter of time before they find us."

He moved his head back and forth. "But *he* will get here first. It's almost time. He's always on time." Clay hitched his head toward the door. "I'll just hang around out there in the woods so I can see his reaction when he finds you here." He laughed. "I wish I had a camera. A bittersweet family reunion. Now sit," he ordered Addy.

She kept her hands up as she dropped to her knees on the floor. She sat back, drawing one knee up in a stance that would allow her to shoot to her feet more quickly.

"Good." Clay reached down and snagged the flashlight. "I'll be watching." He ran the beam of light over the floor until he spotted her weapon and cell phone, picked both up, and shoved them into his waistband. He gestured to Prescott then Arnold. "Doesn't look like they'll be going anywhere." He focused on Addy. "You could leave them to fend for themselves and run before the bastard gets here," he offered. "You might even get away. I'm not the best shot in the county. It's a risk you might decide to take. After all, that's what you do, isn't it, Addy? Run away from your trouble."

A shadow blocked the moonlight filtering through the open door. Adeline's heart lurched. Clay, apparently, recognized the danger at about the same time she did. He wheeled around, actually squeezed off a shot.

Something sliced through the air, slammed into Clay's

temple. He lurched sideways, then crumpled to the floor. A baseball bat clanged down next to him.

Adeline lunged forward. Two hands rammed her shoulders and shoved her backward. She landed on her ass. She scrambled to a better position. The flashlight had rolled across the floor, its beam highlighting the bastard.

Tall, bald, and looking furious, Daniel Jamison surveyed the situation as he dragged a gun from his waistband. "Thanks for making this easy," he said to Clay's motionless body. Then he looked at Adeline and the others and smiled. "All the princesses in a row. Perfect."

He kicked Clay in the ribs to see if there would be a reaction. Clay's body bounced with the impact but he didn't grunt. Just lay there.

Clay had taken her weapon. Damn it.

Jamison dropped the bag he carried on the floor and motioned to Addy with his gun. "You. Get up."

She pushed to her feet, squared her shoulders. "I don't know why you think it's necessary to finish your father's work. You saved us once. Why would you do this now?" Reason likely wouldn't get anywhere with this guy, but the longer she could keep him talking, the more time she had to formulate a plan.

He laughed. "You were too young to remember how it was, so don't pretend to know what you're talking about. You have no idea." He took a step back and pointed to the sports-type bag he'd dropped on the floor. "Open the bag."

Addy moved toward him, took a long hard look at the man who was her brother. He'd rescued his sisters as a child, surely some part of that good still survived deep inside him. She lowered to her knees and opened the bag. More chains and shackles.

"Get the key from the bottom of the bag."

She dug around, found the key.

"Now put on a pair of those cuffs."

She pulled the length of chain from the bag. Seven, eight feet long. Three sets of cuffs were attached to the length of chain. He was going to shackle them together. Shit.

"I've been watching you for days," he told her. "Trying to find the right time. Imagine my surprise when asswipe over there did my work for me. Looks like I'm not the only family member who had it in for you."

Her fingers cold as ice, Adeline ignored him and slid two of the iron bracelets onto her wrists then clicked them shut. She lifted her gaze to his. "Yeah, yeah, the story of my life." Then she dared to smile. "Maybe I'll have the pleasure of doing to you what I did to asswipe's brother." The front of his hand smacked across her face. Adeline rode out the wave of pain, licked the blood from her lip. "You know, if you were a real man you wouldn't have picked on a poor old lady in the hospital." *Bastard.*

He laughed. "I did that just for you, little sis." He smiled. "I knew you'd love it."

Fury bolted through Adeline. He was dead.

"Now take the key and release Prescott. Put the next set of cuffs on her."

Adeline lugged the chain toward Prescott. The woman sobbed harder, shook her head. Adeline produced a smile. "It's gonna be all right," she whispered as she unlocked the cuffs already on the woman's wrists. Her wrists were scraped and bloody.

"Put those on her wrists before you release her ankles," the bastard ordered.

Adeline did as she was told, the whole time whispering reassurances. When she'd finished with Prescott, he ordered her to do the same to Arnold. As she obeyed his order, she watched him remove her weapon from Clay's waistband and store it in his own. Damn it.

"Now stand up and make a line."

Adeline moved toward him, the other women in tow.

He pointed the gun at Addy's chest. "I want you at the back of the line."

She shrugged, circled around behind the others so that Arnold was closest to him.

Arnold dropped to her knees sobbing, the sound choking around the gag in her mouth.

"Get up!"

The woman curled into a ball, her sobs pitching to a new frantic level.

"Get up!" He kicked her in the back.

Adeline started forward.

"Don't move," he ordered. Keeping an eye on her, Jamison dug around in his bag and pulled out three tiaras. He placed one atop each woman's head.

Arnold sobbed even harder. Adeline wanted to demand that he remove the women's gags but she was afraid if she brought it up, he'd shove one in her mouth. Someone needed to be able to scream.

"Get her up," Jamison ordered Prescott. "Or I'll kill her here and you can drag her to the river."

Prescott reached down, helped Arnold to her feet. Jamison grabbed the end of the chain near Arnold's cuffs. "Now, stay in a line right behind me. Anybody falls down or stops, I'll blow your damned head off." His mouth cut into a grin. "Be hard to wear your tiara then."

Flashes from her dream swam in front of Adeline's eyes. He was taking them to the water. Nichols's words bobbed to the surface of those churning memories.

The women are being held close to the water. If you don't find them soon they'll be under the water.

Adeline glanced longing at her stupid ass cousin as Jamison dragged them out of the shack.

Poor Clay. He hadn't gotten to enjoy the show.

Think, Addy! The metal cuffs chafed her wrists. The December air was chilly. The full moon hung low in the sky. The distant hum of Singing River grew louder, threatening. Jamison tromped through the brush and saw grass, leading the way toward their doom.

The panic started deep in her chest.

The water would be cold and deep.

The hands clutching at her in her dream were her sisters'. They would be looking to her for help.

And she wouldn't be able help them.

Adeline's throat closed as the panic clawed its way there, urging her to scream.

But there was no one to hear. Wyatt and his deputies would be back at the other location…where she'd sent them. She prayed they would discover Clay's truck, search the area until they found her Bronco.

She swallowed back the defeat. She could hope.

The roar of the water was louder now.

They were close.

Too close.

Adeline kicked back the fear. She wasn't going down without a fight.

Not tonight. Not ever.

He broke through the tree line and stalled on the river's bank. The water was dark and wide, its song whispering to the air.

Arnold fell to her knees, making those god-awful sounds. Prescott knelt down and tried to comfort her. Adeline ignored the tugs on the chain. She wasn't getting on her knees again for this bastard. He'd have to shoot her first.

"When I discovered you had grown up here," Jamison said to Adeline, "I realized the setting was perfect. I had to get you back here. I knew when Arnold wouldn't cooperate, Prescott would come here looking for you. All I had to do was wait and follow her here. I wanted to do this *here.*"

"How clever of you." She spat the words at him.

"You don't understand, do you?" he jeered. "The Singing River. 'It murmurs a tragic tale,'" he recited, evidently from something he'd read.

"Yeah, yeah," Adeline said, "I know the story." Who could grow up here and not know it?

"Those sweet, kind Pascagoula Indians were about to be enslaved by the Biloxi tribe." He shook his head. "Rather than be taken, they joined hands and walked right out into that dark water. Chanting a death song the whole way. The Singing River hums that song to this day."

Prescott and Arnold sobbed louder with his every word.

"Amazing," Adeline tossed at him. "You see yourself as some kind of warrior or something? You need to prove you're more powerful than us?" She rattled her shackles. "I think you pretty much proved that already."

He shook his head and made that annoying tsking sound. "You don't understand at all, Detective Cooper. The story revolves around a *princess*. It was her goddamned fault that all those people walked right out there," he pointed to the murky water, "to their deaths."

He was right. The Biloxi princess who'd fallen in love with the Pascagoula chief. That was why it had to be here. He saw them as princesses...it was destiny. But whose? What had they done to him? How had they intruded into his territory? It didn't make sense.

He motioned to the river with his gun. "Now. Get in the water."

Arnold and Prescott wailed even louder, the sounds strangled.

"Why?" Adeline asked him. "What's your point in making us get in the water? Why not just shoot us right here? Dead is dead. Who cares about a stupid legend?" He rushed up to her, shoved the barrel of what she recognized as a nine-millimeter into her face.

"Because this is what was supposed to happen all those years ago when you were just a tiny little baby."

"Your father killed your mother," she reminded. "He tried to kill you. But you hid us where he couldn't get to us. Why kill us now? What happened back then is over. You don't have to do this. Where's that hero who saved his three little sisters?"

He laughed long and loud. "That's not what happened." He snickered. "That's what *they* thought happened. But that wasn't the way it happened at all."

"Tell us then," Adeline challenged, "how it really was. I think we deserve to know before you kill us. Otherwise your whole ritual will have no meaning."

He stared at her a moment, his blue eyes—the ones exactly like hers—narrowing with suspicion then relaxing. "Why not? A bedtime story to put you to sleep."

Haha. He was a comedian. Right now she just wanted him closer and distracted.

"For six years it was just me." He banged his chest. "My parents loved me so much. Everything was about me. It was perfect." He glowered at Prescott. "Then you came along and you were all they talked about. I had to share everything with you, especially *my* parents. Their little *princess*," he snarled.

He shifted his attention to Arnold. "Then you." He kicked her in the side. "By then they didn't have any time at all for me. The babies needed them. Especially that bitch mother of ours. Their little princesses were so sweet in their little pink dresses and bows." He jerked Prescott to her feet. "I tried to get rid of you. Tried to drown you in the bathtub but that bitch caught me. She was so stupid she thought it was an accident."

Adeline eased a little closer to where he stood.

"And the princesses just kept coming!" He released Prescott and whirled on Adeline. "That bitch just kept spitting 'em out. You cried all the time. I made sure. Mommy," he said in a squeaky childlike voice, "just couldn't figure out why you cried all the time." He rushed closer, nose to nose with Adeline. "It was because I tortured you when they weren't looking."

"Sucked for me," she muttered, scarcely able to contain the urge to hurl herself into him. But she wouldn't when the gun's barrel was turned toward Prescott.

"Finally," he snapped, "I'd had enough. My father kept telling me not to worry, that it was still me and him. He would laugh and say the princesses ruled our world. I knew he was miserable, too."

Adeline dared to ease a little closer to him.

"I made a plan," he said, seemingly lost in the memories. "I promised to take you on a picnic. The bitch thought we were all sleeping, so she'd fallen asleep in front of the TV. I carried you," he said to Adeline. She halted her incremental movement toward him. "And the rest of you followed right behind me just like you were in a parade." He smirked. "It was so easy. I led you right to the water. It wasn't far from our backyard." He stepped back. "Then I persuaded you to come into the water with me. It wasn't more than knee deep. We all sat down, laughing and having fun. Then I pushed you under the water, put my knees on your chests," he said to Arnold and Prescott.

He shot Adeline a sideways look. "I held you under with one hand."

Adeline quashed the panic that tried to swell in her throat. "But our mother caught you again, didn't she? Did she punish you?"

He lunged at her, grabbed her by the jacket. He pulled her face to his and shoved the gun under her breasts. "No, she didn't punish me. She was afraid of me. She convinced my father that I needed to go away." He shoved Adeline away. "So I killed her." He looked from Adeline to Arnold, then Prescott. "I would've killed all of you, but you," he snarled at Prescott, "took the others and hid from me."

"Our father caught you, tried to stop you, and you killed him, too," Adeline surmised, the scenario unfolding in her mind.

Jamison's face blanked.

Realization dawned on Adeline. "You wanted it to be just you and him. You didn't intend to kill him. That's why you wouldn't talk afterward." His world had been over. *Shit.*

"Get in the water!"

The strangled wailing started again. Adeline knew she had just one shot at escaping certain death. All she needed was a little bit of luck.

They waded into the icy cold water. Prescott and Arnold clung to each other; Adeline lagged as far behind as the chain would allow.

"That's perfect."

He was right behind Adeline. She couldn't see where the gun was . . .

"Now," he said, "sit down in the water."

CHAPTER FORTY-SEVEN

Tuesday, December 28, 12:18 a.m.

Adeline shivered. The water was up to her neck. Beside her Prescott and Arnold were clinging to each other, still sobbing, but the sounds were weaker now.

They were beaten.

Jamison waded back and forth in front of them, his movements sloshing the cold water in their faces. He was singing some bizarre song he'd clearly written about death and princesses. Fury burned low in Adeline's belly. She was going to kill this bastard.

But before the bastard died, she had to know what he'd done with his son.

"Too bad Danny found out what a monster you are."

Jamison stopped, turned to her. "You don't know my son. I've protected him from bitches like you."

Adeline laughed. "That's not the impression I got when

I visited him and your wife in the hospital. He said he never wanted to see you again." Jamison bowed down to put his gun in her face. "He wants to live with his grandparents now." She just kept right on talking. "He *hates* you."

"You're a liar!"

She shrugged. "Sorry to be the one to tell you, but he told the police exactly what you did to his mother. He might pretend to like you to your face, because you scare him, but he hates your damned guts."

"Liar!" He dropped the gun, bent down, and grabbed Adeline by the throat with both hands.

She sucked in as much air as possible before he cut off the flow completely.

"He knows the lies they've told! He's going with me." He crushed her face to his, his grip on her throat like a vise. "He's waiting at home for me right now."

Bingo.

Jamison's fingers tightened a little more. "You'll go to hell for lying, princess."

Adeline opened her mouth wide and clamped down on his nose. He screamed. The harder he struggled to get loose, the harder she ground her teeth. Blood spurted in her mouth. Her hands shot up...felt for the weapon in his waistband—her weapon.

He shoved her back, tumbled on top of her...they both went under the water.

Paralyzing fear shot through her veins.

The others' hands were grabbing at her hair...her arms.

She clutched at him...tried to find the weapon. Tried to break free of the hold he had on her throat. Panic burned in her lungs.

Don't breathe. Don't freaking breathe.

He banged her head against the rocky river bottom. Pain shattered through her skull.

More weight pressed down on her. A foot caught her in the jaw.

The fear ignited full force...her lungs threatened to burst...she couldn't move...couldn't breathe.

Adeline stopped struggling.

CHAPTER FORTY-EIGHT

"Sheriff! Over here!"

Wyatt ran forward, cutting through the knee-deep saw grass.

Two of his deputies were crouched down...someone was on the ground.

Oh hell.

He lunged toward the huddle.

Clay Cooper lay there. He was talking. Wyatt surveyed the area. A shack—the one his contact had said he used for making drug deals—sat in the distance.

Wyatt shoved his deputy out of the way. He grabbed Clay by the shirt and shook him hard. "Where is Addy?"

"He..." Clay shook his head as if to clear it "He took 'em to the river. He's gonna drown them. He's got a gun."

Wyatt dropped the bastard, drew his weapon, and started forward. "Fan out, head for the river," he shouted to the dozen deputies running toward them.

"He's crazy," Clay called after Wyatt. "I couldn't stop him. I crawled out here and tried to do something, but I passed out again."

The river's song buzzed louder and louder in his ears. Wyatt's heart thumped harder and harder. His feet wouldn't move fast enough. He had to hurry! He couldn't be sure how long the bastard had been gone with her...with them.

The crash of water reached his ears. He adjusted his direction...held up a hand to let those behind him know to go silent.

Muffled cries or wails were coming from the water.

He pushed through the brush and saplings. The moon's full glow spotlighted the tangle of figures struggling in the water.

Wyatt took a bead on the tallest of the tangle. One of the women shifted into the firing line. "Dammit." The women...Prescott he could make out and maybe Arnold...were fighting against Jamison's efforts to shove them back under the water. The way they were moving...tangled up...he couldn't risk taking the shot.

Where was Addy?

Wyatt counted the bodies again. One...two...three...

Fear jammed into his throat.

He ran toward the water.

Jamison whirled around, dragged Prescott in front of him. "Stop right there!" He held something against the back of her head.

Shit. Wyatt couldn't tell for sure if he had a gun. Clay said he had one. "Don't move, Jamison," Wyatt ordered, inching closer.

"One more step, Sheriff, and I'll blow her head off."

Prescott kept screaming or crying...hell, Wyatt couldn't tell. The sound was muffled by whatever the bastard had stuffed in her mouth.

"Where's Detective Cooper?" Wyatt demanded. He

divided his attention between Jamison and the water's murky surface.

"She's dead, Sheriff." Jamison laughed. "You're too late to save that princess."

The water suddenly split in front of Prescott.

Adeline rose like a ghost, her arms leveled in a firing posture.

The discharge of the weapon echoed through the night.

Jamison's head jerked back. He fell backward. Splashed into the water and sank.

Wyatt rushed forward.

Addy jerked at something that looked like a chain, took two steps toward where Jamison had fallen and unloaded the weapon into the water.

Two…three…four…five and six shots resonated, shattering the river's hum.

The women surrounded her, hugging her against them. Wyatt had to push his way between them to get to Addy.

She turned to him, her face pale, her teeth chattering. "I told you that bastard wasn't killing me." She sucked in a shaky breath, then fell into Wyatt's arms.

"You were right," he whispered as he held her tight to his chest. "And you're no princess, either. You're the best damned detective I know."

CHAPTER FORTY-NINE

Once the women were on dry ground, Addy removed the socks stuffed into their mouths. Sullenger found the key Addy had told her about and released their shackles. The women hugged some more. One of Wyatt's deputies had called Wiggins and Hattiesburg to let them know the victims had been found and were alive. Wyatt had also called Sheriff Henley to let her know to look for the boy at the Jamison residence. Henley had just called him back to relay that the boy had been found and was safe.

Thank God.

Wyatt kept an arm around Addy as they moved toward the shack. She shuddered every time she thought about how close she'd come to giving up under that water. But she'd remembered telling Wyatt that Jamison wasn't killing her. She'd felt around the river bottom and found the weapon Jamison had dropped.

Clay broke free from the paramedic treating his injuries. "Addy! You're alive!" He rushed to meet them. "I was worried sick. You okay?"

Addy pulled away from Wyatt and took the three steps

that separated her from her cousin. "I'm fine, Clay, which is more than I can say for you."

Confusion claimed his face. "What?"

She drew back and slammed her fist into his jaw. Clay staggered back, wailing like a little girl. Addy turned back to Wyatt. "Arrest that piece of shit for conspiracy to commit murder." She shook her hand and winced.

Wyatt pulled her back into his arms. "I think that's called police brutality."

She smiled. "I learned it from a guy I used to know."

Wyatt tilted her face up to his. "You scared the hell out of me, Cooper."

She searched his face. "We have a lot to talk about, Wyatt. It's time we got over the past."

Before he could ask her what that meant, she walked over to where the paramedics were checking out Prescott and Arnold.

The investigation was pretty much over. The victims were alive and seemingly well.

With the investigation done and her mother gone, Addy had no reason to stay.

Wyatt wasn't ready for that. Losing her once was more than enough.

CHAPTER FIFTY

Forrest General Hospital
Hattiesburg, 4:22 p.m.

Adeline smiled. Amazing. A beautiful baby girl. A little light at five pounds and six ounces, but absolutely beautiful. A head full of dark hair.

Just amazing.

Wyatt moved up beside her at the viewing window. "You'd better watch out, they say this is contagious. Next thing you know, you'll be wanting one."

She smiled. "I think I'm immune."

"Maybe so." Wyatt chuckled.

Adeline liked it when he laughed. He hadn't done that often since she'd been back. With good reason. But that was behind them now. She made a mental list of the things she needed to do, including the arrangements for her mother's funeral. Adeline would miss her so much. There were things she wished she had said. In time she would come to terms with what she hadn't said and done.

Cyrus had high-powered attorneys all over the charges

against Clay. Womack and his buddy up in Laurel were facing charges of evidence tampering. Both would lose their badges. Sad thing, but there was nothing worse than a dirty cop no matter the excuses for his or her actions.

Prescott and Arnold were safely back home with their families.

Lydia Jamison had awakened from her coma at eight this morning. Her water had broken three hours later. Allison Renae Jamison had come into this world via Cesarean section at two this afternoon.

Adeline was an aunt several times over.

She smiled at her nephew, Danny. A nurse had dragged a chair over so he could stand in to admire his new baby sister beyond the glass. He was a little shy, but Adeline had already decided they were going to be friends.

He didn't know just yet that his father was dead. When his mother had recovered sufficiently, she would talk to him about that. The grandparents couldn't stop doting on the new granddaughter. They hovered around their daughter the way Wyatt was hovering around Adeline.

That was something else she had to take care of. And there was no time like the present. She was never again going to be guilty of failing to share her true feelings with the people she cared about.

"You never trusted me to take care of myself on the job," she said to the man beside her.

Startled, his gaze collided with hers. "Are you kidding?"

She shook her head. "What you did nine years ago is proof positive that you thought I wasn't capable of doing the job. Don't even think about denying it." He'd already admitted as much.

Wyatt sighed. "You're right. I was afraid for you. I loved you so much and I couldn't bear the thought of you being in that kind of danger. If I'd had my way you would have stopped being a cop altogether." He gave his head a bow in acquiescence. "But I was wrong. You were and are a damned fine cop, Addy. I'd go through a door with you anytime."

A smile pulled across her lips. "Thank you. I am a damned fine cop."

Say it, Adeline! "I was wrong, too," she confessed, not an easy thing for her to do.

Wyatt inclined his head. "Do you care to elaborate?"

"Leaving for a while was a good thing. There was too much going on around here. Going was good." She surveyed the activity, nurses and newborns, beyond the window. "But when things settled down, I should have come back." She looked into Wyatt's eyes. "And I should have listened to what you had to say. I shouldn't have allowed what happened to destroy what we had. You deserved the benefit of the doubt, and I didn't give it to you."

"Wow." He glanced around to ensure no one was paying attention to them. "Does that mean you want to give us a second chance?"

She pushed her arms around his waist and leaned into his chest. "That means that I'm through running. I'm going to stay here and take care of the house and other things. And, while I'm here you and I will see where things go. I can't say that I won't end up back in Huntsville, but I want to take the time to be certain this time. No mistakes. No misunderstandings."

One of those killer smiles spread across his face. "Fair enough."

He kissed her. Didn't matter that they were standing in a public corridor in a hospital. Adeline savored the kiss as long as possible before drawing back. His tendency to be overprotective was going to take some getting used to.

But he was worth the trouble. A lot of things about life were worth the trouble, she had decided. Like standing her ground here, where she belonged—at least for a while. And letting Wyatt back into her heart.

Truth was, he'd never completely been evicted.

No more walking away—running, actually. She was here to see this through. If she returned to Huntsville it would be a mutual decision with no things left undone or words left unsaid.

She patted his chest so he wouldn't notice her fingers trembling. "I need to check on my nephew. He's all alone over there."

"I'll be right here," Wyatt promised. "You can always count on me."

That was one thing she understood completely.

She pecked Wyatt on the cheek and walked down to stand by her nephew.

Danny watched the baby sleep. Her pink gown and cap were so sweet. Wyatt was right, this stuff could be contagious. But she wasn't anywhere near ready to admit that out loud.

"Hey, Danny." He flicked a glance her way before turning his full attention back to his baby sister. "We could go get some ice cream or something," Adeline ventured. "If you're bored hanging out here, I mean."

He didn't say yay or nay, just stared at the baby on the other side of the glass. Adeline wondered if he had any idea how much his life was going to change.

She had that problem, too. Getting used to not having her mother to talk to or to visit whenever she took the notion was definitely going to take time. Holidays would be hard even though she'd never been a big holiday person. Plus she had two sisters and several nieces and nephews to get to know.

Adeline sighed as she watched that tiny infant. Life went on. Living proof was right there all swaddled in pink. "She's beautiful, isn't she?"

Danny nodded.

The baby took a big breath and shivered. Adeline smiled. She really was gorgeous.

"She isn't just beautiful," he said.

Adeline looked at him. "Oh yeah?"

Danny nodded. Then he looked around as if to ensure no one else was listening. He leaned toward Adeline and whispered, "She's a princess."

Did you enjoy this book? If so please leave a review! If you'd like to read more by Debra Webb be sure to browse her titles on Amazon and follow her to hear about new releases! Just a simple click to Amazon will take you there!

ABOUT THE AUTHOR

DEBRA WEBB is a USA Today and Amazon Charts bestselling author with more than ten million books sold in numerous languages and countries. Debra's love of storytelling goes back to her childhood when her mother bought her an old typewriter in a tag sale. Born in Alabama, Debra grew up on a farm. She spent every available hour exploring the world around her and creating her stories. She wrote her first story at age nine. It wasn't until she spent three years working for the Commanding General of the US Army in Berlin behind the Iron Curtain and a five-year stint in NASA's Shuttle Program that she realized her true calling. Follow Debra at Amazon or visit her at www.debrawebb.com.

Printed in Great Britain
by Amazon